At Od Each Other

A Novel

Ben Suhrie

outskirts
press

DEDICATION

This novel is dedicated to all the poor, sick, lonely, elderly and vulnerable, and to those everywhere suffering from environmental problems.

ACKNOWLEDGEMENTS

I would like to thank my family and friends for their ongoing support and encouragement, in addition to Bruce Carter and Douglas Cooper for writing Water Wars, the main inspiration for this novel.

Nicknames

Barnyard Boy – Chase Reinhold
Black Train – Daniel Verny
Boiler Brain – Evan Stroop
Buff Face – Brian Garrow
Deep Throat – Isaac Norman
Elephant Man – Jon Wyganti
Encyclopedia Brown – Kevin Swaney
Fly Fisher – Adam Chiocchi
Happy Bunny – Brianna Yachin
Idiot Scumbag – Sam Polan
Lazy Loafer – Jocelyn Reical
Mister Suckup – Ronald Giarto
Old Man – Elias McCullough
Pale Egg – Halley Towser
Racecar Dude – Bo Milako
Running Ninja – Kyle Heshfield
Savvy Socialite – Alyssa Cale
Shadow Guy – Mike Matthews
Silent Soldier – Terrence Hasinger
Soft Tongue – Candace Meakard
Steam Head – Henley Strankop
Sunshine Lady – Amy Lane
Tender Toucher – Jenna Braubach
Total Wreck – Mindy Davison
Zombie Woman – Lisa Misteak

Acronyms

AOI: Area Of Interest
DEP: Department of Environmental Protection
FOP: Flow Origination Point
GPM: Gallons Per Minute
HSW: Hydrologic Surface Waters
JHA: Job Hazard Analysis
MSHA: Mine Safety and Health Administration
SCM: Stream Current Monitor
SDS: Safety Data Sheets
STP: Stream Termination Point

Table of Contents

PART SEVEN

Part One

CHAPTER 1:

New Directions

The vice president neither had dark hair nor wore dark clothes, but he bore a dark countenance, and I imagined a shadowy figure whenever I thought about him. He resembled Ganondorf from *The Legend of Zelda* series.

On his right side sat a short rotund woman in her late thirties, a little younger than he, whose perpetual smile shone like the sun, radiating the simple bliss of many a day spent in the outdoors. She shared the puffiness and optimism of Nintendo's Kirby, but was more of a slow female King Dedede.

At the end of the long wooden table, they faced away from the door nearest to which they had claimed their places. Two windows on the wall opposite the door provided an outside view for them, but not for me.

It's not that Shadow Guy was incapable of summoning a picturesque expression on necessary occasions – though that left much to be desired – but he had never been able to find the grace to simply look like a pleasant person.

Likewise, Sunshine Lady could not conceivably appear stern to anyone, which belied her role as project manager, much the same as a red robin can be described as anything but threatening; it was only fear rather than peace in her faraway glare by which she could be distinguished from a baby bird.

Their yin-and-yang contrast threw the vibe of the

Conference Room perfectly off balance.

"What are some of your weaknesses?" asked Shadow Guy, maintaining eye contact.

"I guess my biggest disadvantage is that I don't know how to do the job yet, though I am willing and able to be trained for this type of position."

They nodded to each other. He shrugged and stuck out his lower lip, while she giggled and nibbled on her long, painted nails. The ball quite nicely rolled into its pocket.

"Where is the University of Prestonsburg?"

"About twenty-five minutes north of here near Lakeland."

"What did you like about geology?"

"The outdoor field experiences."

"Why did you earn only magna cum laude?"

"I was too busy with extracurriculars to try for *summa*."

"What is the course 'Environmental Templates'?"

"A class where I created models of different parts of the earth using R Programming."

"And what is R Programming?"

"Computer software that enables the user to code with input and output variables."

"And what is this...College Tutoring Central?"

"A location on campus for students needing help. I was a math and science tutor."

"Indeed. Now for you to perform some calculus problems!" Sunshine Lady burst out in laughter, and he exclaimed, *"Just kidding, we won't make you do that! But you must like math, then? That's quite unique here."*

Her head soared through clouds of possibilities as her lips and tongue moved in sync. "What *do you like to do* for fun?"

"For fun?" I hoped my sigh of relief wasn't audible. "I do lots of stuff for fun – *especially* as it relates to this job. Hiking, biking, rock climbing, reading, traveling...and amateur astronomy. I was in the AAAP for several years – the Amateur Astronomers Association of Prestonsburg."

A clap pierced the room. *"Excellent! It's good to know you've spent time looking up instead of down. We do need more of that, I suppose...."*

Sunshine Lady reached across the table and grabbed my hands, hair and jewelry sparkling. "Now, in *this job you* will spend *most of the time* outside. Is *that okay* with you?"

"Absolutely. The last thing I want is to be chained to a desk all day."

"Well *thaat's* good. Do *you have any questions* for us?" Her voice reached a high octave while she opened her arms.

"How has the vision for this company changed since Jack Murray resigned last year?"

Consumed wholeheartedly by a fit of giggles, she gestured to her accomplice, who rose to the occasion, stretching. *"We've learned a lot from ol' Jack, a fine fellow and faithful great-grandson of our pioneer...but we've decided to take things in new directions, let's say."*

"What kind of new directions?" I kicked myself.

He smacked his palms on the polished wood. "Very *new directions.*"

Shadow Guy's handshake placed his own hand on top.

Sunshine Lady turned away from the flowers hanging in the hall and sneezed. "Lots of *pollen this time* of year. I *must have* allergies."

CHAPTER 2:

Murray and Affiliates

Images of rocks, trees, and rivers accompanied the website. The company described itself as an environmental consulting firm dedicated to clients' interests.

Michael Matthews and Amy Lane offered to connect through LinkedIn. Amy was a former botanist with a background in biology, while Mike held a professional geologist license and was the king of himself; his eyes seemed to look in a direction different from which his mouth spoke.

August 15, 2018

Dear Richard Amradale,

After careful consideration among all of our candidates, we believe you are the most qualified. We are pleased to offer you the position of Field Technician for Murray and Affiliates, Inc. Please keep in mind that your employment is contingent upon undergoing a background check in addition to completing a physical at your primary care provider. By signing the electronic form below, you agree to avoid employment with competitive businesses for twelve months.

Sincerely,

Candace Meakard
Human Resources

To the Reply address I sent the following:

It's Armadale, NOT Amradale.

Among notable literary works, there stuck out from my bookshelf a Kopen picture book about caring for nature. A hiking trail with trillium flowers was illustrated on the front, and on the back a short lovely poem.

I rested outside listening to music under the setting sun until evening gave way to night. A mild itchiness crept upon my skin, but I brushed away the buzzing. When the breeze had blown away, the trees held their branches still. My iPhone played 'Fireflies' by Owl City as soon as fireflies emerged from the grass and bushes.

CHAPTER 3:

Elephant Man

The two-story building was composed of bricks, one part square and the other longways rectangular, and in the top floor of the former portion was Waterstone Surveying and Mapping. At the intersection of both components lay a fully-sprouted garden. The parking lot was shared with a four-story rectangular building composed of white stone and laced with rows of blackened windows.

The president was noticeably less active in business and financial affairs than the vice president. Whatever his official duties, his functional role was that of an overseer, aided by his physical height. Spacious, double-bridged silver-rimmed glasses illuminated his otherwise dull complexion and gave him an impression of ever-watchfulness; nary a stray pen nor a loose paper escaped his circumspect attention.

Jonathan Wyganti was an observant, portly man around sixty years of age whose monosyllabic vocabulary betrayed the dignity of his office. All the words he never spoke were stored deep inside his potbelly, which hung dangerously over his belt buckle, and despite being tall his poor posture caused him to stand like an elephant.

Elephant Man walked as slowly as a green-shelled Koopa, yet with the regular rhythm of a Goomba about to make contact with Mario.

Bum, ba-dum – ba-dum, *ba-da-da-da*-dum da-dum, da-*dum.*

I arrived at eight-o'clock and passed Mindy Davison, the receptionist, who greeted me in the midst of her frenzy. Maps, charts, and graphs hung on the walls and alongside the cubicles. On the far side of the complex was a framed geological map, and beside it a photograph of the earth from outer space, also framed.

Jon was standing in front of the cubicle complex.

"Good morning!" I said.

"Mm hey. Lemme show you 'round."

The maze of cubicles was intersected in the center by restrooms, one which displayed a flower vase, and the other to the right in which a sports magazine lay folded by the sink.

All the entry-level employees had their own cubicles, while higher-ups had offices along the perimeter of the main room. Most of the employees appeared to be in their twenties and thirties.

He led me to my own cubicle covered by a tinfoil banner with my name misspelled. I crumpled it and tossed it in the wastebasket as I examined my immediate surroundings. I sat in the swivel chair and shuffled the computer mouse.

"Giddup. You know where your place is, now we're goin' over here."

Around the corner was a portrait of a waterfall with exposed bedrock at the drop and an overhanging canopy. At the bottom right corner was the signature *Monet.* Its frame was positioned on the edge of a kitchen stool, and an upper corner was wedged into a groove in the wall plaster. Several types of rocks surrounded the bottom corner, pointing to the center.

To the left were two tall glass doors. A plaque beside them read MEETING ROOM. I grabbed the metallic handle; the door was heavier than I expected.

"This is the meet up room."

It appeared much the same as the Conference Room, only the table was positioned at an angle, and a wide projector screen hung on the opposite end.

"Now I'm gonna take you through what you do in this job. Siddown."

He flipped the light switch and pressed a button on a white projector nuzzled against the windowsill. When it failed to start, he grabbed a wrench from his pocket and smacked the side. The machine buzzed before the screen brightened. Jon grabbed a chair from the side of the table while I watched from the back.

But as soon as Elephant Man found his place, he stood up again. With a small remote he paused the video; the screen turned a heavy blue.

"Wait here, I gotta go git my coffee."

As he left the Meeting Room for the kitchen directly across the complex, I noticed his gray fuzzy slippers.

He brought back a large mug filled nearly to the brim. Drops spilled out and sizzled my skin as he lumbered by. A puddle of hot liquid had formed on the table when he set it down.

"Let's begin."

The video covered the impact of hydraulic fracturing on stream subsidence. I kept tabs on Jon just in case his elephant nature made him leave the room again; I made way to escape his tromping path. A persistent beeping noise came from behind a windowsill. He stretched and fumbled for the cordphone barely within his reach.

"Mm hey."

The jibber-jabber was loud enough to hear, but too coarse to understand.

"What's still sticking out?"

He stared in my direction.

"Quiet down, I'm with the newbie."

I smiled and waved, but Jon rolled his eyes.

"I'll try to remember. It's no big deal, no one will look for it."

His left arm flailing towards the door urged me to step out at once.

Sunshine Lady lingered by, tossing a pile of maps until they landed *plop* inside the recycling bin. She raised an arched eyebrow.

"Is *it already* over?"

I shrugged. "Apparently so."

"Well *thaat's* good. All I *need you to do then* is sign that you've *completed the training* for Environmental and Hazard Awareness."

I signed three Certificates of Training from Amy.

During lunch I observed a magnet which read FRIENDS OF COAL underneath which a train spewed out generous heaps of anthracite. The refrigerator was filled with plastic bags, most of which bore people's names. A brief episode of scrounging enabled me to find a few unlabeled ones. I formed a meal consisting of ham, cheese, leftover Cheez-Its, bottled water, and a Klondike bar.

Shadow Guy burst into the kitchen, one hand on the door handle and the other on the shoulder of a lanky young man wearing a neon-green polo shirt with blue jeans. His straight black hair spoke volumes about his bleak expression.

"*Richard, I'd like to introduce you to my pal, your co-worker, Henley.*"

Mike prompted him, but he remained silent.

"*You'll be going out together tomorrow; he's your very first trainer, and you'll be shadowing him.*"

I cringed as he spoke that word.

"*You chumps have fun out there – but not too much fun. And stay safe – but not too safe...otherwise you wouldn't have fun.*"

He winked and left the kitchen.

"Nice to meet you," I said shaking his hand.

After a long pause he replied, "Sup."

CHAPTER 4:

Steam Head

The company provided three-hundred dollars' worth of equipment oriented towards rural expeditions. I received hiking pants, wool socks, and flannel shirts, along with a bump cap with safety glasses for protection and muck boots, as well as a fifteen-foot tape measure. My rain jacket and rain pants were stowed away for such weather in a locker.

The neon-green bump cap matched the safety vest worn as the outer layer, onto which were sewn velcro and zipper pockets for storing technological and other items: an old-fashioned walkie-talkie known as the InReach near my left shoulder, a black R1 GPS receiver near my right one, and a yellow Rite-in-the-Rain field notebook on my lower left side with a customary waterproof pen to the right.

At the end of the day, all these bequeathments could be stowed away for safekeeping in my locker, onto which *ARMADALE* was printed and taped below the top hinge.

Having dressed, I became acquainted with the person in the adjacent cubicle, a gentleman looking upward and spinning counterclockwise. Evan Stroop, a Level-Two technician, was thirty-five years old but looked slightly older and acted half his days younger, a merciful assessment.

"Be sure to get napalm at Field and Stream (you'll need it)."

"*Napalm?* Why in the world would I need that?"

He grinned, raising an index finger. "Frogs get in the way sometimes (even poisonous frogs, and some that would really freak you out). When I was crossing Sharmin Creek last year, I needed to get the best quality sample of water underneath. But there were frogs, lots of them (some had brown spots all over), and they were hopping around on lily pads, getting in my way. So I threw a bunch of napalm at them and they all died (or at least went away)."

"Napalm. I'll write that down."

"Are you coming or not?" called Henley.

I grabbed my purple water bottle and brown paper-bag lunch.

The parking lot beheld a sea of gray vehicles – a few sedans but mostly pickup trucks. The label *Murray & Affiliates: Groundwater and Environmental Professionals* was fixed along the right-hand side of each one, with the phone number underneath, all parked in reverse to facilitate a speedy getaway in case of 'unfortunate catastrophes.'

"Hi there!" said a short fellow with messy brown hair and circular piercings to his ears. "I'm Adam. My girlfriend and I go fly-fishing on the weekends."

"Cool," I replied. "All I know about fly-fishing I learned from that one movie..."

"*A River Runs Through It.* That's my favorite movie. Do you know how to do fly-fishing?"

"Only regular fishing."

Henley's truck, parked right outside the locker room, flashed when he pressed the keys. With a rapid round of clicks, all doors were unlocked.

"Have you ever driven a pickup truck before?"

"Can't say I ever have." I stepped to the front door and held out my palm.

"You're not driving – I am. I don't want you to mess this up. I was just wondering."

"When do I get to drive?"

"Not today. But eventually. Normally when you start going out on your own."

I reclined in the passenger's seat, content in being paid for doing nothing.

We turned left to depart and then made an immediate right onto Fieldlands Boulevard, where the posted speed limit was twenty-five miles per hour, but everyone else was traveling faster and it seemed ridiculous to drive that slowly given the nature of the terrain.

We turned a sharp bend and came to a three-way traffic light. Another right brought us to the exit ramp for Raylee L. Shafter Highway.

"This is the way you'll usually take when you go out."

"Where exactly are we going?"

"The closest site is called Eblen. That's where we're headed."

Green hills and meadows of southeastern Kentucky rolled past us, interspersed with farmland of varying acreage. I admired the landscape while Henley focused on the road. Given his manner, he operated the truck with remarkable smoothness. Our conversation cruised through the getting-to-know-you questions quite seamlessly, though Steam Head seemed too probing of my personal life.

"How come it took you an extra year to graduate? Did you basically take time off?"

"You could say that."

We merged onto Route 60.

"What made you want to play piano for twelve years?"

"I just enjoy playing for family and friends. If they have weddings or funerals and they ask me, I play. Sometimes I play at nursing homes."

"What kind of music do you play?"

"Usually classical, other times baroque."

Steam Head scoffed.

Past a BP station, South Passage Street was the first truly rural road we experienced, replete with bumpiness and narrowing lanes.

We crossed by bridge a stream flowing parallel to the road. A winding gravel track disappeared into pine and oak trees rising in accordance with the topography. Friction of tires grinding on pebbles lasted a minute before Henley pulled onto the grass.

CHAPTER 5:

My Eureka Moment

The breeze, by which chirping birds flew, swept through the glen and softened the noonday late-August sun. Its rays illuminated the stream water bringing currents to which fish swam in rhythm.

Steam Head was still straightening his socks by the time I had donned my muck boots.

"Not like that," he spat.

"Not like what?"

"Take your boots off and tuck the ends of your pantlegs into your socks."

"What for?"

"Because that way water won't get into your pants – duh."

He stomped with his second boot, ready for action.

Henley climbed through tall grass, weeds, and cornstalks toward the streambed with a half-open gray bag of angular equipment slung over his left shoulder. Whenever I forced down the taller and thicker stalks, they smacked me in the face.

He brought out a black sensing probe attached by cord to a blue rectangular piece of plastic resembling a large phone. He placed the sensor under the stream's surface and glided it from the left bank to the right one in ten to twelve intervals, stopping for five seconds at the end of each interval.

"So why do we do this?" I asked.

"I'm taking the flow."

"I mean, *why* do we take the stream flow?"

"To see how well the stream is flowing," he said flatly, staring me down.

My mouth was not quite closed. "What is the equation for flow?"

Steam Head placed the device in his bag; the sensor was hanging out when he zipped it. "You don't need to know that."

He grabbed a small black device shaped like a thermometer. "Come close so you can see what I'm doing."

Henley removed the cap revealing a rounded, perforated surface. Numbers on the device's flashboard ranged from 6.0 up to 6.5 and around 7.0, occasionally up to 7.5 and back down to 6.0 again.

"Let me guess: You're getting the pH reading."

"Yup."

Then he pulled out two glass jars and handed one to me. He screwed open the lid and held the jar steady in the midst of the flowing current. Turning around he directed, "Do what I'm doing."

"And what is it that we're doing?" I asked with a tinge of sarcasm.

"We're taking samples."

I unscrewed the lid and let water flow into the jar. "Oh. Water samples, of course."

"*Not* like that."

I smiled. "What did I do wrong this time?"

"You have to unscrew the lid *after* you've placed the jar underwater. Plunge it down about halfway and aim it upstream. Make sure the water flows directly into the jar."

"I get it now! We're collecting stream water from the middle of the stream halfway across the streambed because that's where water flows the fastest, which means that's where we get the freshest water to use as a sample. We unscrew the jar *after* it's underwater so no air bubbles get inside, which means I should screw the lid back on while it's still underwater, *before* I bring it back up. And we're collecting this data, such as the chemical content, rate of flow, and pH from this particular stream of many because we're employees from an environmental company doing fieldwork." I gasped for breath.

He furrowed his brow. "Yeah, I guess so."

When we had almost returned to the truck, Henley stopped in his tracks. "Crap, I forgot the pH meter. Where was it?"

"I'll go get it."

I hurried back.

It was halfway underwater, a small trickling current trapping it against a piece of weathered shale. I grabbed it deftly.

I ran back to him.

He brought it up to eye-level. "Where's the cap?"

"There was a cap?"

"It had a cap, where is it?"

"I didn't see a cap, at least not when I went back to find the meter itself."

He sighed, looking down and shaking his head. "Oh well, I guess it doesn't matter."

CHAPTER 6:

Only Wealthy People

Henley turned on the radio to NPR as we ate our lunches. I munched on a ham-and-cheese sandwich while he bit into a large apple.

"Well that was fun so far."

"One thing I forgot." He handed me a piece of paper. "Review this sheet and sign at the bottom if it looks okay."

I skimmed through a page of boxes with jargon and placed my signature below the bottom margin.

"No, turn it *over* and then read *this* and then sign *here*." He flipped the page for me and pointed at the bottom line.

On the back were several more boxes which he initialed next to field indicators. Below that was a paragraph, and I signed on the bottom line. I flipped the page and stared at the front. Henley grabbed the sheet.

"It feels good to rest now," I said. "My legs are tired from going through that cornfield."

"You're already tired?"

"Good thing I work out several times a week. But this is different."

"You'll get your stream legs. Make sure you drink water so you don't get dehydrated. I haven't seen you drink any water."

"I have water with my lunch."

I ate on listening to the radio, which featured a journalist discussing drug use in America. The discussion of hard-core addiction among America's youth gradually turned to musings about alternative medicine.

Henley lowered the volume and cleared his throat. "Pot should be legal," he declared, his posture filled with confidence.

"You mean for medical purposes?"

"For all purposes."

"Even recreational?"

"Let me put it to you this way." He leaned back and folded his hands. "You know how you have to be eighteen to smoke and twenty-one to drink? I just turned twenty-seven. But I say that everyone who's twenty-four or above should be allowed to use marijuana for whatever they want."

I raised a finger. "So teenagers and college students may not be able to handle it. But by your laws, I could be a full-fledged legalized pothead in six weeks."

Henley smiled for the first time. "Don't let anyone tell you what you can or can't consume. Pot should be legal everywhere."

"As more states legalize it, that very well may happen."

Steam Head grimaced. "No, I mean all at once."

"...to cure diseases everywhere."

Scorn filled his face. "Everywhere, period. Think of how much debt our country could get out of if people started buying and selling it on a mass scale!"

"Well, we are twenty-trillion dollars in debt, last I checked." I opened my palms. "Whatever it takes, I guess."

He sighed and munched on kettle chips. "Look, I've been having a problem. My right leg's been hurting for about three months now. Last winter, I was lugging around heavy equipment while crossing a steep bank. I slipped and fell. I've been to several doctors, but none of them really agree about what's going on with it. One said it might have something to do with my back. Mainly, it hurts whenever I'm walking up steep hills."

"I'm sorry to hear that."

"It may have had something to do with the fact that I was really busy and wasn't eating enough. My calf was just skin and muscle – it was pretty disgusting. My girlfriend became concerned."

"So you have a girlfriend!" I released a chuckle. "I'm sorry. Please go on."

He swaggered his head. "She's actually pretty awesome looking. I do, in fact, have a girlfriend. You probably don't," he said, pointing at me.

"Out in the field, I wouldn't have noticed that your leg is a problem. It doesn't seem to affect your driving. Have you tried chiropractic? I've heard that helps for issues originating from the spine."

"That's an idea…. Wait – do you support the coal mines?"

"We get paid to monitor coal mining activity. If coal mines didn't exist, then I wouldn't have this job. So maybe to that extent, yes."

"I didn't know you were wealthy."

I wrinkled my brow. "I'm not wealthy."

Steam Head glared at me, disdain dripping from his voice. "My dad supports the coal industry because *he's* wealthy. I don't know what *you're* doing supporting coal mines when you're not wealthy. Only wealthy people support coal mines, and wealthy people are the only ones coal mines are looking out for. It's just the rich who work for them anyway."

He maneuvered onto South Passage Street and headed in the opposite direction from which we had come. "I'll probably just tell everyone working here that you're receiving lump sums of money from the coal industry." He elbowed me, but his face held a pained expression.

We remained silent for the half-hour ride.

CHAPTER 7:

Shot At, Not Shot

The primary individual I noticed when we returned was Brianna, a twenty-nine-year-old geologist outside the locker room jumping in her muck boots while chatting with female coworkers. She was an Eight, and her long smooth light-brown hair and wide toothy smile contributed to her rabbit-like appearance.

"Thanks for training me, that was really helpful."

"We're not done yet," he grunted.

As he unloaded the truck, I headed towards the door to converse with the jumping bunny.

"Are *you* the *new* guy?"

I introduced myself; we graduated from the same college in different years.

Happy Bunny stopped her vertical motion and faced me. "So *you* went to Prestonsburg *too?*" She also wanted to know if I studied the same program.

"What did you think of Doctor Smith?" I asked. "He's now the head of the department. Everyone thinks he's the greatest professor ever. He's definitely entertaining during lecture, but some of his tests were incredibly hard."

"Wally! You know what? *Yeah,* he can be a tough grader at times, but I learned so *much* from him when I was there. He really *is* a great guy."

The truck door slammed shut. Henley passed through our group and unlocked the entrance with another set of keys. I held the cold metal door open with an extended arm.

The floor of the locker room was a dusty gray concrete. To the right, beige vertical lockers were aligned in rows organized with linear precision, indistinguishable from those of a high school gym. The back door was half-open, revealing the edge of a shower curtain submerged in a shallow puddle. A laboratory straight ahead beheld a half-dozen men jostling each other and spurting insults.

I followed Henley into the lab; he offered a sleight-of-hand to his fellow homies.

"Watch what I'm doing."

"What is it that you're doing?"

Steam Head set the jars by the sink and turned on the water. He brought out a measuring cup, a stirring rod, and a beaker from an overhead cabinet. A wheeled cart behind us provided him with a bottle of an opaque, watery substance onto which a piece of white masking tape was affixed with 'NOx' printed in magic marker.

The banter distracted me.

A thirty-something-year-old man was the tallest and widest. "So then – so then he goes across this guy's property, the landowner we didn't know yet, and he's only looking around for the mouth of the downhill stream which..."

I lost the trail of his words amongst several side conversations now brewing.

"...just being alone near the barn and barely any trees around. He should have heard the 'get off my property' threat, or maybe that was never said at all, but continues on and next thing you know, *bang,* it blows right by his head!"

Laughter arose.

"And that's how he got shot," said Fly Fisher.

"Shot *at,*" corrected the bigger gentleman, nudging him.

"THAT'S NOT WHAT HAPPENED TO EMILY THOUGH,"

said a long-haired individual sporting chains around his neck.

"No Sam, she was fired when they realized she messed up the computer system from going on naughty websites," said the big man.

Sam inclined his head. "I'M PRETTY SURE THEY SAID SHE COMMITTED SUICIDE AT AGE THIRTY BECAUSE SHE DIDN'T WANT TO LIVE IN A WORLD WHERE HER BEAUTY WAS DECLINING."

"Wait a minute," I interrupted. "Who got shot at?"

The group turned to me.

"Hey, it's the new kid in town, Richard!" exclaimed a comrade wearing a ball cap and square plastic glasses.

I joined the group, and he gave me a noogie.

"I'm Kyle," he said, shaking my hand. "And this is Adam."

Fly Fisher held up his hand. "I go fly-fishing with my girlfriend on the weekends."

"I think you already told me that."

"And I'm Ronald, but you can call me wrong," said the storyteller.

His friends laughed and patted his back as he shook his head; even Henley snickered.

"I mean, you can call me *Ron*."

I shook his hand, a well-padded bear paw. "Ron, I just wanted to know who got shot at?"

"HE ACTUALLY GOT SHOT, BUT DON'T TELL ANYBODY," remarked Sam, hand cupped against his cheek.

"Well maybe, maybe not," Ron surmised, head and hands shifting in balance-scale mode. "But the official story is: Jacob's GPS got messed up, so to figure out where he was going, he ended up crossing over the land of someone who just so happened to be a Second Amendment champion. And this guy fired a warning shot, not meaning to kill him. This company," he emphasized, pointing downward, "decided the risk was too great of him getting himself killed or severely injured. They let him go."

A young dark-haired lady with sunglasses on her forehead walked by, carrying a tray of test tubes. "So if he's not *dead,* why hasn't anybody *heard from him?* I know some of you tried to *call."*

They stared at one another.

"Maybe he changed his number," said Adam.

"Or maybe he just moved on," added Kyle.

"Or maybe he's in jail," I conjectured.

My acquaintances stood with their mouths open, but I headed to the other side of the laboratory.

"Don't listen to what she says, she's just crazy," Ron teased.

I said to her while gesturing to Henley, "We just got back. What do people usually do once they've collected water samples?"

"I'm testing for *harmful chemicals.* That's what you guys are supposed to be *doang too."* Her leather-gloved hands fingered the test tubes. "I'm Alyssa *by the way."*

"Were you a chemistry major?"

"Chemistry *minor."*

I went back to Henley tightly wrapping in plastic several glass containers filled with a variety of colorful substances. "Are we all done with the chemical testing?"

He placed the supplies on a lower shelf. "For now. One last thing."

We washed our hands and headed through a set of double-doors into a broad hallway and over to the cubicle complex.

"I enjoyed the area we visited," I said nonchalantly. "I might want to move around here someday."

"Honestly though, I don't know how well you'd fit in – no offense. These are farmers who live here. They don't play classical piano."

Henley's place was to the right-hand corner, a cubicle with nature photographs on the side and technical manuals on the shelf.

"No offense...."

He opened an upper drawer for a folder from which he grabbed a data-entry form.

"Check to see that nobody's watching."

Everybody was absorbed in their tasks.

"This is something I've been wanting to do for a while." He wiggled a mouse to reveal an Excel spreadsheet full of names, phone numbers, and random decimal numbers. "And since you need to have everything explained to you, I'm going to tell you exactly what I'm doing with this."

Kneeling, I pointed to a PERMISSION FROM heading with an underline following the words. "Don't you need to write someone's name here?"

"I don't know what you're talking about."

I turned around to stretch, both hands on the back of my head. "Nevermind then."

CHAPTER 8:

Sunshine of My Day

Vines of ivy circled around the inside of Amy's office, with plants positioned on her desk and bookcase, on which a Buddha bobblehead leaned to the left. The upper wall displayed her academic accomplishments: a bachelor's degree in biology and a master's in environmental studies – but her master's degree was from Mark Park University, one of the easiest and worst colleges in the country. The side wall presented a hanging banner which read GO VEG. The last empty space on the right side displayed a poster reading FOUR RIVERS SOCIETY OF WOMEN ENVIRONMENTAL PROFESSIONALS.

Kyle tumbled down the aisle, colored graph in hand. When I saluted, he whipped me a smacking high-five, jolting my wrist. I stepped into Amy's open office to avoid Running Ninja.

"Don't tell me we're out of Red Bull!" I hollered.

Sunshine Lady came around the corner. "Wha-what *are you doing* there, silly!"

Her open-mouthed dog smile indicated she was tame. She sported a flower dress and carried a lilac pocketbook over her shoulder and wore high-heeled leather boots.

I stepped aside.

She half-hugged me as she slid into the room.

When I told her to guess who had been darting about, she

gave a nod of instant forgiveness.

"According to the schedule, I'm going out with Evan, but he said you're training me today."

Amy plopped in her armchair. "Yep, *that's* right! The schedule got changed up *juuust a bit* last night." She bounced on the cushion seat. "We're *going out* together."

"When do we leave?"

"Hmm...." She tilted her head upwards and brought a finger to her chin. "I have *to get dressed* first, and I'm always *the last one* to get ready. Say...*about an* hour!"

I leaned inward. "An *hour?"*

"Well...*half an* hour." Her head restored its original position and she folded both hands on her lap. "No, *twenty-five* minutes. Does *that give you* enough time?"

"Yes, plenty."

Amy sprung out of her chair and hopped over to the restroom, while I hid in the kitchen.

A plethora of scratches marked the iPhone 8.

I stopped surfing the internet when she reappeared.

She held a large sugar cookie and was dressed much the same as I was, in mostly outdoor clothes, which included a Greenpeace T-shirt.

"Kyle *brought these* today. Would *you like* a cookie?" she asked with a sparkle.

"I am quite fine right now, but thank you for asking." Blast! Why couldn't I just act normal for once and learn the Common Speech?

"See, I told *you I always* get ready last."

I held the tips of my index finger and thumb together. "You mean, you're always the *last* to get *ready.*"

"Ha." She tapped my back with her rainbow folder. "Well *okay,* mister!"

My shoulders dropped as my head sagged forward. "I'm just saying."

Despite uniform design across vehicles, I firmly believed Amy's would be painted a bright yellow. It wasn't, but she did drive a car instead of a pickup truck.

"Alrighty *now, let's* see if I can *get all snug* here. I need to *scoot up a* couple notches..." She shifted the driver's seat closer to the steering wheel "...because *I'm* short."

I should have asked about side-bumpers, since she was also fat.

"Make sure *when you drive your* vehicle, that the *seat is just right* for you."

She proceeded on the same route as Henley.

"I'm a *pretty slow* driver, but we'll *get there in pleeenty* of time."

Amy closely followed the 25 MPH speed limit. At least she was consistent when it mattered most.

"I'll turn on the radio so *you don't have to tolerate* my awkward silence." A grin crept onto her face as she held her fingers on the dial. "What *kind of music do you* personally enjoy?"

"Owl City," I responded. "I like – I like the lighthearted style they have."

Sunshine Lady slowed down on the highway. *"Aww...."* Facing back to the road she said, "Alexa, *play:* Owl City."

She drove a steady sixty in the right-most highway lane while that smirk remained. 'Bright Eyes' was the randomized selection.

At the BP station where Henley had made a left, she turned right. Suburban traffic gradually gave way to countryside meadows. She commanded Alexa to play a children's tune:

"Zip – adee-do *dah, zip* – adee ay! My oh my, what a *wonderful day.* Plenty of *sunshine...*headin' my way. Zip – adee-do DAH, zip – adee ay!"

We arrived at an isolated house where a winding stream flowed across the front yard and under a narrow bridge to a low-lying river.

Amy bestowed to me a 'baggie' of goldfish for our 'Little Adventure.'

Birds chirping in the heavens sang of our arrival. Cumulous clouds floated in the true-blue sky. The noonday sunrays reminded me to bring my water bottle.

CHAPTER 9:

Back to the Beginning

I stretched before stepping onto the mud-soaked grass and pointing at the house. "Are these the people whose groundwater we're going to help fix?"

"Well...*no, not* exactly. We just needed *to get permission* to go on their property. The *first HSW point* is over there, right *next to their* driveway." She aimed her finger to the left side of the yard. "Come *on, I'll* show you."

It was actually I who led her, considering that I was, in her terminology, 'fast.'

She set her backpack on the grass and unzipped it, pulling out the same blue device as Henley. "This *thing is called* the Hawk. You *went out with* Henley, so you *already know how to take* flow measurements, right?"

"Yeah."

"Or do *you need a* review?"

"Yes, definitely a review!"

"Okay, *show me what you* remember first."

I grabbed the Hawk, hurried to the stream, and moved the sensor across the water.

A power button was right below the blank screen. Four directional indicators surrounded a large 'OK' button. There were small rectangular buttons for all ten numerical digits. The engravement HACH-950 signified it was named after the inventor.

Her grin was wiped away. "Okay, *okay, let's start* at the very beginning." She waved her hands crosswise.

"A very good place to start."

"Now *these are called the* metersticks." Amy reached into her backpack, and when her hand came out it was wrapped around a series of yellow measuring sticks bound together like an accordion.

She placed them in my open palms.

"You know *what to do* with these."

Two bundled metersticks lay in my hands; the rickety edges felt nice to my fingertips. "What exactly am I supposed to measure?"

Amy sighed. "Okay, the *first thing* you want to do is *measure the stream* width. I'll record it." She brought out an iPhone 8.

I unfolded one of the sticks and lay it across the streambanks perpendicular to the current direction.

"Make *sure you're facing* upstream!"

I rotated the metersticks one-hundred-eighty degrees parallel with the ground. "About five-and-a-half."

She wrinkled her brow. "Five-*and-a*-half??"

Sunshine Lady came over and leaned down without bending her knees.

"So, *you've measured it* by feet. We *need it to be* in meters. That's *why I called them* metersticks. Silly!"

I flipped the *metersticks.* "One point seven."

She wagged a finger. *"Be* careful!"

The water level was up to my ankles. The right end of the meterstick lay on the edge of a flat rock. "One point eight." I bit my tongue.

"I need *it to two* decimal places."

"One point eight..." I strained forward "...two."

"That's better." Her thumb jabbed the screen. "Now *for the* depth."

The depth was to be measured multiple times across the

stream and was determined by width; wider streams required more depth measurements. I held the main part in my right hand and positioned the sensor with my left at each depth measurement. The display screen showed 0.00 before I put the sensor in the water. After ten seconds, the average velocity would appear.

The mouth, sixty feet from this point, was out of sight on the other side of the bridge. I recorded the data, per her instruction, in my notebook.

We followed the stream behind the house. A barking dog scurried onto the deck. Amy shared my affinity for animals. As I walked alongside the stream, she skipped beside me.

Then she dropped out of sight.

Sunshine Lady was standing in the middle of the stream on a large dome-shaped rock which appeared as though it had protruded from its home underground. Its wrinkled brown-gray surface made it look like it had been scorched by a flame.

She swayed while humming and mouthing the lyrics to pop music.

"Do you *know what this is* caused by?"

I stared at the extruding bedrock.

"I'll *give you* a hint. Think *back to the video* you watched *with Jon on* your first day."

"Mining! It's caused by mining."

"Well *of course* it's caused by mining, but what *is the word* for the thing I'm standing on?"

"Lumping."

"Close. This *is called* heaving, remember?" Next to her head she wove her finger around in circles.

My eyes followed her finger. "Yeah, that's what I meant, heaving."

"Okay, *good,* you know that."

She grabbed a black-and-red checkered ribbon tied in knots around a twig attached to a tree branch.

"If you see this – *this tape* – you know that the AOI *has already been* marked, that *someone already* spotted it."

"And AOI stands for..."

"Area *Of* Interest."

CHAPTER 10:

A Slow Person Indeed

A metal garden fence blocked our passage. Its wires were thin but stiff. I hopped out of the stream and onto the back yard. The fence, about half my height, continued until it reached a shrubbery-laden hillside. I saw an identical fence several yards away. In between was an exhibit of large green plants which had grown beyond the height of the fences.

I climbed over it and landed nimbly.

Amy tumbled.

I held out my hand.

We shuffled through the plants. At the other fence, I grabbed her hand before she had crossed it.

"It's *been a while* since *I've been* out." She caught her breath. "I used *to go out* a lot, but *not so much* anymore!" Sunshine Lady laughed and patted her midriff so heartily she nearly toppled. Then she cleared her throat. "Like *I was* saying, *fieldwork is* outside, but *project management is* mostly done indoors, which is *why I'm* so slow. I'm probably the *slowest one* of everyone here. Whenever *I do* go out, I *always finish* last."

She trotted on the shrinking grass.

"It's good to be thorough. You're a tortoise among hares."

"Yep." She smirked, and we hopped into the stream.

To the left came a smaller stream trickling into the one we followed.

"Since we're *running short* on time, thanks *to* me," said Amy, batting her eyelashes, "we'll *catch the trib* on our way back."

"The tributary."

"You're smart. Now let's see *if you know what this* next thing is."

Further upstream came a stretch of water diminishing to a trickle.

"It's a dried streambed."

She walked onto a section of sagging bedrock thoroughly cracked and splintered. "Do you *know what* this is?"

"Breaking."

"This is *what we call* fracture. It's best to *know these terms* when you're *out in the* field."

She reached for a tree branch. "Since *it's not marked* yet, I'm going to put *our special tape* here."

The branch bounced back to its original position once she secured the ribbon.

"Do you know *what other AOI* we need to record? You *sort of already* mentioned it."

"Lumping?"

She shook her head. "Whenever *the stream dries* up, we *call it* 'No Flow.'"

The stream turned to the other side of the dell.

I jumped across migrating point bars while she navigated the outer bend.

Hidden behind several pines we discovered a dilapidated wooden swing, where we rested in front of a large pond.

Amy gave me a short lecture on stinging nettle.

"Is this a sign of stinging nettle?" I showed her two stray red marks on my arm.

"I *wouldn't worry* about that."

We ate lunch as we swung. I thanked her for the goldfish. The ring on her finger meant she was not completely insane.

"The *next part up ahead* is treacherous, so we *might not*

get all the way through it."

"But the more difficult it gets, the more fun it will be."

"Well then *you're perfect* for this job." Amy beamed.

I hesitated. "That's what I was thinking, I just didn't want to say it."

She giggled, and I ate more goldfish.

Amy munched on a cheese stick and pineapple bits. "If you *don't see me* eating meat, do *you know why* that is? It's *because I'm* a vegetarian."

"Oh, really?"

"But I *did go to* Burger King recently."

"Burger King sells hamburgers."

"I got *the Impossible* Burger."

I widened my eyes and nodded.

"You *know, Richard,* if you *really enjoy* this kind of work and we feel you're an *asset to the* company – well, we're willing to *pay for further education* and training for employees who excel. Professional Geologist certification, GIS certificate, *master's degree,* you name it. Some people even go to *swamp school* to learn more about *this terrain in* detail."

"I thought only alligators went to swamp school."

She laughed.

"What did you say HSW stands for?"

"Hydrologic *Surface* Waters." She pointed to a tributary flowing out of a thicket of woods. "There's *another one* coming up. We should be able to *take the next flow* there even if we don't make it *all the way through* today."

The stream led to the right and up a gentle slope; the bed became deeper even as the water level remained the same. I leapt off the bank and skidded across the bed without falling.

Amy looked like she was afraid of heights. "Hold on *just a sec* there, let me get down..." Her legs dangled "...on *muh* butt."

Sunshine Lady slid into the water and became soaked.

I stood with hands on my hips. "Need a hand?"

She declined and righted herself.

"Are you okay?"

"I'm fine. I just *feel pretty disgusting* after that fall."

"I might end up enjoying this line of work more than you do." I bit my lip and tasted blood.

Sunshine Lady wiggled my cheek. "I saw you *pull that stunt* back there, you *little* superstar."

Uphill we went, I leaping across the stream and she trudging in a quagmire.

We followed a tributary into a grove with a green canopy providing shade. I swigged water. The HSW lay around the bend.

After another minute of hiking we discovered our point trapped in a zone walled off on all sides by plastic orange fencing ten feet high. To both sides it stretched along steepened banks into denser tree clusters.

"What *the hell is* this?"

I appreciated it when people in authority swore, as long as I didn't swear, because it gave me the Upper Hand, just in case I needed the Upper Hand.

"Are we *even allowed to go* through?"

Bushes with red and blue berries lined the stream along its left edge. "Maybe someone is trying to keep deer away from their gardening project."

"But *why* here?"

Sunrays poked through leaves and branches, yet the stream had grown dim. The sound of acorns dropping accompanied that of squirrels chattering. Ahead lay several hills with plants and trees slumping off edges carved by secondary tributaries, or 'tribs of a trib.'

Amy held her mouth agape. "Let's *go* back."

I took the flow outside the orange fencing; she called out measurements as I recorded them.

We returned to the clearing. Tire tracks marked both sides of a grassy path, and below appeared the landscape we had navigated.

Her backpack was smaller than most others. From the top she pulled a long plastic tube with a nozzle that she placed in her mouth.

"What kind of backpack is that?"

"It's *called a* CamelBak. It has a *pouch inside* where *you can store* water."

"Just like a camel's back."

Hedges appeared on both sides of the path, which soon became one of cobble. A black lab with its tongue hanging out ran off a balcony concurrent with the driveway.

Amy reached down to pet it. "Hey *there, little* fella."

I rubbed its fur, and it sniffed me.

"Barkla, come back here!" commanded a woman hidden behind a newspaper. "Don't worry, she's friendly."

"Rarf rarf!"

I smiled. "I can tell. Don't worry, we both love animals."

She folded the newspaper. "Where are you from?"

"We work for Murray and Affiliates. We were just down below your house, making sure the streams were flowing properly for everyone around here."

Sunshine Lady bared her teeth. Her giggle was nearly inaudible.

She nodded and smiled at the woman, who continued reading. "That's nice to know."

We passed mailboxes as a road came into view and the trickling sound returned. Her car was parked alongside the curb, two wheels on the road and two on the grass.

"Well, we *got a little bit* done."

"Don't we have more to do?"

Amy shrugged. "I'll tell them *I was training* a new recruit." She nodded.

I leaned forward with my arms open. "Tell whom – I mean, tell who?"

She opened the door. "I'll *make the phone* call. You *stay out* here."

It was four-o'clock. Sunshine Lady blabbed on with all manner of expression for minutes on end. I recuperated on a wooden bench across the street, content in my twenty-three twenty-five overtime payment.

Part Two

CHAPTER 11:

Sleeping to the Sound of Metal

With the coming of September, almost everyone was bustling about; Henley's desk was clear. CartoPac, an application of stream maps, had both a desktop and a cell phone component. CartoPac lacked a search-and-find feature, so I sometimes switched to ArcGIS.

Evan, whose computer save-screen image was the black hole of the Milky Way Galaxy, was my next trainer. His shelf held a plethora of topics related to the outdoors: forestry, fishing, kayaking, hunting, and survival skills. After spinning around, he faced me. He was wearing a Slipknot T-shirt and had a glazed look in his eyes.

"I wonder what happened to Henley? Maybe he quit when he realized he would be training me."

Evan shook his head. "He was laid off last week."

"Did he get tested for pot use?"

"No (it was because of his leg injury)."

"He could walk just fine. Is the company going bankrupt?"

He lowered his voice. "We're not supposed to talk about it."

The mystery alarmed me.

"Oh boy, Amy is crazy."

"Why is that?"

"I was just talking to myself," he said. "Your phone looks

pretty scratched up there. You can ask them for a screen re-placement (I forget who was here before you). Also, make sure you bring your JHA with you."

"My what?"

He handed me a copy of the same sheet Henley told me to sign. "Your Job Hazard Analysis. It's where you write any physical risks you come across (and what you do to adapt). For example, it's hot out today, so you'd write 'Heat' as a po-tential hazard (and 'Water Bottle' as the adaptation)."

I filled out preliminary information and folded it inside my notebook. I buckled the lower strap of my CamelBak.

Headlights flickered at the end of the parking lot.

"I bet you didn't have as much fun as I did this weekend," said Evan.

"What did you do?"

"Isn't it obvious?" he asked, arms outstretched.

"Congratulations on joining Slipknot."

He pumped his fists. "I was in the front-row seat (their concert was awesome)!"

I held the door handle of the passenger's side.

Evan dangled keys in front of me; I brushed them aside. "C'mon man, you're driving."

"How come?"

"I'm tired," he yawned. "It lasted all night (but it was well worth it). I only got a few hours of sleep."

Screaming startled me. He adjusted the dial. "I guess you can't get enough of them, huh?"

"This is actually Black Sabbath. Know the different kinds of bands (it'll help you get along with people here)."

The vehicle lurched. I shook, and the truck vibrated to the music. The gas pedal felt too sensitive and the brake too unresponsive.

The truck swerved.

Evan leaned his head against the window and snored.

The music's tempo hastened the truck's momentum, as the

reverberation of clashing metal suggested a physical collision with a nearby vehicle. I shifted into the right lane and tapped the brake, certain the onslaught of honking was directed at us.

"Could you please turn the volume down? I'm trying to keep us safe."

Boiler Brain was tranquilized by his lullaby.

"Evan, wake up!"

He blinked rapidly. "What'd I miss?"

"Turn the radio off. It's very distracting."

"The radio's not on."

"Turn the *music* off!"

"I need to keep it on (so I'll stay awake enough to show you where to turn)."

Tires screeched as I melded my toes into the brake pedal, desperate to keep my distance from the back end of a delivery truck.

"You were already fast asleep, trust me."

"Exactly!"

"Can we at least listen to something else? Some other kind of music maybe?"

"No problem." He turned the dial.

The next station played even more jarring music.

"This is the same thing!" My knuckles turned white as my fingers became iron clamps around the steering wheel.

"No it's not. Slayer – ever heard of them?"

"Anything but death metal," I demanded through clenched teeth.

"This isn't death metal (it's thrash)."

I raised my shoulders as the highway came to a bend.

"Dude, why are you going so slow? I thought we'd be there by now."

"I don't even know where we're going! It's dangerous driving while this music is playing, so I'm going the speed limit."

He flicked his hair to the side with a headbang. "Uh, *yeah,* that's called going slow."

I re-engaged the gas pedal.

"Dude, what the hell is wrong with you? Live life and stop being so old (you don't need to drive Grandma Style)."

I sighed. "Look, I just want to listen to something where these kinds of guys aren't screaming. It's just not good driving music."

"These aren't all guys, you know (some female singers do hard rock). Want me to prove it to you?" He motioned to the dial.

"No thanks."

"So you're saying you're sexist?"

I took a deep breath and lowered my voice. "Look, now that you're wide awake and we're miles from where we started could you at least direct me?"

Evan fell back into the reclined truck seat. "Whatever."

CHAPTER 12:

Boiling Over With Ideas

The trip to Harvon took twice as long as the one to Eblen. Evan directed me to park in a small abandoned gravel lot with a humming generator in the center. The buzzing drowned out everything he told me as we assembled our gear. The country road I had driven cut across the rising hillside. Across the valley, a school bus with broken windows and flat tires was sinking into a swamp.

I finally heard him once we approached a jungle-like neck of the woods with a gushing stream.

"...so that they know that we didn't monitor that length of the stream." Boiler Brain looked at me like he was prompting me to do something.

"I'm sorry, all I heard you say was that this length of the stream is not monitored."

"Exactly. So you want to record the mouth to here as 'Not Monitored' on CartoPac."

With iPhone strapped around my left wrist, I stared at the open app displaying an intricate map.

Evan inspected the screen. "The mouth is point 0 (so you want to mark that with the green reticle). And you see how it lists our present location as 3452? That's how far upstream we are in feet from the mouth (you mark *that* with the red reticle). And you identify that segment as 'Not Monitored.'"

"That's the best explanation anyone has given me so far."

"You're welcome. Remember to record that in your note-book too; that way you'll have a backup in case something happens to your phone (and vice versa)."

I wrote in my notebook, using the abbreviation 'NM'. When I closed my vest pouch, I turned my attention back to my first legitimate trainer.

"What do you think we do next?" he prompted.

"We walk along the rest of the stream."

"You want to record a new section at 3452 and label that as 'F' for 'Flowing.'"

Some abbreviations on my handheld schedule still puzzled me. "What does *gurns curr* mean?"

"Pardon?"

"The spelling is 'G-r-n-s-C-r'."

"That's the abbreviation for Greene's Creek (where we are). Usually 'Creek' is abbreviated with just a 'C'."

We followed the stream into the fullness of the woods. Woodland creatures called out to each other amongst dwell-ings therein. Tree branches reached out above, bearing leafy green surfaces ascending stepwise throughout the vale and into the sky, effectuating a high canopy. The stream flowed in twists and turns along the dimmed passage.

We came to the school bus sitting on the hillside. "What could've happened there?"

He shook his head. "It's been up there for a while (ever since I started working here six years ago). I wonder how many dead children there are."

My boots splashed in the watery trenches. Evan stepped across the bank a few paces ahead.

"Hopefully none. Do you not like children?"

"I hate children," Boiler Brain replied. "I've hated them for as long as I can remember."

"What was your childhood like?"

"Pretty chill for the most part (I guess)."

Stumbling, I hurried along the outer embankment. "If you remember your childhood and you've always hated children, then you must have hated yourself when you were young."

He halted, boots covered in mud. I was a few steps ahead of him. "Yeah (pretty much)."

He caught up to me.

"I'm glad I don't have any kids (they're such a nuisance). And they're so much responsibility that they take all the fun out of life."

All the water from cascading tributaries became part of the main channel.

"What does your –"

"I'm single. Women are nice at first (but then they start to suck your life away). I value my freedom (so I can do everything I ever wanted as a kid)."

"Like this, what we're –" I slipped on a patch of wet moss and skidded into the stream like a baserunner as the cold water soaked my hiking pants.

Evan stepped back and laughed. "Especially this. Nice one!"

I righted myself.

Leftward, we followed an intersecting tributary much narrower than the main stem with a less active current. A soft light-brown glow accompanied the reflection of light from sunrays barely peeking through the overbrush. The stream wound up to the road.

"What do you notice about this stream?" he questioned.

"It's a different color."

"That's right. I've been recording this as 'Orange Staining' (one of the preloaded comments in CartoPac)." He tapped his phone several times before scribbling in his notebook. "You also have to indicate whether each AOI is new (but only if it's over five-hundred feet). And you keep reporting it until remediation takes place. In the Field Review (which can be incredibly slow sometimes) you want to make sure there's the letter

'T' next to the term 'new no flow' (indicating that it's *true* that you're reporting it for the first time)."

"But what if it's an AOI other than a No Flow?"

"It's labeled that way because No Flows are the most common kinds of AOIs."

Bright light shone as we emerged from the woods to a broad grassy floodplain.

"The stream just stopped," I observed. "What a coincidence, a No Flow!"

Evan nodded. "So, record it. We're at 4757. And make sure you create an SCM table for these distances at some point (every stream over a thousand feet needs one)."

"Stream – Current...Monitor!"

He smiled.

"Why is there orange staining back there?"

"Orange staining can be caused by two things."

We quickened our pace.

"It could be caused by mining (specifically acid mine drainage). It could also be caused by iron-oxidizing bacteria. The orange coloring back there was definitely the second."

"What does the first one you mentioned look like?"

"It's really obvious if you see it. It will look really unnatural (almost like thick shining paint)."

A series of logs from fallen trees appeared. We traversed them one-by-one, and the stream began flowing on the other side.

I updated the SCM table accordingly. "Seems like you have a knack for science."

"I love science."

Evan kicked the deepening water with many splashes.

"Especially because it's interesting and useful (but also because it's the enemy of religion). Remember what happened to Galileo?"

"Is there a particular religion you especially hate?"

"Nope (just all religion)."

He swung himself over a large block of sandstone.

I executed the same move.

"When I was fourteen, my grandmother was really sick, so I prayed my ass off that she'd be okay (but she ended up dying anyway). I figured there's no point to it."

Evan stepped slowly across several rocks, his head bowed low.

I tested the deepening waters accumulating beside a pile of bramble. "Do you think if she stayed alive longer you'd be religious?"

He stopped again. "No (that experience was just a catalyst for getting me to think for myself). It's easier to think clearly when you don't assume that things happen because of unexplainable forces."

I waded into a rapid descent of the bed. Water filled my boots and rose into my pantlegs as I realized I forgot to follow Henley's advice.

When he saw me scrambling, he climbed onto dry land and reached out his hand. Thanking him, I rolled onto the grass where we settled down and opened our lunch bags.

"See, if I believed in life after death, I'd just leave you there to drown (knowing you'd be in heaven). But I helped you. My rational worldview is what makes me a good person (most religious people I've met are stupid hypocritical bigots)."

I gave a subtle nod while tasting the small grains of salt on the chips crumbling in my mouth. "So then you'd never consider the possibility of an afterlife?"

He furrowed his brow and stared at the rushing water. "Only if scientists seriously investigated the possibility of multiple dimensions and experimentally proved the existence of them."

"You should see what they're doing at CERN." I explained the acronym as he thumbed his phone screen.

"Why do you think religious people don't believe in evolution or climate change?"

"Because people from certain denominations believe that their doctrine is authoritative on both the natural world and a spiritual world," I said. "But in my experience, it's evolution and the big bang that are dismissed."

"But millions of religious people are climate skeptics," he said chewing a granola bar, "which makes some politicians not want to do anything about it."

I reached for my CamelBak nozzle and took a long fresh swig of water. "And you think politicians *should* do something about climate change?"

He dropped his peanut-butter-and-jelly sandwich and spat out the bread. "Absolutely! Even if it turns out not to be true, they should do something just in case. I actually want to pay more in taxes (so I can help the government fight our climate catastrophe)."

"I wish I could be in your place and make whatever amount of money you make. I really do, but you know my position only pays fifteen-fifty an hour."

Unzipping a bag of chocolate chip cookies, he replied, "The federal government is awesome, dude (the jobs are so slick)! I've considered working for them so I can serve our country. I want to do high-level research (probably on environmental issues so we can clean up all this pollution). I have a lot of great ideas and I'm actually a genius; I'm just too lazy to put things into practice (but I'm pretty sure I could solve the problems of the universe), and if I was better at math, I'd do research in astrophysics. But I'm cool with watching Neil DeGrasse Tyson (who, of course, teaches about the big bang theory)."

"I've seen Carl Sagan's version of *Cosmos* as well as his. Tyson was supposed to have a sequel coming out soon, but it got cancelled for some reason."

"It's actually *not* cancelled (which means science is on its way to completely replacing religion)." He crumpled his trash and stowed it inside a compartment of his red Spider-Man backpack.

Boiler Brain propped himself up and stretched. "I hope someday there are no more self-righteous bigots telling us how rock and roll is sending us to hell. Heck, even Jesus never said anything about rock music (then again, he lived his whole life without ever contributing to scientific research), if he was even a real person."

I nearly choked on saliva as I got to my feet. "What do you think happened in the year zero?"

An episode of laughter overwhelmed him; he buckled over and groveled. "Sorry, what you just said was so funny and it reminded me of a hilarious movie with Jack Black (it's called *The Year Zero*). You should totally check it out!"

My eyes sifted the landscape until he recovered from his laugh attack.

CHAPTER 13:

Red Piercing Eyes

The stream wound to the other side of the floodplain, where tributaries trickled from the hillside forming a swampy environment. Evan told me we needed to take a flow measurement, but that it was impossible to do so.

"Couldn't we try to measure whatever water is still running?"

"Whenever it's difficult to do so because it's barely flowing, you want to record that as a Non-Measurable Flow that's too Low for a Flow (or 'NMF-LF'). What did you notice about the trib right behind us?"

"Which one are you referring to?"

"See all that water?" He pointed all over the place. "That's actually a stream which (for some reason or another) has begun to settle like a swamp. When it's spread out like that, we refer to the condition as 'Diffuse.' Now let's make sure the rest of this trib is flowing (come on)."

The tributary led to the edge of a hillside. Steep rocky banks flanked the trickling trail.

When we arrived at the guardrail beside the road, Evan raised his head to the remainder of the hill. "You know what, let's look for an FOP near the STP where it ends (when we come back around the other way)."

We sped down in half our ascension time.

Onward, we crossed a metal pipe spewing water into the channel; below and around the pipe, the sod was overturned, and large gray rocks pointed toward our feet. Soon enough, we reached a soft grassy field, and a long red line appeared on my screen.

"That's the buffer (where we stop monitoring). Each day you'll see a red box on the computer part of CartoPac (which designates the area we monitor). Go ahead and record that it's flowing up to the buffer."

I tapped the stream and marked it with an 'F' up to point 6031.

"Good (tell me what else you need to do)."

"Record that it's flowing on the other side of the buffer?"

"But normally we don't bother with that (anything beyond the buffer zone). What did we do when we first started?"

"You said something about 'Not Monitored.' Of course, the stream on both sides of the buffer is not monitored."

"There ya go."

A curved stone lot with parked trucks merged into the eroding hillside.

We marched upwards, where Evan directed me to take the lead finding the tributary segments we missed.

"How come we passed them?"

"I told you we were going to catch them on our way back. The stream starts from up there (flows under the road) and goes all the way down to the mouth." His finger followed the path.

I took the lead. We walked single-file alongside the curb. My GPS showed a stream labeled GrnsCr-3L. If I turned around, all the streams on my right would be designated with an R. I ignored a distant rumbling.

We climbed onto the streambed, which now carried a diminishing flow. Soon it became difficult to determine if the stream was flowing or merely wet.

"I knew it, this Flow Origination Point is below the Stream Termination Point. Select 'FOP' but not 'FOP-A' (the 'A' means

'At the STP')."

"Why do we need to go all the way to the STP?"

"Just to make sure it doesn't start flowing again."

The bed merged with the rocky ascent.

As Evan followed close behind, I grabbed the tree branches, which I followed to their trunks and used them to propel myself upward. Near the summit lay a small alcove with a mound of dirt piled against the inner side.

"There's one more stream we have to check," said Evan, drinking from his water bottle, "but it's on the other side of the valley we came through." He saw my expression and added, "Which is why I parked down below here."

I placed the keys on the hood and stood by the passenger's side. When he started the car, I turned down the volume.

Our final destination presented a narrow but deep stream channel in full flow. Although lower in gradient, this hillside was wider and longer, covered by patches of farmland interspersed with hemlocks and evergreens.

"Let's go!" I exclaimed.

"If you didn't notice, there's actually an HSW just up from the mouth."

He hovered his meterstick over and along the surface waters.

"Can't you just put it down and take the flow at any of those lengths?" I asked. "They all seem close enough together and close enough to the indicated point."

He looked sideways. "I'm measuring it at a width of one-point-one meters. For some reason, the technology is designed so that one-point-one gives you the fewest number of flow measurements (much fewer than, say, one-point-oh meters). The other lucky values are two-point-one, two-point-six, five-point-six, and twelve-point-one."

Evan winked, and I grinned. "You're quite the connoisseur for efficiency."

He turned his palm outwards. "They get paid for completing the job (whereas we get paid per point)."

As various farms came into view, I spotted cattle, horses, and other farm animals grazing and trotting. Halfway up, we encountered a long, dense line of trees.

Evan made no hesitation in entering the thicket. The oncoming stream splashed beneath our boots. He raced forward only to stop at once, standing straight and scanning the terrain. I stepped in front of him but was knocked over by a barrier.

His bemused expression blocked my view of stratus clouds drifting far above the treetops. He extended a hand. "You alright there, dude?"

I inspected our surroundings for some evidence of the force. I counted five thin gray wires running like lines of latitude on a Mercator projection. A *boing* came forth when I plucked the middle wire.

He knelt and inserted into the soft earth a pointy metal probe, which was attached by a delicate wire to a plastic handheld object with a curved metal hook. It resembled a black shaver in its shape, but not in its intended use. He placed the curved hook around the lowest wire. "It didn't light up (so we're good to go)."

Evan placed both hands on a cylindrical wooden post and swung himself over the top.

I dropped my CamelBak over the top wire and wiggled my way under the electric fence. Brown goo crept onto my hands; I wiped my fingers on my damp pantlegs.

He trudged through, heading to the right.

I looked over my left shoulder.

The creature was still sleeping. Snorting, it had heard something that disturbed it. It was definitely not a beast; it was a thick log. Or maybe a large brown rock. Some rocks have horns anyway. There was another beside it, also moving. The first one strode near us, but not toward us. The second one lumbered to the side of the first one and could not see me.

My left leg plunged into a pit of light gray matter thicker than the mud pit. The stench was terrible. I wrenched my knee upward, to no avail. I was literally trapped in a pile of bullshit!

Boiler Brain was vanishing from sight.

I tried freeing my leg again, lifting harder. My sock popped out, but the boot was sinking. I stood on my right leg and grabbed its outer cuff.

The snarling creature was closer.

I tugged with all my might and fell flat on my back, arms around the boot. Red piercing eyes of the ninth one met mine, or perhaps they belonged to the eighth.

Hopping on my right foot, I slipped the boot on; it felt heavier. I hobbled to the corner of the arena and caught up to him. I stepped to his right side. Evan sat on the corner post, swiveled around, and dropped to the ground.

I held the wires steady. With a sudden jolt, my arms flung to the sides; I yelped.

Boiler Brain continued onward.

Numerous tree rings wound their way around the flat circular surface of the post. The area was just big enough for my palms, one on top of the other.

"Hyah!"

I swung my scrambling legs, landing with a commando roll on the unforgiving ground. Standing up, I brushed myself off. Now I could see what those savages were doing.

They were bored out of their minds.

I ran to a picket fence, where Evan clapped slowly. "Way to go, Link (lots of people lose their boots there)!"

"You could have told me you were taking me into a bullpen!"

"But then you would have opted out."

"Wasn't there a better way?"

"Not really."

I opened my dirty hands to the side. "Thanks for sticking by me."

"No problem, soldier." He patted me on the shoulder. "You should have taken the outside edge."

"And you should have taken the inside way!"

He tore aside a loose wood-exposed unit of the fence. I slipped through, into the great beyond.

"I can sort of see the STP from here (I think it's flowing). We can go there (or I can mark it as 'Flowing' and call it a day)."

"Let's call it a day."

We weaved our way like skiers down the grassy scarp.

"Did you just call me Link back there?"

He patted my back. "I heard what you yelled when you jumped over the fence. Like I said, you're a soldier (a hero)."

"So you're a *Zelda* fan too."

"Played every game (well, almost every game)."

"I always enjoyed throwing the chickens around and helping villagers with their weird complaints."

Evan nearly slipped as we reached the end of the slope. He opened a rickety gate and jumped onto a grassy knoll near the side of a road. "Yeah...I wouldn't do that kind of stuff while you're working here."

"I won't throw anyone's chickens."

CHAPTER 14:

Pick Up the Race

I filled the blue plastic water pouch of my CamelBak halfway because filling it to the brim made it too large to fit inside the main compartment. A shadow above the kitchen sink hovered as I washed my hands; resting on a long cylinder was an oval with a triangle pointing slightly downwards, a form reminiscent of half a diagonally-cut ham sandwich.

"You know," came a cartoonishly nasal voice more bothersome than nails on a chalkboard.

A slim but unathletic figure towered into the stratosphere. His body was perfectly straight, save the crick in his neck. If this awkward monument looked up just once, a satisfying crack would sail along his vertebrae as the myelin sheath therein glided up to the tip of his spine and aligned his head with the rest of his body, correcting his kyphotic posture. He was as tall as Elephant Man, but his body stayed within its proper confines. He could have been anywhere from twenty to forty years old.

"You know."

His Adam's apple bobbed with the fluctuating pitch of his voice. He held a narrow bony finger in the air longer in any direction than the fist from which it protruded.

"I was just going to tell you, that if you perhaps wanted to make things more convenient for yourself, you could fill up your jimjam there the previous afternoon, before you head home, and place it in the refrigerator, so that by the following morning, you would have a fresh pack of water to bring with you, and you would be all ready to go."

My right eyelash twitched. If Encyclopedia Brown here wanted to tell me how to do the least important part of my job, he could have instructed me from the very beginning.

I stood there petrified, grinning awkwardly. "Thanks."

"You are quite welcome. If you need any more advice, just come to me."

I extended a hand. "What's your name?"

He grabbed my fingers and wiggled his elbow up and down. "My name is Kevin."

"Cave in? Where are you caved in?" I pried away his skeletal hand.

Shaking his head back and forth repeatedly he replied, "N-no, listen carefully. My name is: *Kevin.*"

"Nice to meet you."

"I am a project manager."

Running Ninja burst through the kitchen door. "Hey Richard, Amy wants to – hey Kevin, good to see you bud! – she wants to ask you something, if you have a minute."

Kevin disappeared like a paper mâché when he turned to the side. As they exchanged high-fives, I seized the opportunity to slink past Encyclopedia Brown.

I passed an empty office and found Amy scanning a pile of JHAs.

"Well *hi,* Richard! Was *that guy* named *Kevin talking to you* over there?"

"Yeah, he was sharing his expertise with me."

"*Oh,* okay. I just *wanted you to* know *I'm here to* help, sweetie. Is there *anything you need* that would *make this job* easier for you?"

"Could I get some of those vine clippers? I got scraped pretty badly by thorns yesterday. And it would be easier, even while I'm being trained, if I had a Hach of my own."

Amy smiled, holding her hands together. "I can *definitely get you* clippers, but the Hach isn't available *for individual purchase* anymore, and it costs us *six-thousand dollars* to get a new one. There *is a much* cheaper brand I *could get you* though."

I thanked her as I left to examine the picture, still balanced on its corners. I held each rock circled around it and placed my hand on the frame.

"I wouldn't touch that if I were you."

"I didn't know I was working in a museum."

"We're not supposed to touch it."

I released my hand.

The serious expression on the thirty-year-old's face was complemented by a head of spiky dark-brown hair, its middle strip receding. He was almost average in height and about an inch shorter than I was. "What's your name – kid?"

"Richard. But who are you to ask for my name?"

"I'm training you today. You all ready?"

I shoved the pouch into my CamelBak. "Almost."

"Come on – let's go."

The stranger took me by the hand and led me to his 'pick-up.' He zipped out of the parking lot before I had buckled my seatbelt, and drove towards Baylor.

Driving was his artistic expression; he weaved through narrow spaces between vehicles, swearing under his breath. Although he strongly preferred the left lane, he would shift into the right one if a car was traveling too slowly, and all of them were. Breaking forcefully before slamming into trucks in the right lane, he then shifted into the left one, mistiming his flick of the turn signal, and regained his velocity once again, never forgetting to curse the driver who made him slow down, blasting more honks than he received.

"What did you say your name is?"

"Bo."

As he swerved around every sluggish obstacle, I examined him. Bo was a gruff individual, rough and rugged to the very core, either gruff because he bore scruff *or* decidedly scruffy because he was gruff.

Under the handbrake lay his notebook, two letters consuming the front cover. Occupied by the challenge before him, Racecar Dude didn't notice me snag it.

His first and last name were printed on the inside. Bo's notes were largely unreadable. Swift black strokes filled the pages, eating up every line and rendering the margins nonexistent. Every letter was capitalized, and almost everything was an abbreviation. In columns of numerical values taken to the second decimal place, he omitted the 0 where expedient.

He had fallen silent on the empty country roads before us, where he was the only driver. Racecar Dude reduced his speed very little from the exit, and with no one to yell at, he had nothing to say. Indeed, he spoke more in expletives than he did in plain English. Every twist and turn he handled expertly. And as I interrogated him, I realized the one thing I hated more than the driving of Bo Milako was his tone.

"What's the speed limit on these roads?"

"Fifty-five."

"But you're going seventy-five."

He glanced at the dashboard. "Yeah."

"Have you ever been in a crash or gotten a ticket?"

"No crashes – many tickets."

We approached the backside of a small buggy traveling the speed limit. Racecar Dude screamed and honked relentlessly, raising his finger, raising his voice, doing everything in the road rage playbook. Verbally harassing the slow grandma made her turn into a guardrail, providing a speedy getaway for us.

Upon a near-collision with a parked police car he reassured me, "Don't worry – they're always empty."

"Why don't you drive a *little* more slowly, just this *one* time?"

"I'm driving *defensively* – that's when you drive in a way that minimizes the risk of crashing."

"Right...."

"And I suck at driving slow."

"You sure do."

Bo slowed down to fifty-five as we came into town and zoomed past a flashing '25 MPH' school zone sign. I closed my eyes.

CHAPTER 15:

Thwarted Expectations

The parked vehicle leaned over the curb, creating a shadow over the entrance to a wooden ramp leading up to someone's front porch.

"Can't you park somewhere less embarrassing?"

"This is right where we need to be – the people down the street are assholes – and the wheelchair guy here doesn't have the backbone to stand up to me."

I developed a case of the hiccups.

He tore out two pieces of paper and handed one to me. "I divided the schedule so it's fair knowing you're a newcomer – this one's mine this one's yours – we start out together then split up."

"Why did you – *hic* – only give yourself three?"

"These are much longer and all of yours are really short – you actually have less total walking."

Bo handed me a large rectangular box with a black top and a shoulder strap. "You can borrow this extra McBirney."

When I turned the power on, the device was instantly prepared to record. "Can we trade? I'm used to the Hach."

"I'm using a McBirney too."

"Why do you prefer the McBirney?"

"It's one-handed and much faster."

Racecar Dude knocked aside the trashcans on the driveway

and barged forward. Behind the trees and along the edge of the back yard lay a large pond connecting two segments of stream water, around which tall crabgrass rose from green-gray muck.

"Are ponds considered AOIs?"

"Ponds are flowing – need me to explain why?"

I thought about a pond in the reserve of my own neighborhood. "No, I understand."

Although using it was convenient, carrying the McBirney was unwieldly. It was fastened inside a small black bag with a long strap, and it was heavier than the Hach. It strained my shoulder, so when one became tired I reversed the strap and held it by the other. When I sped up, it dangled and banged against my knees. I pried it out of its bag and stowed it among Bo's items. The plastic box barely fit inside the second pouch of my CamelBak, which added a few pounds to the load. I tightened the straps, transferring the weight to my upper body.

He lunged into the stream water on the other side of the pond, and the impact created an airborne splash that soaked my hair. I marveled at the precision of his footsteps and the efficacy of his gait as he waded upstream, jogging alongside him on the relatively dry bank.

"Are you by chance a fan of NASCAR?"

"NASCAR sucks – they go too slow." He ran up escalating rocks of a miniature waterfall.

"Too slow?" I started crawling.

Bo marched on the leveling ground and jumped over a fallen tree trunk, two feet at once, landing squarely but never stopping. "They have technology that can make cars go five-hundred – but they're not using it because they don't want to lose their fan base – the older generation who can barely handle two-hundred."

Stream segments similar in width and velocity quickly spread away from one another.

"This is where we split up – you take the left one." And

with a flash he sped away, a light beam traveling from Earth to the deepest reaches of space.

I strolled alongside the first stream on my list. The bank grew higher and higher, forming a small gully, and roots of red oaks climbed the soil-ridden sides. Periodically, I checked both the GPS and the stream list. Hardly ten minutes passed before I realized that HerkC-49 had scrolled downward only a tiny bit on the screen. I reviewed the list of streams assigned to me.

I directed my steps to our starting point, jumping down the waterfall and traversing around the pond.

Relaxing on a wooden bench hidden by a clump of trees just beyond the property boundary, I used my CamelBak as a pillow; my legs dangled through the arm rest at the other end. The modest logwood house filled the background as I punched in numbers for every velocity, depth, and width. For reference, I could also view previously recorded flow values and stream issues.

I righted myself to the sound of a creaking door followed by approaching footsteps, and greeted the woman on the freshly pollinated back yard.

"Excuse me," she said softly, raising her hand, "I don't know if you happen to be associated with Murray and Affiliates…"

"I am, and that parking job was not mine."

"Well, my son needs to catch the bus for school any minute now. It would be great if you could talk to the person inside that truck."

"Is he trying to highjack it? Who's inside the truck? There's not supposed to be anyone inside!"

I tromped across the yard and ran up the stone steps at the side of the house and onto the porch. The window was down, and smoke billowed out, with a few orange sparks inside. I crept across the wooden ramp, trembling. My muck boots squashed as I peeked into the vehicle.

Racecar Dude was lighting up another cigarette. "Looks like you went the wrong way – partner! You alright with maps?"

I coughed and pointed at the expanse of trees. "I'm great with maps. We're supposed to be out *there* doing fieldwork, not in *here* doing drugs."

"Cigarettes aren't drugs – I thought you'd be smart enough to know that."

"I also spoke to the lady who lives here."

"What did you do?!"

"She says the school bus is coming, and that her son needs to get on so he doesn't miss it."

He leaned back with smelly socks resting on the dashboard, and shrugged, cigarette sticking out of his mouth. "Forget it – go back to your work."

I clenched my open palm in front of him. "It's *our* work, and if *we* don't finish what we started, I'm telling Amy about your truancy."

Bo licked his scruffy lips tauntingly, and I chuckled at the ongoing irony. "Good luck with that – I've been here for seven years now. I started in your lowly position seven years ago when my parents got divorced – when you were just a measly dork in high school. I've been here longer than almost any other technician. I'm their most trusted asset – and if you so much as raise one of your cute little fingers at me – I'll accuse you of what I've been doing!" The pointer finger of his thrusted arm was directly in my line of sight.

I smiled and nodded, tapping on the door, and climbed into the seat.

A teenager came rolling out of the house. He was pale and gaunt, and he wore a white shirt. His backpack hung on the back of his wheelchair. The graceful smile spoke volumes about years of trials patiently endured. Out of all the handicapped people I had ever met, he was the fastest when it came to spinning the wheels forward.

Racecar Dude gave a passing glance.

He approached the end of the ramp. "Hi there!"

I leaned through the open window.

"I don't mean to bother you guys if you're taking a break from some really important work. But this is my last day to make up a class, so if you could please move the truck forward a little, that would be terrific."

"Hang on – hang on." Bo grabbed the base of my skull and turned my head inward. "Listen – this one's all on me. Just say what I tell you to say – and I'll help you get promoted."

"Yeah, sure."

"Tell him if he doesn't roll back inside – I'm gonna blow his f**king brains out."

The boy waited. "I just need you to move a little so I can get out, and then you can back up to where you are now, I promise."

"Okay, but like you said, it's all on you," I whispered. "You're the one who would supposedly have it and shoot –"

"Right right now tell him before it's too late."

The long yellow figure traveled leftwards in the distance, then disappeared, then came toward us.

"Hey kid, what's your name?"

"Timmy!"

"I'll tell you what, Timmy, I need you to do something simple, I need you to..."

The bus engine grew louder.

"Yes?" The corner of his lip twitched.

"Tell your mom that if we don't move right now, she can sue us!"

"What?!" Bo's voice quavered.

Timmy opened his mouth wide and laughed as he wheeled his way back. "Thank you so much!" He closed the door.

CHAPTER 16:

Fiery Tears of Rage

Grasping the steering wheel, he shifted into drive and floored the gas pedal; the engine revved with his own rushing adrenaline. The back tires flung patches of over-turned grass onto the windshield, so he karate-chopped the wipers into full speed, creating a mess that only cleared when abundant wiper fluid drenched the glass.

Racecar Dude maintained his speed, heading further south, GPS raised above the steering wheel.

He shook his head. "Just what the hell do you think you were doing back there?"

"I don't think it would help my case if I tried to explain."

"No – it wouldn't."

I clenched my teeth, concerned about his reddening complexion. "Sorry, I was just under a lot of pressure."

Bo scoffed. "You sure don't handle pressure well."

The delicate silence gnawed at my chest. I disguised my breathing under his outburst.

"So much for the promotion I generously offered you – see if I ever give you a good recommendation!"

He nearly slammed into the side of a roundabout.

"It takes two years working in your position to get promoted but I could've had you working at my level by the end of the year."

Without sacrificing speed, he glared at me with a loathsome expression, the pinnacle of disdain.

"Don't think I've taken my eyes off you just because we're going faster than you can handle. I see you sitting there proudly – you little good-for-nothing do-gooder!"

His voice shook near the end of that slight, and the glint in his eyes manifested fiery tears of rage.

"You're such a goody two-shoes! I bet no one actually likes you or thinks you're cool – I bet your parents are still together you silver spoon loser!"

"Bo, look. I'm fine, you're fine, and the people back there are fine. What's the big deal?"

He sped onto an alternate highway.

"The people back there – the father – he was the lawyer responsible for my parents' divorce when my dad didn't know how to fix the water – and *he* still gets to keep his wife! And then you come along and almost make them sue our company – I can't believe it."

"Oh!"

"Do you know what would happen if we got sued? You'd lose your job! Even worse – *I* might lose my job."

"I shouldn't have been so stuck-up back there. I guess I really do need to chill out more."

"Yes – now you see."

He shifted left and right, and left again in his usual pattern, muttering insults and curses under his breath, his lines well-rehearsed.

Then he cracked a smile. "It's good you realize that about yourself so someone else doesn't have to tell you."

"If Timmy's father is a lawyer, why don't they have a bigger house?"

"It's a long story. They actually just moved there as far as I know and they had to pay a shitload during the lawsuit – but no amount of money can replace the relationship my parents once had."

I leaned back, and Racecar Dude accelerated on the empty lane.

"What about the stream data we're supposed to collect?" I wondered.

"Did you collect any?"

I winked. "Let's just say when I saw the list you handed me, I took a few creative liberties."

He waved his hand. "Just plug stuff in and look back to make sure it fits with the rest of the data. If anyone says anything – I know how to talk my way out of it."

"Did you actually finish your list?"

"Sort of – but I more or less ended up doing the same as you."

As I typed in digits, I viewed the houses of suburbs perched on rolling hills, some with flowing streams. "What would you say the purpose of this job is?"

"We do environmental consulting for energy companies."

"Which companies?"

"Conrad Power and CNG – but this is supposed to be confidential."

"Everyone knows about Conrad, but who's CNG?"

"Conrad Natural Gas – they're a branch of Conrad Power which focuses on coal."

"So both are basically a single organization. Any others?"

Racecar Dude swerved away from a line of stationary orange cones, slamming the horn with an ear-piercing honk that startled a highway patrol officer wearing a bright yellow vest.

He flattened his brow. "Not that I know of."

"What would happen if we didn't do this job? Or if this job didn't exist?"

"Sometimes energy companies and the government will get in bed with each other – they'll start paying the government to ease off regulations a bit – that's why according to law there has to be an independent third-party agent to give an unbiased report of environmental conditions. That's where we come in."

At a traffic light that turned green at precisely the right time, he veered left onto an intersecting country road, dismissing the right-of-way of oncoming traffic.

"Since we also provide remediation services the streams wouldn't be fixed – they would eventually recover after a really long time but peoples' wells would dry up and might even get contaminated."

"From pollution?"

Bo bobbed his head back and forth. "You could say that but not exactly – there are always pollutants in the water – the issue is how much? The remedial part of Murray puts augmentation units into the ground – or AUGs – which bring up more groundwater into the streams to dilute any contaminants."

Ribbons of streams wove throughout homelands. "The ideal situation is to have every stream flowing freely with fresh, clear water."

Bo shrugged.

"I have an unrelated question, Bo. And I don't want you to take this personally. But I was just wondering if we are in some kind of hurry?"

"I have to work here on Sunday – it's Friday which means I only have a one-day weekend. I need to get an early start to relaxing so I don't burn myself out working too hard at this job."

"That won't happen to you. Do we ever work on Saturdays?"

"Rarely – if we do we get the following Monday off. You might have to work one Sunday every month or two and you'll get the following Friday off."

"But you are aware that you drive faster than pretty much everyone else, right?"

"So? What's your point? Everyone knows the speed limit is the lower limit anyway – which only grandmas drive."

He decelerated behind an oiler truck traveling the lower limit.

"Whose grandmother do you think is ahead of us?" I asked.

Racecar Dude performed his entourage, rhythmically combining insults, profanity, curses, and gestures with flickering headlights and honks, both smooth and staccato. I bounced in my seat to the symphony of lights, sounds, and dialogue starring a hero rescuing his one-day weekend from the loss of a few hours.

Our guest made a right turn. Perhaps it was too ornery for the elderly.

The truck lurched down a winding road and careened along the curve, tilting sideways in the air. The brief rotation forced my body against the door.

Clink!

The back edge of the truck struck against the inner guardrail.

"Slow down!" I demanded.

We landed on four tires like a cat landing on its four paws. His vehicle lost traction under screeching brakes, and an oncoming vehicle slammed *crunch* into the left headlight.

The seatbelt wound around my waist as airborne shards of glass clattered onto the hood of the recipient's car. The truck was halfway across the yellow lines.

Bo reached across me and opened the glove compartment.

He communicated with a man shorter, thinner, and older than he, a fellow sporting a gray mustache and a farmer's hat. Racecar Dude explained away his mistakes, his mouth moving at the speed of his own driving, and I was rooting for him until the other man's shoes were no longer touching the pavement. His tongue was sticking out as Bo grasped the collar of the man's plaid shirt in one hand and in the other a clenched fist.

The victim hurried into the car and sped away, faster than when he had front-ended us.

Bo slammed the door shut.

"You're an asshole!" I exclaimed.

He appeared embarrassed but shook his saved fist. "You were distracting me with your retarded questions! You remember what I'm gonna do if you tell them anything about me I don't like?"

His speed became a right-sided parabola about to grace the limit.

CHAPTER 17:

The Truck's Locker Room

The following Monday, I arrived at work with pen in hand as a reminder to label personal items. I passed Elephant Man as I navigated to my cubicle.

"Good morning, Jon!"

He grunted.

I twirled the pen and flicked it upward; it ricocheted off the ceiling.

Elephant Man grimaced at me, and stared at the pen. He remained preternaturally silent, his face sagging.

"What's wrong? Everything's okay. Are you okay?"

"Pickit up."

I knelt down, hand on the pen, and rose, his glare following me as smoothly as a cat would watch a swinging pendulum. "Ta da."

He grunted again.

When he was out of sight, I placed the pen in its former position.

I headed for Amy's office.

"Did *you and Bo* have a *good time together* last week?"

"Great time. He said I did very well for a rookie."

"Well *thaat's* good. I *wasn't sure* you two *would be a good* match, so I'm *glad it* worked out. While *you were out* and about, did a kid come up and *smash his truck* with a baseball bat?"

"What? No. I mean yes, yes. I just forgot because it happened while I was far out in the field, and Bo being a little faster – he just got back first so maybe he saw it."

She nodded and smiled. "In *that* case, the company *will pay for all* the repairs. And since *you two seemed to have* so much fun together, I'm going to *send you out together* again."

"What!"

"There'll be *someone else coming* with you, of course."

"Right, of course, someone else. Someone else would help us have an even greater time."

She stepped out halfway. "Chase! I have *someone for you* to meet."

From a nearby cubicle came a lad about my age and build with brownish-red hair and a dirty open grin.

"Chase, *this is* Richard, the guy I've *been telling you* about."

Chase lifted his hand in the air, and I flinched before I realized he was about to give me a high-five; his hand landed on top of mine as he sang out, "Sup, *dude!*" with atrocious intonation.

"Very good day to you sir, I'm pleased to meet you." He scared me so badly I didn't have time to translate my thoughts into the Common Speech.

Bo, looking like he had a miserable weekend, approached him from behind.

"Do you *all know what* you're doing?"

"We're a-gonna have a good-good time!" announced Chase.

"I'll show them how to do permitting," said Bo.

As we were leaving, Sunshine Lady wobbled up to me. "I forgot *to tell you* I've gotten you *a very special* gift. It's *a key* fob. I'll put it *on your desk with the clippers* and the McBirney. It opens *both the front* and side doors."

She began to walk away, evermore cheery-eyed.

"Thanks." I closed the side entrance.

The smashed headlight was almost carved out, revealing the underlying gears.

"I'm gonna drive you two knuckleheads out to Eblen today."

"Wo-ho!" exclaimed Chase. "Look at what happened there. What was it that you two were doing last week? Smashing into people's mailboxes?"

He got in the front passenger's seat.

"Let's just say that somebody –" said Bo, giving me a bare-knuckle noogie "– thought he knew how to drive better than me."

I buckled up before it was too late.

"Nah – better than you?" replied Chase.

Bo started the sputtering engine.

"I never seen any drivers better than you."

"Bo's quite the champion," I said as we left the parking lot. "You should see how he drives," I added right as I saw that he was driving normally.

I shifted my body to the center of the truck and felt a smooth bar of wood wedged into the seat.

"I thought – I thought you said you drove faster," complained Chase.

Bo chuckled at length. "Let's just say someone here likes his trolley – well..." He pumped his fist back and forth.

"Not Grandma Style!" Chase exclaimed, looking back.

"He was being so old you wouldn't believe it."

"Look, I just have to warm up a little," I argued.

Chase rolled his shoulders. "Let's get this baby rollin'. How 'bout we play some music?"

He fiddled with the radio dial for a few moments, and as the beat picked up I recognized the style as that of AC/DC. 'Highway to Hell' started playing as we rode down the highway. Racecar Dude and Barnyard Boy sang along; Chase bumped his fists against the headliner while Bo honked the horn to the sluggish tempo.

Ignoring the banging trashcans, I zoned out to things I learned as a child from school and television. I never forgot

George Washington's famous advice, or perhaps it was Bugs Bunny himself who coined the phrase: *If you can't beat 'em, join 'em.* Having heard enough to predict the next stanza, I prepared to join in on the refrain, modelling my voice on the singer's dialect.

"Sounds like Dumpy Son back there finally joined in," said Barnyard Boy.

"Richard – I have to admit – you are actually a pretty decent singer," added Bo. "Why don't you pick the next song?"

"After 'Highway to Hell' is over, why don't we all listen to 'Stairway to Heaven' – Lynyrd Skynyrd anyone?"

Chase jabbed his thumb backwards. "I like the way this guy here thinks."

They conversed on the array of topics of interest to the average American male, and even got around to teasing each other.

"Knock it off dude – only my mom calls me Arebo," said Racecar Dude.

Chase combined observations and factoids among the infinite range of relevant subjects. His words made Bo respond in a socially proactive manner. Whenever Racecar Dude's interest began to wane and his hands began to twitch, Chase would say the simplest phrases and recapture his attention.

"It's true," said Bo. "My parents actually wanted me to become a baseball player – almost went pro too – just wasn't quite good enough. Could've been with the Reds – Sonny Gray man – almost met him."

Amidst automobiles, music, sports, celebrities, and the weather, eventually the tides turned to the topic of all topics.

"I didn't get no women over the weekend," said Barnyard Boy, "so all I had those two nights was an old fashioned F.D., if you know what I'm talkin' about. I should really just stick to Lissie to meet my needs."

Racecar Dude chuckled heartily and elbowed him. "Some guys with women still have F.D.'s though – which obviously means they need a better wife or girlfriend."

Chase laughed along, and both their guffaws became synchronized.

My jaw dropped as they spoke at length about the most offensive scenarios.

"Hey Richard, you've been pretty quiet back there," said Bo.

"Yeah, would you let a lady into your place if she came over dressed like that?" Chase inquired.

"I dunno man, I respect women."

They both turned around instantly.

Bo slowed down and pulled onto the grass. The truck stopped in front of the sequoias.

"Did you hear...what he just said?" asked Chase.

"I think he just said he respects women," Bo clarified.

"Can we please just get back on the road?"

The tires rolled on the grass.

Only the engine's low hum could be heard.

Chase broke the silence. "Are you...uh, not *interested* in women then?"

"Of course, of course I am. I'm not what you're thinking. I'm more like you guys than you know, really. I love women." I put on a cheesy smile and held up both thumbs.

"We thought you mighta been a freakin' faggot," said Barnyard Boy, "but we still woulda treated you the same. Lemme guess, your *mom* told you to respect women."

"Yeah, so?"

"It's time for some yo momma jokes!" Racecar Dude declared.

"Your mom's so stupid it took her two hours to watch *Sixty Minutes*," said Chase.

"Ha ha ha – good one," Bo responded. "How 'bout this one – your mom's so fat when she steps on the scale – it reads 'To Be Continued.'"

Chase gave him a high-five. "Aw huh huh, nice dude! Your turn Richard."

"Hmm okay.... How about this one: Your mom is *so fat* she can be in *five* states at the same time!"

They looked back at me. "WAH-HA-HA-HA-HA!!" they laughed.

"That's a good line right there," said Bo.

"Duuude...nice," Chase agreed.

"So anyway – what *type* of woman are you looking for?" asked Racecar Dude, eyeing me in the review mirror.

"Who's that blonde lady preparing coffee for everyone in the kitchen each morning?"

"You mean the one with the big dopey brown eyes and the shiny white teeth who's always smilin' at people and huggin' everyone?" asked Chase.

"Yeah, that's her," I replied.

They turned to each other wide-eyed, then turned back to the rural roads.

"Her name is Jenna," said Racecar Dude.

Barnyard Boy bounced, almost jumping. *"Aw yeah.* You'll reeeally like Jenna, trust me on this one. She's a real nice girl, so good to be with."

"Amy is a kind, thoughtful person," I said. "I imagine that if I were older, or she were younger, I might consider asking her out. But Evan said she's crazy. What did he mean?"

Chase brought a finger to his lips. "Crazy fun! In lotsa ways. Oh man, she *loves* goin' eighty five down the highway."

"We're here," said Bo.

The truck stopped in the middle of the countryside.

CHAPTER 18:

Working with Fire

"Wait in here – I have to go check the area first." Bo slammed the door.

"Where's he going? And when is he coming back for us?"

"You like to ask lotsa questions, I see," said Chase. "Why don't you go on and catch up to him?"

He opened a duffel bag for electrical equipment.

The cigarette lighter in his right hand met in his left a series of three wires – one red, one blue, and one yellow. The copper was sticking out of the plastic tape by about an inch. The scent of burnt toast wafted in the air. Sparks graced the tips of the wires.

My left hand was on the door handle. A flame appeared in front of Chase, and I stepped out. A dinging sound came from the inside as I held the door. He trembled and, opening a canteen, drenched his contraption in water.

I climbed inside. "What the hell are you doing?"

His face was frantic, and his arms, jerking back and forth, tried to explain his behavior where his vocabulary failed. "I thought you were – I thought you were out with him!"

"Bo said he was going to check the area first."

"Right, but I thought you were goin' with him and he was just talkin' to me."

My expression was dead serious. "You thought you were

AT ODDS WITH EACH OTHER

alone, so you started playing with fire."

"Not playin' – workin'."

"Who taught you to work with fire?"

"Well I'm just like you, just like you said you were more like me than I know. I started out in mechanical, but then finished my degree in lectricle jeneerin."

"*What* did you study?"

"Ee-lectrical engineer-ing."

"Where did you study electrical engineering?"

"My grampa's basement. What's the matter? You look like you never seen a young guy play around with tools in his old man's basement."

"How did you get hired here? I thought this job required a college degree, as stated in the online job description."

He put on a sullen smirk. "None of your business how I got hired. I can tell *you* went to college, just by the way you talk and act. But you think that makes you better than me? And I'm not as stupid as I sound, which is prolly what you were thinkin' of me at first."

Chills ran up my spine. "What are the company's hiring policies?"

Chase opened his hands. "Does it matter? You think they actually give a shit who's here? They just hire and fire at will, good deeds be damned. You're not special just cuz you got the job. And you know what," he said sitting up, "I bet I got more real world experience in just one week than you got in your entire life."

I coughed twice. "But why were you playing – I mean working – with fire? I was back here; I saw the lighter, the wires, the sparks. I see that stuff right now on the floor in front of you!"

Barnyard Boy closed his eyes and smacked his lips. "See, this is what's wrong with you. You think I don't even know what I'm doin' just cuz I don't meet your narrow definition of smart."

"Well, no offense, but you don't!"

"I just been practicin' what I been trained to do."

"You have the same position as I do; I saw it in the emails."

"I been workin' this job 'bout a year now. And lemme tell you, you can't be a robot all the time and do what everyone expects. You gotta be handy with tools, with gear, you gotta know what you're doin' when you're out here, it's all about survival, you know!"

A knocking sound came from behind; Bo's face was pressed against the window. I opened the door. "Richard – get out for just a second. Chase – stay in there."

He pulled me to the opposite side of the road.

"I thought you were coming with me," said Bo.

"You told us to stay in the car."

"I told *him* to stay in the car – and I assumed you were following me and just being really quiet. I was trying to get you away from him so I could show you permitting."

"But not show Chase?"

"No! He's dangerous."

"And you're not?"

"The difference between me and him is I know what my problems are – okay?"

I pried myself loose from his grip. "Has he ever played with a lighter and wires?"

"He does that all the time – Chase is a dumbass. I've been trying to get rid of him ever since he's been here – and I saw him tricking you with his usual bullshit. You better snap out of it!!"

He struck me on the face. I grabbed my jaw and raised my fists.

Bo disengaged.

I relaxed deliberately.

I examined Barnyard Boy sitting in the truck, finicking with the wires. "You mean you tried to get him killed?"

"It's not murder if he ends up burning in his own mess.

You can talk to him and work with him and even be friends with him – but don't trust him. I know him well – so just leave it to me. Or else."

Chase opened the truck door. Birds chirping one-to-another knew nothing of the ground. I stepped back to view the sloping vista, trees, field and brook.

CHAPTER 19:

Holes for an Excuse

The narrow path wound through the woods on a downhill gradient, weaving with a diminutive but unfailing stream in a crisscross pattern.

We walked the dusty trail. Bo led the way leaping among bushes and bramble. Whereas I opted for safer yet longer avenues, Barnyard Boy barged through each obstacle.

"Whadda ya think of this job so far?" asked Chase.

"It's enjoyable for the most part. I appreciate the opportunity to explore nature."

"I only work here because they pay me," said Bo. "I was making a shit-ton of money as a mudlogger before this but then got laid off."

"What would be your ideal job, Bo?" I inquired.

"Sitting on my ass playing video games! Anyway – right now we're basically just checking out the area to report any pre-mining issues."

"Where does this stream end?"

"We don't use STPs in permitting. Does that make sense?"

"Yup," said Chase.

I raised a finger weakly. "Not entirely."

Bo slowed his pace. "There's a split in the main channel just up ahead – I'll let you two knuckleheads catch the trib. When you're done we can meet back here."

"Will do, pal," said Chase.

I clutched the phone in my pocket.

The tributary led to a quiet countryside road with a drainage system. An HSW appeared on the GPS, but the arrow-cursor surpassed it.

"It looks to me like the point itself is underneath the road," I said. "Maybe we should identify it as 'No Access' so they know to revise the map."

"Nah man, we'll just take the flow right next to it."

I pointed at the road. "But that would be dishonest reporting. They ought to know we can't possibly dig or crawl underneath and measure it from underground."

Chase sat down, boot kicking the stream. "Don't worry about it, we can just take the flow right here. Looks like it's barely one point one."

I dunked my sensor in the brown dusty water. The flow rate was 1.043 gallons per minute, which I rounded to 1 GPM. "CartoPac gives us an option to describe stream conditions as other than 'Clear.' I'm going to mark it as 'Turbid.' That seems to be the best description."

"Whatever." Chase rested with chin in his palms. "It doesn't really matter, you don't have to get obsessed with it. Save your energy if you want this job to work out for you." Then he lay on the ground. "I bet you were homeschooled."

"There's no harm in getting obsessed with it; we collect data, while they interpret it."

The land rose as we entered a patch of woods, a high green source of shade overhead. Chase's pace matched mine, and we slowed down at the rise of a more demanding gradient.

"So you got anything cool to talk about?" he asked.

"Would you classify Pokémon as fantasy or science fiction?"

"It's definitely not science fiction."

"So how is it fantasy?"

"I dunno, why don't you explain your ideas first?"

"Well, Pokémon is about creatures, or fictional animals, who battle against each other and have certain traits, abilities, strengths and weaknesses. Ecology is the science of relationships between living things, especially animals, in nature. Therefore, Pokémon is science fiction."

"It's not about advanced technology though."

"You're saying it's not science fiction, but you haven't explained how it *is* fantasy. And though this is not the central point, it does involve advanced technology in some parts. Just like the advanced technology you were working with back at the truck, remember?"

At the coming of a rusted brick wall, we sidestepped behind a small square shed and climbed over a low wooden fence.

"Why do you keep makin' such a big deal about that?"

The sun's rays waned against the side of the rise, and the shade grew cooler.

"They did that kind of stuff in holes anyway."

"In holes? What are you talking about?"

I leapt onto a long flat rock protruding from the hillside and grabbed a tree trunk. He went around the drop and met me behind a defunct orange tractor.

"In *Holes*, my favorite movie. The characters did electric experiments all the time."

"I don't remember that at all."

"They do it all throughout the movie."

"No they don't. Do you mean in the book?"

"Never really got into the book."

Climbing a high bank, we lost sight of the stream and backtracked, then sidetracked until we came to a steepening rise.

"It's been a long time since I've seen that movie," I said. "The only thing I remember about it is that they all have to dig holes in the desert as some sort of criminal punishment. And then there's the part about surviving on onions near the end."

He stepped ahead of me, speeding up as we arrived at an

abandoned picnic table.

"You remember that? You sure have a good memory, man."

A fallen tree branch lay parallel and on top of a diminishing current, thick branches extended laterally. The trunk obstructed the flow as the high end descended into a ravine.

"You go on ahead first," said Chase. "I'll go my own way and catch up to you."

CHAPTER 20:

The Least Fun Person

On ahead I went, my first priority to surmount and surpass the fallen oak. I selected 'No Access – Blocked by Vegetation' for the length of the stream obstructed. Thick yet spidery roots twisted out the other end, and below lay a gaping hole lined by soft brown dirt.

The gully upstream lay barren, with little to no vegetation amidst its side or surface, so I marked the upcoming track as a 'No Flow.' The woods grew thicker as well as higher. The trickle reappeared and grew to a volume of appreciable girth, where I marked the territory as 'Flowing,' only to merge into a thick wall of thorny vines overhanging a sharp ledge.

I grabbed relatively smooth parts of the vine and, pinching them together, snapped away the offending tangles, and crawled through the low passage.

Leaning backwards, I sat on the brink of the ledge and proceeded to search for the STP. A pipeline, sticking out and downwards from a rock impasse, dripped into a low wet gorge. "Chase! Where are you?"

I arrived at the fallen oak and jumped onto the base of the trunk and, though first stepping about wistfully, reached a point where the narrowing width met a steep ravine and a high drop.

Sitting down with the trunk between my legs, I scooted little by little.

The rocky narrow passage was thoroughly covered in every bit of root and twig, brush and bramble, not to mention thorn bushes circling across the entrenchment like curly hair on a grown man's leg.

"Drop from there!" he called.

"I can't, it's too high."

I inched my way like a spider caressing its web, then stopped, steadying myself and balancing my weight on both sides of the thinning cylindrical wood.

"Drop from there, you pussy!"

I made no verbal response.

"Come on, just jump down!"

My own hesitations were concomitant with his insistent remarks that I should plummet, and when I kept moving, his promptings ceased. The trunk became branch-like, and I had to use both arms and both legs to progress, like a crawling cat defending its balcony.

"Whatever, just stay up there, you big sissy."

Grasping the extended branch tightly, I swung my legs underneath, back and forth, imitating Tarzan, or perhaps a child climbing the monkey bars. I grasped the dwindling bark, shifted sideways, and landed on both feet by the edge of the streambank.

I ran over to Barnyard Boy, now joined by Racecar Dude. "I need to get a stunt double."

"Richard, you are prolly the least fun person I ever met," Chase informed me.

"We were waiting here for hours," added Bo.

"Thanks for helping me out."

"Why do you have to be so boring?" Chase complained. "We coulda taken a video of you and put it on YouTube, or even showed it to Jenna, and then you'd have her for real."

"Dude – we really need to take you out somewhere cool," Bo advised.

"Sure, wherever you guys want to go."

We hiked our round trip.

CHAPTER 21:

Unlimited Shadow

My late devout grandmother had always told my cousins and me that it's human nature to worship, that everyone worships something knowingly or unknowingly. If she had known my supervisors, she would have said that Sunshine Lady worships the environment, in light of her green-oriented décor and personal choices. Amy Lane was as beautiful as a goddess, and indistinguishable from Mother Gaia herself. And if Grandma Armadale had known Shadow Guy, she would have been concerned for his eternal salvation, because he worshipped money, the root of all evil; and so his punishment in the afterlife would be to lie face down with limbs spread at the bottom of a barren rocky hillside in a dried streambed under a starless dark sky.

In more ways than one, a lump of coal in his stocking would be a generous gift. His malice knew no bounds, and if he were a celebrity, those who knew him would say he was one of the evilest people in the world. His black aura was limitless; those who got sucked into his trap would be lost in abysmal darkness. No one whom he sacrificed could ever escape, and after being swallowed, those victims would never be any less miserable.

Mike was one of a dwarfish nature, who, if he was heated by a sullen fire, would become monstrous. The man was a blackguard, crawling towards darkness, going backwards in life, using his expertise to increase his own deformity, and becoming steeped evermore in viciousness. This is the case with Shadow Guy.

The man would have been a puzzle to a physiognomist. I only had to look at him to distrust him, for I felt his darkness in two directions. He was restless to those in his past and threatening to those in his future. I could answer no more for what he had done than what he would do. The shadows in his eyes gave him away. Hearing him utter one word, or seeing him make one gesture, I caught glimpses of secrets in his past and mysteries in his future. All would be well for a season, but at a certain time, he would spring from this shadow, as from an ambush.

In my off-hours, I listened to the following lyrics to put him in context:

"When you *FEEL* my heat, look *INTO* my eyes. It's where my *demons hide, it's where my* demons hide. Don't *get* too... close. It's *DARK* inside. *It's where my de-mons hide,* it's where my de-mons hide.... They say it's *what – you – make. I say it's* up – to – fate. It's woven *in – my – soul. I need to* let – you – go."

Whenever I passed his office, I heard Shadow Guy engaging in grotesquely detailed conversations about money, sometimes right down to the nickel. He was shredding green pastures into paper dollars, constantly working for the destruction of the planet; every pebble, rock, and stone could be transmuted into dimes, quarters, and dollars, even if the earth itself must wither away and everybody else must die. Mike scooped up the land like he was digging through a bucket of unlimited ice cream, and in that way, he was not a geologist in the true sense of the profession; he was a profoundly corrupt businessman with a passion for hatred.

I avoided him whenever possible. This is his premise: Stay in business at all costs, and *always* use safety as an excuse. I didn't blame him for using objective monetary values; everyone needs certain criteria for their decisions. But there was no justification for what he was doing! Unlike Hitler, Shadow Guy lacked a rationale for his motives.

There was a method to his madness, but also a madness to his method. Out of the greatest anger and the greenest greed, and in a crude manner of black torture, he would yank a magic carpet from underneath someone's feet if it was the only way to take that person out; and because the carpet touched his hand, all the magic would die away, and every lily of the field would start to cry. All the earthquakes in America meant nothing compared to his gold penny, which to him was as the Ring to Gollum. He could never play devil's advocate, because it's already who he was. Mike Matthews was a wolf in wolf's clothing who listened to the demon on one shoulder, but also to the other demon on the other.

But perhaps the most frustrating thing about Shadow Guy was that I could not decide whether he was most likely a Republican because he kept track of finances, or a Democrat because he was close to Sunshine Lady.

There I leaned against the linoleum wall right outside Mike's office, his door propped open; we were both looking at the towering bookshelf, wedged into a corner in front of his desk, that almost touched the ceiling. Lining its shelves were used and weathered field notebooks, mostly yellow ones but also blue and orange ones, volumes of records on environmental conditions spanning many decades.

"How much would it cost?"

"Rip up their property!"

"Let them drink poison...."

I started to slink away, lest my overhearing soon qualify as eavesdropping.

"Richard!"

Heaven forbid he discover my stealthy ways, for it seemed

too ominous that he might have seen the tip of my shoe, or heard my fingernails gliding lightly against the wall as I propped myself upright.

I innocently revealed my presence. "Hi Mike, I'm right here."

"Sorry, I thought you were at your cubicle. Why don't you come in and have a seat?"

The chair had a cushion seat with wooden arms and legs. At the left-hand side of his desk was an orange barrel with white letters spelling out DO IT RIGHT OR DO IT AGAIN. I did not at first notice the area behind him, the bare carpet and walls; the open backdrop of nothingness complemented his face in the foreground, comprised of everything sinister, and shame was the only thing in his eyes.

"I was going to call you in earlier, but Jenna came to me early this morning – with an unrelated issue. I just want to know how you like working here."

"Can't complain. I've learned a lot so far, and I'm enjoying the work."

Mike smashed his hands together; a clap echoed throughout his chamber. *"Excellent! Now, do you know why I've called you in?"*

"To ask me how I like working here?"

"This is a man-to-man talk. We need to discuss your behavior around women."

His expression bore disappointment when he saw my unresponsiveness.

"Go on...." I bowed my forehead toward his.

"Well, I just wanted to know if you've been having any fun with women lately."

I tilted my head. "Sure, I'm having fun...with them. But not too much fun. I play it safe, but not too safe – just like you said."

He suppressed an emerging grin, his mouth poorly concealed by fingers brought to his tightening face. *"I'm glad to* hear it. *I just wanted to let you know that you'll be going out with Alyssa today."*

"You've arranged something between us?"

Mike closed his eyes and snickered. *"Good one. But no, she'll be training you in the field today."* He motioned to the door and said, *"You can come in now."*

Alyssa had been lurking outside his office, just like me, only waiting behind the door.

Her movements were so graceful that she made no sound until she spoke. "Hi," she said softly, facing more towards Shadow Guy than towards me.

"Richard is pretty up-to-speed on his techniques and knowledge with everything. I've asked you to go with him to Eblen just in case he needs a few brush-ups."

Alyssa greeted me with a radiant smile and deep blue eyes. She was wearing a white headband, and a yellow daisy was fixed upon the back of her head. Her ears were pierced with loopy silver earrings.

I stepped aside, letting her out of the room.

Shadow Guy waved us goodbye. *"You two have fun out –"*

"Yeah, yeah, we know how it goes," I interrupted. "Try to have the right balance of fun and safety, or safety and fun, never sacrificing one for the other, or either one."

Even if he had something different in mind, I wanted to be spared the torture of his riddles.

"I see you're ready to go," I observed of her. "I just need a few minutes to get ready."

She closed her eyes and then reopened them.

CHAPTER 22:

Savvy Socialization

Alyssa was not short for a woman, but she approached me so closely I had to bend my head down to see her. "Ready-to-*go?*" she asked, three words melding into one. Her breath smelled like strawberry mint.

We crossed the lot to her truck, parked very close to the center.

She turned on the radio to NPR.

"Thanks for driving me," I said weakly.

Her stillness filled the atmosphere with enchantment.

Facial symmetry is one of the greatest components of attractiveness, but causes a disturbing feeling in its extreme form. I never fully understood this concept until I met Alyssa; looking at her was pleasant and unsettling simultaneously.

The journalist stated that a two-year-old girl had been kidnapped earlier that morning.

"That's terrible!" I exclaimed.

Alyssa's eyes followed the highway bends, her driving as smooth as her own skin.

And it came to pass that words and phrases I uttered every now and then caused her to finally speak, or perhaps she opened up of her own accord. She told me that her close friends call her 'Lissie.' In a melody of her voice, all the notes would be to the right of Middle-C on the piano.

"So how did you get into environmental consulting?"

She pursed her lips. "When I was *growing up,* fracking messed up our *family's farm.* The cows were *acting funny,* and our water supply was *harmed.* I wanted to understand what was *going on.* What about *you?*"

Many well-meaning men of average intelligence had told me that extremely good-looking women are annoyed by anything *au contraire* one might say of the well-established, mainstream fashions in the upper echelons of society, and I sensed Alyssa lived the High Life. More concerned with mastering the basics of this job than with acquiring a date, I rebelled against this wisdom and spoke my mind, though still tried to make my voice sound impressive.

"I grew up addicted to video games, which I enjoyed because of all the adventure and exploration your character could do – in the main adventure as well as the side-quests. While taking an earth science class in high school, I realized you could do in the classroom what you could do in video games. In college, it occurred to me on the geology field trips that I could do in real life what I was doing in the classroom. My parents were so glad I was finally going outside more. But really, it all goes back to video games. The way I see it, video games are about jumping across platforms, and geology is about jumping across platforms, so there's really no difference between the two."

Catching my breath with my throat tight, I turned my head, resigned to whatever awaited me.

She was already looking at me, well and alive. Her open mouth was upturned in a smile and her eyes were beaming with admiration. "That's *awesome.*"

"Did you play outside a lot then?"

"Yeah, *sometimes.* Mostly to play around with my dog when I was a *kid,* since I was *pretty lonely.* Then I got into tanning later on so people would *notice me more.*"

After the familiar exit off the main highway, Alyssa drove a route that passed by a countryside school building. "That's where *I went,* MacGuffin *High School."*

"No kidding, that's my middle name."

"Guess who was the first girl there to be prom queen *twice.*"

"I'm drawing a blank."

She looked at me like the answer was supposed to be obvious. "Me."

Traversing the rolling hills, the truck neither slowed nor buckled, but always followed the natural contour.

Within the slot below the right door handle was a crumpled, closed plastic cup labeled STARBUCKS with melting ice inside and a green straw sticking out. Beside the cup and wedged into the front corner was a thick book with hard red binding. I pretended to examine my shoes. Inscribed on the spine was the title *Adepts, Ascendants, and Ancient Masters.* An author was listed neither below nor beside the title.

"Do you have a degree in something like philosophy or psychology?"

"Nope, environmental studies from *Prestonsburg.* I did *soo* many things in college and had such a *great time."*

Her glimmer shone more brightly than sunrays beaming through the windshield that made her earrings sparkle.

"I was the vice president of my sorority *Beta Phi Epsilon,* as well as the fundraising director of the Prestonsburg *Dance Marathon,* and the spokesperson for the Green Fellowship *Advisory Board."* Her voice grew giddier with every word.

I experienced a clenching sensation in my neck. "I don't know if I could ever keep up with that."

Savvy Socialite grinned and brushed her tongue against her teeth. *"Ooooh,* what did *yooou* do in *college?"* she mooed.

The truck came to a stop-sign before a mount.

"I was a member of the Geo Club and the Newman Club."

"Pssh.... You weren't in any sort of *fraternity?"* She looked

at me squarely.

"I was too busy with academics for so much involvement in extracurriculars."

She continued driving when two more cars approached the three-way stop.

"Aw, that's too *baad.*"

Tears dripped from her words.

"You graduated just a year *behind me!* We could've had *sooo* much *fun together.*"

We descended on the far side of the mount.

"Sorry to take away your fun," I replied without a glance her way.

"*I* had plenty of *fun.* I meant that *you* could've had fun with *mee,* not the other way around, since *you're boring.*"

"Well, good for you."

We drifted through a low pass covered by a roof of leaves.

"We're having fun right now, right?"

She rolled her eyes.

"I will have fun. With this job, with you."

Savvy Socialite reached over with her right arm and squeezed my left shoulder, her left hand still on the steering wheel. *"That's* what I like to hear, *smartypants.*"

NPR now the prominent voice, we fell silent drifting into the heart of the countryside.

CHAPTER 23:

Memory of an Impending Lawsuit

The road split, and the truck followed the right fork, whereby we came across a small-domed bridge on our left and on our right a barn with a red roof, brown wooden sides painted white on the long ends. The east side showed the words CHOW MAIL POUCH TOBACCO: TREAT YOURSELF TO THE FINEST.

"Don't go on their *property*. They're not very *friendly,* and they might try to *shoot you*. Their property was torn up *last year,* and we had to fix up the stream to avoid a *lawsuit,* which took *forever.* Jacob ended up there when he *got lost."*

"Thanks for letting me know. The ideal situation is to have every stream flowing freely with fresh, clear water."

She smiled, but her brow was furrowed, wrinkling for the first time her icing-smooth complexion. "Cute."

"Well come on. You know how the poem goes: 'Every drop of water, Every breath of air, Every ray of sunshine, Is part of what we share.'"

She tilted her head back and forth, her dark hair flapping against the sides of her head. "You sure are *one-of-a-kind.* I bet you'll go really *far in life."*

We parked on a small dirt lot with a rectangular gate barring entrance to a dirt path along a grassy hillside. Next to the lot, positioned like a mailbox, a rigid pole stuck out of the ground, onto which was fixed a plastic canister with a long plastic measuring cylinder about an eighth full of water.

Alyssa removed it from the canister, examined the water level, then emptied it onto the ground. "This is the *rain gauge.*" She twirled it in her fingers. "There's another one *farther south*. Most of the time we have to stop by one of them and measure the water level before *nine-thirty*. This is also a good place for us to *park*, to monitor the streams *assigned to us today*."

She brought out two sheets of paper equal in length from her own CamelBak and handed one to me. I quickly compared my list to hers.

"Just stop by here when you're *done*, and we can have *lunch together*, just *you and me*."

Savvy Socialite winked and smiled upon our departure.

ShrC-24R-1L, a secondary tributary, was the first stream I found included on my list. Its water flowed out of a long steel culvert underneath a brick-lain bridge. I walked through, keeping my head low enough to avoid tarnishing my bump cap with whatever slimy drippings hung from the top.

Coming out the other end, I recognized the barn she warned me about; the stream flowed directly across the surrounding land, which sloped downward to meet the road. After putting my iPhone in my left pants-pocket, I strode slowly along the stream, arms held high.

A middle-aged woman came sprinting up the hill, her gray hair blowing in the late-summer breeze. I discontinued my plod, only letting my arms down when she stopped beside me, panting.

"Wait, are you from Conrad?"

"Murray. We check up on their activities."

The woman let her guard down. "Okay...good."

She walked to the barn more slowly than she had come.

On the other end of the field and through a patch of woods came a gentle flow of many small streams interlocked with several dried beds on which they might have once coursed. I could not tell if they were a system of interwoven braided streams or many meandering streams in one area.

The flow of streams depicted on my GPS conflicted with the physical layout in numerous ways. I noticed discrepancies when I compared the stream distances on the screen to those on paper; for several given lengths, CartoPac contradicted my portion of the schedule.

It took perhaps thrice as long to navigate them all to their ends as it would have if the map had concorded with reality.

I returned to the rain gauge. Alyssa brushed her hair, with the mirror in front of her face. She flipped it and placed the daisy in her hair. I grabbed my paper-bag lunch resting on the passenger's seat. She had already started the ignition.

"How long were you waiting?"

"About...*ten minutes*. Did you get *lost?*"

"Not really, just had a little bit of frustration with some streams all bunched together. It's nice to know you're concerned about my whereabouts."

"Just in case you get *lost,* let me give you my *number.*" She held out her phone, leaning in so closely I could smell her breath.

A text arrived: 'Lissie.'

"I have just a few questions."

"We can discuss this stuff on our *way back.* Let's have lunch *together first.*"

She drove along the lot's circumference and flashed the left turn signal.

"I thought we were going to have lunch."

"We *are.*" Alyssa opened a dark green lunchbox with black straps and pulled out a plastic bag; she drove with one hand as she ate Cheetos with the other.

"So Baylor is south of Harvon, which is south of Eblen, where we are, correct?"

"Yep," she chirped.

"And now, when the phone app doesn't match up with how things look, physical reality takes precedence over the GPS, which takes precedence over the schedule, right?"

"Yep."

Then she turned on the radio to the following song:

"Hey, I just *met* you...and this is *crazy*...but *here's* my number. So *call me* maybe!"

CHAPTER 24:

My Lackluster Performance

Because the weather was growing cooler and the bushes were becoming pricklier, I started wearing long-sleeve shirts.

The schedule for the following week indicated I was to be trained by Terrence Hasinger, whom I briefly spotted working each time I circled by the main entrance; he was the most thorough of all the employees.

"Good news!" Sunshine Lady raised her arms in the air. "Someone *wants to trade you* the Hach for the McBirney. You'll have *the one you* always wanted, isn't *that* great? Just remember to *clean the sensor* regularly so *it doesn't get* contaminated."

"It'll be good to have the easier one for the first day on my own."

"Actually, this is *your last day* of training. But you'll *be doing everything* by yourself. Terrence will be *working alongside you* just as a backup."

He was nowhere in the office.

On my desk I found a schedule of stream names, one edge of the paper uneven.

It was my first day taking my own vehicle; the keys to a 2016 Toyota Tacoma hung underneath my name on the outside of Amy's door.

The truck was empty of all items, save a short orange cone in the rear. Sunshine Lady's words came to mind, her squeaky voice reminding me: 'Make sure *when you drive your* vehicle, that the *seat is just right* for you."

The seat was too far back from the steering wheel. There was no lever for raising the seat; in its place was a knob for producing support in the backrest. It strained my back, so I turned it all the way counterclockwise. To compensate for the lack of height adjustment, I reclined the backrest for a wider view.

I started the ignition and turned on the radio to the Prestonsburg Symphony Orchestra. The truck moved forward faster than I expected, and I immediately steadied it with the brake.

Before I left the parking lot, Ron came running out motioning for me to stop. I rolled down the window. Huffing and puffing he said, "I just want to make sure you know how to drive this thing."

"I've driven the same kind before."

"Do you know what the dial next to the steering wheel does?"

"No, I don't."

"H2 is when you're driving normally on the road, H4 is when you're driving through a bunch of shit, and L4 is when you're stuck in a bunch of shit and need to get out."

"Thanks for making it simple."

The drive would not be too long since I was assigned to Eblen. I flicked the left turn signal and waited until the road was completely clear.

I stuck to the 25 MPH speed limit on the first road.

A right turn at a traffic light required me to shift into three different lanes to reach the leftmost one, but since I needed to make an immediate exit onto the highway, I illegally merged across all of them at once and guided the truck into a left turning lane.

The green arrow was on, so I turned onto the highway exit ramp.

Now I was driving with the big leagues – the slow trucks in the right lane. I took account of every sign and landmark, aiming for the general area of my training visits. To find my assigned location near Terrence, I had to look at the GPS.

At a slow point in traffic, I wedged my iPhone into a space inside the steering wheel so that below it was the horn and above it the top rim. I zoomed out to get a general idea of the area, then zoomed back in on my location.

I merged right onto Route 60 and flashed the right turn signal for Exit 12, Taybortown, then turned left onto South Passage Street and headed towards Prospire.

I continued driving along South Passage Street for several miles and then turned left onto Mounds Ravine Road, where a broad valley extended for many acres. The neatly terraced grass grew in shades of off-color green variants of tan and yellow. Bushes dotted the mostly clear area, while lumps of browning green tree leaves graced the hillsides.

A gravel path connected Mounds Ravine Road to another road across the valley, and a Murray & Affiliates truck was parked halfway along the path. I positioned my truck so that both vehicles were parked bumper-to-bumper.

I stepped out and laughed at the comical symmetry; it appeared as though either one was about to take off in either direction.

A figure in the distance came hustling by. Terrence raised his right arm as he passed.

"I need to know if you finish early if –" I started, but he turned around and ran backwards at the same pace, waving goodbye.

CartoPac guided me to my last turning point, where a broad stream flowed alongside an inclement rise. The sun above illuminated the pebbles, plants, fish, and macroinvertebrates, a lively riparian habitat. I stepped onto a protruding shelf of limestone and hopped into a shallow landing; my muck boots eased into coarse-grained sand.

As I slopped upstream through crisp rushing water, I developed a straightforward safety priority: I would not step in a spot where I could not see the bottom.

An orange-tipped stake stuck out of the streambank immediately before water flowed into a wide bowl-shaped depression. An HSW marked on the map was located in the middle of this pool.

I stopped and took the flow on a relatively shallow cross-section. The width was well over six feet, which required many more measurements of depth and velocity. I placed a block of wet granite on each end of the meterstick to prevent losing it to the fluctuating rise of the current. I grabbed my other meterstick, and after measuring each depth at every quarter-meter interval, set it by the bank.

With the iPhone strap dangling from my left wrist, I grabbed the sensor with my right palm, keeping the main part of the Hach wedged between my right arm and thigh, while holding another meterstick with the fingers of my right hand.

As I dragged the waterproof case through the water from one measurement line to the next, my phone swept from side to side, and I dropped the sensor in favor of the phone whenever I recorded velocity data.

The meterstick buckled under the current and sank to the streambed, where I held it in place with my left muck boot. I continued eyeballing the increments, visualizing where they had been, and dogmatically dragged the sensor across the water's surface.

Drops of water on the screen made typing in the numerical values quite difficult, and I pressed harder and harder until I realized that I could no longer work the touchscreen at all.

I scribbled the measurements in my notebook.

I tried turning my phone off, then back on again, as well as pressing the Home button as rapidly as I would have the 'A' button on a Nintendo controller, but all to no avail.

My first job out of high school was that of a kitchen-knife salesman. The company for which I worked during those long summer months had convinced me that their products were scratch-proof. I thoroughly believed this claim until I presented the knives to an eighty-one-year-old client who had survived the Great Depression as a lad and was quite unwilling to purchase even the cheapest item in the company catalogue.

A retired and divorced elderly man, he told me he had worked in the steel industry, that all claims about scratch-proof steel were misleading, and that such steel was only comparatively scratch resistant. I knew in my heart of hearts he was right, that I had been deluded into believing I was selling invincibly sturdy household objects, more durable than gold itself.

But I acknowledged, sadly, that the great many number of common items are simply not held in the kiln of purifying fire to withstand all types of damage for ages and ages. Such was the case with my waterproof phone; it was not water-proof, simply water-resistant.

I crawled out of the stream and gathered my equipment, then ventured uphill alongside a tributary surrounded by many trees, which soon blossomed outwards into an endless array of woods.

Resting on a grassy hillside with a large oak tree to my back, I nibbled on the contents of my lunch. I took account of all my belongings, both personal and company-issued, electronic as well as basic. Because my physical location was off the grid, I received no cellular service.

By the time I had consumed the better part of my lunch, I remembered the company policy requiring field technicians to send a safety signal to the managers every two hours they were in the field, in order to make sure their workers were on track and out of danger. There was also a pre-written message that things were not okay.

The interface of the InReach presented very few digital commands. There was a circular button with four directional arrows, and two smaller rectangular buttons: one with an X and another with a checkmark. The screen was smaller than even a prodigiously tech-savvy child would have tolerated. The letters of the keyboard onscreen could be selected only by moving the cursor one step at a time, reminiscent of a worm struggling to obtain every last bit of soil.

Minute after minute, I persisted in spelling out the briefest of messages that would convey the essence of my dilemma, and was satisfied upon finalizing my entreaty: HELP PHONE PROBLEM. The recipient, Jocelyn Reical, had been pre-selected by the time I was ready to send my message, but I could also add another, simply by typing the first few letters of that person's name.

Five minutes passed before I heard the InReach emit a *swoosh*.

As I finished my lunch, I mused on the proper pronunciation of the last name of my final trainer. 'Hasinger' was a simple enough surname, but the spelling suggested four possible pronunciations given by the two-by-two matrix inherent in combining a long or short 'A' with a hard or soft 'G'. I spoke out these pronunciations to hear which one would be correct by virtue of sounding the most melodious:

"HAY-singer, HAY-sinjer, HAA-singer, HAA-sinjer."

I checked my immediate surroundings to make sure no one had heard me. A chipmunk scurrying along a thick branch stopped and looked to the side, as a falling acorn struck the back of my hand.

Although I never needed to do this myself, I recalled how friends and siblings had cocooned their cell phones in bowls of dried rice after dropping them in swimming pools.

Emerging from the shade, I observed that the wide field

on the opposite side of the stream received the better portion of sunrays.

I sped down the hill and leapt across the embankment.

Rows of hedges lined the field. The warm sun was kind to my face, and a natural drying agent to the brown-and-red leaves strewn across the grass.

Gathering each leaf one-by-one, I formed a pile within minutes. I placed my phone face down within the leaf pile so that it was cushioned above, below, and on all edges.

I lay against the bushes, waiting for the water to evaporate from my phone.

Silent Soldier marched forward in the direction opposite from which he had left me. "Sorry about that, these things they give us seem like they're from the nineteen-seventies. I got word you need help using your phone."

I stood up to greet him. "You're Terrence...*HAA-sinjer,* right?"

"HAY-singer," he corrected me in a low voice, his countenance rather surly. His prominent lower lip, downturned eyebrows, and hat-flat hair were redeemed only by a tiny white sparkle, glinting in the early-autumn sun, on the piercing of his right earlobe. "Your phone okay?"

"Well actually yes, it should be now." I reached into my leaf pile. The phone still had watermarks and was unusable. "Water got inside my phone when I accidentally dropped it in the stream. I found out they're not actually waterproof."

"Yeah they are," he said with a quizzical expression. "What are you talking about? Lemme see that."

When I handed my iPhone to him, he grabbed the corners of the case and stripped it off the iPhone itself. Part of the case had a thin, transparent area to protect the surface of the phone's screen. He wiped the screen dry of the water-drops, shook out the case, and inserted the phone back into the case.

It was completely functional again, like brand new!

"It wasn't water damage, you just had water inside the case."

"Oh. Thanks. Do you know what the stakes with the orange coloring at the top are for?"

"That's where you take the stream flow. Most of the points have one. They're more precise than the HSWs on the map."

"I was also wondering, since you probably have so much done, and I have so little, if you could finish off some of these streams for me?"

He ripped my schedule in half.

"Great," I said. "See you back at the office."

He raced into the distance.

I fudged some numbers for the previous flow measurement.

The few streams on my sheet, which could be counted on a single hand, were located mostly along the hillside I had earlier descended.

I ran across the field and leapt across the main stem, aiming myself diagonally up the slope to reach the latter half of the next stream, and I did the same for the following one.

My phone signaled a LOW BATTERY warning.

The trucks were barely visible on the eastward landscape.

I peered upstream, squinting under the photosphere of the sun and blocking out most of the rays with the visor of my bump cap, practicing some sort of visual acuity test. For all intents and purposes, the stream was flowing at the STP.

The battery life dwindled, but the internet connection sprang alive, four of five bars. I texted Amy a question: 'Do we use hsw or stake for flow?'

As I headed back, I received her response: 'I'd go off a combination of both.'

Mere moments later my phone shut off.

My InReach buzzed with a message from Jocelyn, the Lazy Loafer: TERRENCE ON HIS WAY.

Part Three

CHAPTER 25:

Safety Meeting

For my birthday I received a pocketknife from my uncle. I propped open the outside door off the kitchen to a small but comfortable area with several plastic chairs.

I grabbed the back of the blade with the tips of my fingers until the *click* indicated it was straight and sturdy, and swung my arm wildly, practicing fighting moves against imaginary predators, hacking and slashing them to pieces.

"Richard, why the hell are you flapping?" Ron stuck his big ruddy head out at me, looking like I had succumbed to a fit of insanity. "We need to obey our superiors."

"I'm stretching for my fieldwork today, what does it look like I'm doing?"

"Sorry to bother you. Just let me know if you need any help."

I admired my weapon with a cross-eyed glare. I tried closing the blade, but it wouldn't bend; I tried wiggling and pushing it, but it didn't budge.

Mister Suckup had his back turned to me, but now I needed his aid in weapon management.

Wiggling the blade and handle back and forth, I asked, "Is there a way to close this thing?"

"I'll show you. See, you want to shift the blade to the *side* first – hold it right here..."

I held the blade over a crevice in the handle I hadn't noticed before.

"...and then, you see how it can slide down on *this* angle? Let go carefully, and it will close."

It was almost like magic. "Thanks."

Mister Suckup examined his analogue wristwatch. "We need to go to the meeting now since we're both running late, and we don't want to piss off our higher-ups."

"Meeting? What meeting? Are we going somewhere for a big conference?"

Ron offered a glazed expression. "The meeting in the Instruction Room started at nine-o'clock, and it's now nine-oh-five. We meet there every other Monday at this time. You should know about it, now that you're on your own as a field tech."

I smiled. "Okay. Maybe I was just exaggerating a little."

Down the hallway with cabinets on the right side was the Instruction Room, located next to the laboratory and the locker room; near the door, a wooden stand held a large yellow book a little smaller than *Webster's Complete Reference Dictionary and Encyclopedia*.

The room was brimming with all the noise and excitement of being amongst one's fellow workers. Three long black tables formed a double-L-shaped seating arrangement, with a whiteboard at the front, now occluded by a projector screen. The tables were full, but a few foldout chairs were stacked together.

I sat in the far back row between Evan and Kyle, while Ron claimed his place next to Alyssa, who was seated next to Jenna; the two young women were best friends – 'besties.' Chase sat on the other side of Alyssa, calling her by name and tapping her flat back to get her attention.

Along the left wall, Kevin sat between Mike and Jon like a hot dog about to be engulfed by a bun, and to Mike's left sat Amy, beaming.

"Hehehehe," she giggled.

I examined the bookshelf in the back corner, next to Evan rather silent taking in the commotion, and estimated the number of yellow notebooks on each space; the bookshelf was shorter than the one in Mike's office, but the notebooks themselves were more densely packed together, and there was only a single one off-color, which was dark green.

The vice president stood front and center. *"Attention, everyone! Before we get started, I'd like to congratulate Kyle on his new position at USGS. He's given us a ton of solid work the past four years, and he'll be moving on in two weeks."*

The room exploded in applause with cheers and chatter, such that it resembled an animal circus, or perhaps a zoo.

Running Ninja stood up and took a congratulatory bow, receiving accolades for his upcoming transfer to the United States Geological Survey. "Thank you, thank you, you all have been terrific. I for one am pretty stoked to have made it with the big leagues, what can I say?" He looked from side to side with an open-mouthed grin.

"Don't *forget Richard* here," said Amy, "who I would say *should be recognized* for his commitment to safety, since he's the *only one I've seen* wearing his bump cap. You *all should model* him, or he might just *be your safety instructor* one of these days."

"Yes, there he is," said Mike, pointing in my direction, *"let's not forget him. I hear he's also having a great deal of* fun *too, isn't that right, Richard?"*

The cheers came my way. "Thank you all. I'm pretty...uh, *stoked* for...for something...."

Kyle patted me on the back while Evan offered a thumbs-up.

"And now, for the moment you've all been waiting for..." Mike spread his arms outward; he stepped aside and clicked a white remote.

The screen flickered before revealing a PowerPoint presentation; the opening slide was that of a grizzly bear crawling through the woods. The names 'Alyssa Cale' and 'Jenna

Braubach' were listed underneath the title 'Bear-ly Surviving.'

I performed my imitation of Baloo the Bear from *The Jungle Book.* "It's all about...*bare necessities.*"

"Whoa that's really good!" said Jenna.

Bo turned around in his seat. "See – I told you you'd like him cuz he's a good singer. I'm tellin' you – he's gonna be the next Mel Blanc."

"Safety time! Safety time!" Alyssa's mouth moved synchronously like that of an anime character.

Jenna motioned to Mister Suckup. "Ron, we'd love it if you'd join us for the presentation, since you're the most bear-like one of us here."

He huffed like he was the grizzly on the screen. "Fine time if I did, fine time if I didn't. I'm not too prepared right now. Why don't you two ladies go on up?"

"Not all bears look like *him.*" Alyssa hopped up, held her hands over her hair in a teepee, and wriggled her body sinuously. "Some are like *meee.*" She started laughing.

Chase pulled her aside by the waist, which accelerated her laughing rate. "And some of *us* are more aware of that reality than others."

"Yes, why don't you two fine ladies show us what this safety stuff is all about?" Mike advised.

Alyssa and Jenna walked around on either side of the room and met up at the center.

"Okay, you *go first,*" whispered Alyssa.

"No, you go first, you have the first line."

"But you said you – *oh, alright.* I get to go *first then.*"

They performed a brief yet charming vocal ensemble; it was sloppily performed and poorly coordinated but positively uplifting in its own right. When one woman stepped forward, she would sing, and when she had performed a certain line, would step back and let the other woman do the same. This alternating pattern continued throughout their fun little ditty, and while the vocal variety was limited by the number of performers, this fact made it easier to follow, such that it could be suitable for children.

"When you're out in the *woods,*"

"With food and goods,"

"When you see a *bear,*"

"And you're in for a scare,"

"Don't *walk,*"

"Don't talk,"

"Just *stand there,*"

"And look big,"

"Real *big,*"

"Put your arms in the air,"

"Stand *tall,*"

"But don't fall,"

"And walk *back,*"

"With your sack,"

"Breathe *in,*"

"You'll win,"

"Growl and *roar,*"

"And the bear will be no more."

The world fell silent.

Then they spoke together simultaneously. "That was..." Both women spun around on their toes and when each had made a circle, they gave each other a double-high-five "...the bear show!"

Although I was not the loudest, I was the first to laugh and to clap as well.

"Nicely done, ladies," said Mike, grinning.

Jon was smiling; there was a silver tooth near his top right molar.

"Aw," said Amy appreciatively.

Ron finished clapping before he looked at his watch. "It looks like we're almost out of time here. How much is left?"

"How many slides did you put in?" Jenna asked Savvy Socialite.

"About *ten* – you mean including the *questions slide?*"

"We didn't get to any more slides, so let's just go right to the questions."

"Are there any *questions?*" she asked the crowd.

Several seconds later, I raised my hand. "What if we have a pocketknife and we want to kill the bear before it kills us?"

Both women gasped; Alyssa glanced at Jenna, who glanced at her, and they looked sideways and all around before Amy spoke.

"We usually *don't talk like that* in here. But if *you do want to* know, you're not *supposed to attack* the bear. It will get *angry and easily* outmatch you. And we're *not allowed to carry* firearms here."

"It would easily outmatch even me. Anyway," Mister Suckup continued, sitting up, "it's time for company photos."

"Picture time! Picture time!" Alyssa framed her head with her palms on both sides, then top and bottom, then back to the sides. "I wanna go *first.*"

We gathered amidst the chatter, and I was one of the first out of the Instruction Room.

CHAPTER 26:

Touching Tenderly

When Savvy Socialite ran through the hall like she was gaining momentum to fly, her pitter-pattering footsteps made a sound for the first time.

She posed in front of the white wall next to the kitchen door in a freeze-frame ballet style. I had never before seen anyone's professional photograph appear with arms above head. I suppose it worked for her since she was already so photogenic. Her mouth made her look like she wanted something to sink her lips into, while her round eyes and high eyebrows made her seem to want as much attention as a newborn puppy.

Next went Mike, who had volunteered to take Alyssa's picture. I held the camera in front of him, waiting for him to smile. Only half his mouth was upturned, as though he were having a stroke. I waited for the other half to rise as well, but pressed the button anyway, fearing the disease might consume him.

Amy held the camera to take my photo, and I gave off as ordinary an appearance as possible.

But when I acquired my nametag, with the phrases RICHARD ARMADALE and ENVIRONMENTAL CONSULTING – with my picture between my name and industry – I realized I looked far too excited for someone enrolled in a tech job, and wished I had combed my hair beforehand.

About half of all fifteen to twenty vehicle keys were hanging on their respective hooks on the rack outside Amy's door by the time I departed.

Because it was the first time on my own, they initiated my performance in one location with only four HSWs.

A wool blanket stretched beyond the horizon, with only mild drizzle.

I followed South Passage Street and turned right onto Mounds Ravine Road. Instead of parking at the base of an intersection where one road continued uphill, I drove until I reached the downstream buffer.

Upon hopping out of my truck, I sprayed myself with tick-spray and ran through the woods to WidC-37, which was flowing.

The first HSW was one-hundred feet upstream. My ascent was inhibited by a vast swath of nettles, thorns, and weeds, and I cut them with my clippers more than I watched the stream.

I opted for a semicircular route through cornstalks to the HSW.

As I took this flow, a 1.1 in width, I switched the iPhone strap from my left wrist to my right wrist. I held the sensor with my left hand and nestled the Hach between my right arm and chest. My motions and recordings were careful and deliberate, and I recorded measurements to the hundredths place for both depth and velocity.

I crossed through the woods back to my vehicle, parked parallel to the road with two wheels on and two off, and stopped when I reached the next flow point.

After the fourth HSW I lost sight of the stream and found myself trapped in a prickly bush. I surged forward and saw that my vest as well as my hiking pants, which now had a small tear in the seams, were covered with an abundance of green burrs.

Finally, I emerged onto a fresh lawn behind a house.

All keys were hanging except mine.

I headed to the patio off the kitchen, where Chase, Alyssa, and Jenna chatted together over cups of decaf.

"...and when I'm walking up this *hill*," explained Alyssa, "out of nowhere three guys come up to me from behind and say nice...well, *you know!*" She leaned in towards him with her jaw hanging low and her hands outstretched.

Barnyard Boy stood straight, listening and bearing his dirty grin. "Uh huh...."

"Hey look, it's Richard!" Jenna smiled with her mouth open like a sideways letter 'D' and extended a palm to me. "I was worried about you since you were the last one to come back."

Chase turned his head toward me while keeping his body square with Alyssa. "Sup, dude! You been on the prowl mega time, I see."

"What happened *to you?*" Alyssa wondered, finger to her mouth. "There are all those green things on your clothes, are *you okay?*"

"I'm pretty sure they're called burrs, dumbo." Barnyard Boy tilted his head back to Alyssa with eyes following.

"Like you would know, *dropout.*" She lowered her eyebrows and folded her arms. "What were you *doang, Richard?*"

I shrugged. "Exploring, you could say."

"I know who Marco Polo is – was," said Chase.

"I have a secret for you Alyssa," I said, "but you can't repeat it to anyone."

Her eyebrows perked up, while Chase and Jenna donned curious expressions.

I grabbed her hand and took her by the sink, and cupped my hand by her ear. "Okay, here it is: Chase should treat you better."

She backed against the fridge, beaming with suppressed laughter. "Yeah. Thanks for *letting me know.*"

"What did you say to her?" he demanded.

"Nothing," I responded. "It was college people talk."

I wormed my way to the door.

"Richard, where are you going?" asked Jenna.

"Outside to clean myself up from this stuff – where else?"

I sidestepped onto the grass and leaned against the brick wall. I picked off each burr one at a time, then in pairs.

By the time I had cleared away the bulk of them, the door swung open and out came Jenna. "Hey, I just wanted to come out here and give you company so you wouldn't be lonely."

When the door closed, she opened up her arms.

"Thanks for looking out for me. I'm making good progress on these things. I should be back inside soon, and there'll be spare time before I leave today."

She came closer and stepped onto the grass; the center of her eyebrows tilted upwards as she faced me. "Are you sure? Why don't I help you take them off your body – your clothes?"

"I guess it would go faster if you did so." I shook out my hiking pantlegs, spraying loose the stray burrs. "There are only a few left on my pants. Why don't you finish those off, and I'll pick off the ones up here; they'll be faster and easier for me to do."

With great care, Tender Toucher plucked off each remaining burr, scanning up and down, and the scent of her golden hair resembled springtime dandelions. She traced the tear by my calf. "What happened here?"

"Sharp stuff – you know." I observed Jenna's pleasant physique; her figure was slightly fuller in its dimensions than Savvy Socialite's, and her attractive face was well-structured. Her voice was not quite as high-pitched, but Middle-C still had a day of rest whenever she spoke, and what I loved about it was that it carried genuine warmth.

CHAPTER 27:

Sagacious Advice

When considering matters objectively, I was stymied in my decision on whom I would rather be with – Alyssa or Jenna. They were two peas in a pod; I couldn't have one without the other. The decision reminded me of all the times when two new Pokémon games were released for a Nintendo handheld system; they always came in complementary colors or themes. One way or another, I eventually did decide based on an evaluation of the pros and cons of each, and I was always the last of my friends to make a purchase. I suppose I could have bought both together, and often considered doing so, coerced by the relentless command of 'Gotta catch 'em all!'

But here is where the analogy ends, for it was beyond my sensibilities to have two girlfriends at once.

My selection leaned towards Jenna for a number of reasons. Chase seemed more interested in Alyssa, and I found that my conversational style was more compatible with Jenna's, as our discussions flowed smoothly like the streams. I was also concerned about how my romantic ventures would affect my career, and Jenna seemed more stable than Savvy Socialite.

Dating Tender Toucher would be by no means a bad deal. Though she was not quite as groundbreakingly eye-catching as Alyssa, she was certainly desirable in a classical sort of way. My secret list of pros and cons suggested by a small margin that it would be more rewarding to seek Jenna, a hunch that reminded me of the sagacious advice that passed from one crony to another in my early university days: *Would you rather have a Ten you get along okay with, or a Nine you get along great with?*

The matter was settled: Jenna was the right Pokémon game for me.

Barnyard Boy never made it explicit, and although their relationship – or whatever one would call it – had a great deal of edginess, I still suspected they were dating.

However, when I creeped on Alyssa's Facebook profile during work hours, I saw her relationship status listed as 'Single.'

She and Chase lived in the same area of Lakeland, and they rode together in the same vehicle; sometimes he drove, sometimes she. Their friendship was certainly beneficial for both of them, so I set my myopic sights on Tender Toucher, aware that the process of acquainting oneself with a woman is like scaling the Grand Canyon – that one must take a single step at a time, otherwise matters could quickly become disastrous.

Next, I creeped on Jenna's profile, and it seemed from her photos that she had a great deal of fantastic fun with the other two, as they often went out to places of which I could only dream, living the High Life. Based on their mutual eye contact, my hunch that Chase Reinhold was more interested in Savvy Socialite than in Tender Toucher was correct; Chase held her in his arms, and sometimes Alyssa kissed him, while Jenna stood by smiling, but relatively aloof.

One step at a time, I reminded myself, keeping my professional life as the first priority.

My people-researching was over for the day; with butterflies in my stomach, I closed Facebook and recorded a doctor's appointment on my calendar for November. Until now, I had not observed the president's office very closely, but from my vantage point I could keep tabs on Elephant Man while pretending to schedule my affairs.

His room was often dim; only the light from the main complex and from the sun illuminated the thick paperback novel he read while leaning backwards in his chair against a stack of cardboard boxes. Because the window of his room faced east, he read that book only in the morning. Jon turned a page once every four to five minutes, a rate that indicated his reading speed was half my own. His glasses slid to the tip of his nose, and he peered over them periodically to glance at the computer screen.

CHAPTER 28:

The Old Man's Request

An early storm gave me time to prepare a meal of eggs, toast, and bacon instead of my usual bowl of cereal. I dressed into my rain gear because the night showers were still ongoing when daybreak came.

Almost all of my destinations were in Eblen, and it was difficult to plan a route to my next location because the interlocking streams wound through a long valley like a birthday ribbon, and flushed to the thalweg as swirling water. Most of the streams on the schedule were listed in red ink, although some were green and one was black.

"What do the colors mean?" I asked Boiler Brain.

"Pink means daily, the other one means monthly."

"And what about the ones with no color?"

"You only visit those once a month."

A name was listed under the first stream in red. "It says 'Call Mallow.' Who's Mallow?"

"That's just a reminder for Amy. You must've been assigned to Sharmin Creek (that's the big bad one). Good luck out there (be sure to tell her if there are any big mistakes on the schedule)."

"What makes it so big and so bad?"

"Heh, you'll see why."

I listened to the sound of my own ambition by turning on the radio to 'Stronger' by Kanye West, who encouraged me to work:

"Harder, better, faster, stronger!"

Indeed, I would need to increase my capacity in all four of these traits if I desired to make a difference.

Although I didn't *really* regret saving that handicapped schoolboy from Racecar Dude, I still beheld the promise of promotion to a Level-Two technician after two years. I had originally planned to study advanced petrology in graduate school, but my student loans were accumulating more rapidly than I had expected, a twisted sort of fate for having worked so hard. Therefore, I needed to beat Level One and reach Level Two as soon as possible.

Heading further south, I turned left off of South Passage Street and onto Venial Road, a very long and slow drive with a '30 MPH' sign.

Many minutes passed during my descent on the gradual downhill gradient before I found a parking spot by a small short bridge at the end of the road with an entrance gate to a fence-enclosed farm with rolling hills.

I reversed my truck into a circular gravel lot in front of a square house, or perhaps a cottage, small enough to fit inside the lot.

I reached for the orange cone in the back and placed it in front of my truck.

New Scales Road, which intersected Venial Road, continued uphill to the right, much steeper and only a little bit shorter than Venial Road. Across New Scales Road stood a large white barn with a red roof and two square doors, and through the one that was open, I saw two men conversing in front of rectangular hay bales. One man was tall and slim with a white button-down shirt, and the other shorter and stockier wearing a red polo shirt. The taller individual appeared slightly younger and had no mustache, whereas the shorter one had a broad thick mustache, and he was wearing a safety helmet.

The longest tributary off the main channel was SharC-66R, and its mouth lay just past the entrance to the extensive farmland.

When I closed the gate with its long black rubber strap and S-shaped rusted hook, I heard something tick at the rate of a second hand. A wire supporting the hinge of the gate had come loose and emitted bright white sparks. I opened my CamelBak to spill water onto it but missed, and then drank the water itself from the nozzle.

On CartoPac I recorded 'Electrical Hazard' as an AOI in the 'Other' category.

I left the farm seeking nearby help.

"The fence is sparking," I told the tall man.

"Ya mean the one right thar?" he asked pointing to it.

"I saw it near the gate, and was concerned that it might start a fire."

The men turned to one another.

"It ain't a big problem, so it'll be arright," said the short man. His shirt had a large pocket on the right side and on the left the words CONRAD POWER in small black capital letters.

"I trust your judgment. I'll check back later to see if the issue is resolved."

The tall man asked, "But didja come all the way over here jus' so you could talk to us all edumacated?"

"Excuse me??"

Resisting the temptation to call them out as trailer trash, I headed to the fields at once. They probably never learned their three R's, or even knew that only one began with the letter R.

The stream had benefitted from the precipitation; my first flow reading on SharC-66R-01, a 1.1 measurement, was well into the triple digits, and I marked it as 'Turbulent.'

I continued along a bend with a large oak tree at the foot of a short steep slope and came around another bend, and hop-scotched on platforms of grass across a blanket of mud and gray muck. My boot hit the edge of the final platform and I fell *smack* against the substance.

I lay face up in the stream until I felt cool wetness on my skin.

On the other side of the stream where a rising hill became a wall on my left, I held out my palm toward a flock of sheep who fled along a rickety bridge across the stream.

One, two, three, four, *five* dark-brown bulls lingered and grazed. I held out my hand, but they were immune. I tried proceeding between the stream and the pack, but they converged on my trail. I brandished my pocketknife, but went the way of the sheep.

I zoomed up a mound, right next to a light-blue cubic home, and raced down, still moving upstream. I checkmated the sheep against the side of a wooden fence, and they ran uphill to the right.

When I swung over the wooden fence, I broke one of the support beams. The field was empty, save an abandoned shed far to the right. Another wooden fence had a loose pointy beam, which I heaved out of the way, and I stepped across the lower beam. Right next to the stream was a solid blue barrel, the Checkpoint.

My GPS indicated I had crossed the upper buffer.

I stepped onto the barrel, jumped over the fence, and landed on the grass, two feet together.

When I strapped the gate closed, I headed for my truck, but standing near the driver's door was an elderly gentleman, not too tall, wearing a farmer's hat and dirty blue-jean overalls with a plaid shirt underneath.

Old Man appeared mournful, much in contrast to the sun behind him emerging from the rainclouds above the high hill. He could not have been any less than seventy-five years of age. "Can I help you?"

The refinement of old age brought his country twang into

balance. "Well, um, you see...there was a great deal of rain last night, as you might have been well aware. And so it rained quite a bit, but it wasn't only that, but the mine around us came by from there to there this morning as well."

He pointed in every direction.

"And so my wife and I, we woke up, you see; I noticed, well, that maybe the river's running faster than before and a little bit beyond its banks here and there."

"Okay, okay, go on." I unlocked the truck door.

"So you see, we saw the river rushing back here and there, and we think, or at least I think, that in combination with the mine, it sort of messed up the bridge there, you see?"

"But the bridge looks fine. I drove across it."

"Well, I'm no engineer but it seems to me that if one part of the bridge is messed up, and nothing is done about it, well then the whole darn thing might just collapse someday. But I'm sure something will be done about it, eventually, I just want to make you aware of this."

"What part of the bridge – we're talking about this bridge..." I pointed to the intersection while holding eye contact.

"Yes, this bridge."

"Like I said, it looks fine to me; what's wrong with it?"

"Well, you see, it's not the *bridge* itself per se, but the part underneath the bridge, the culvert, but just the one on the left, not the right."

One metal culvert had been squashed to nearly half the height of the one beside it, slowing the steady current. "What do you think will happen to it?"

"Uh...I can't say for sure, but the here-and-now thing that's going on, is that I reckon the combination of the wet weather and the active mine has caused a great deal of pooling on our property. And while the crops did seem to benefit from the extra water, at least at first, well it just seems that there's become too much of it and now they're mostly ruined. I fear we may not have enough food to survive this winter, you see?"

"Pooling, did you say? That's one of the descriptions on my phone app."

I placed my hands on the fence. A puddle grew at the intersection of the main stem and the tributary, drenching grass while soaking the topsoil, which turned the water dark brown as it gathered. Cornstalks floated in the cesspool.

"I see what you mean."

Old Man came up beside me. "So, now that you do see, I was wondering if you could maybe in some way tell them about the pooling?"

"I can easily report it."

"And now one more thing, the last thing, if you could just get on the other side of the bridge over there and take a picture, and make sure you get the area of pooling, the bad culvert too, and my house as well, just so your people know where I'm at and how they can help me."

"I'll do that. But you do need to move so I can get inside my truck."

The farmer waved his hand. "No problem, no worries, sorry to get in your way, it's just something I thought I ought to tell you about; I mean, I'm looking out for my wife as well as myself – and I'm looking out for you too, in a way I guess, because I'm helping you do your job a little better. So thank you."

"And thank *you*."

On the other side of the bridge I angled my camera so the bridge with its culvert, the pooling, and the farmer's cottage were in one picture. The pooling on the other side was the most difficult to bring into view, so I crossed the stream onto higher ground at a better angle and snapped a photograph from there.

At the side of my truck stood a short gray-haired woman wearing a wrinkled white dress with small red roses.

"We, uh, I just needed to tell you that there was raining,

and there was the mine, and there was a great deal of –"

"Yes, yes, your husband told me all about it," I said, one leg already inside the truck.

"But you have to know it's a problem, since it created pooling and we don't know if – well, we want you –"

"He already told me everything you're going to tell me, and I did everything you want me to do."

I had forgotten my lunch, but felt the benefit of extra energy from the larger breakfast. I still had more to do, but started the truck to scare her into fleeing back inside. Then I took off my rain gear.

I crossed the bridge to a large field with tall dry grass and observed the first point assigned on the main stem, SharC-98.

The primary channel diverged around a small island, but one side was stagnant, so I dropped a 1.1 on the other side and obtained a rate of 512 GPM.

Heading downstream, I tumbled onto dry land to record the lower buffer as 'Flowing,' but noticed a discrepancy: CartoPac marked the point as 46,000 FT, whereas the schedule read 47,000 ft.

From there I dropped into the main channel, where I followed SharC-61L through a long metal culvert underneath a broad road with busy traffic.

When I emerged onto the far left side of a courtyard in front of a castle-like home, I edged my way around its outer perimeter, hopped across a bend in the stream, and scuffled my way through brush and bramble to the upper buffer.

Heading back, I left the bramble for a sunny field and crossed the road. I walked diagonally across from one corner to the next, and since they had plenty of land, did not care about the vandalism of my footprints.

At the main stem, I took the flow of SharC-99 on a cross-section near an orange-tipped stake against a tree, where I measured the width as 2.1 meters.

From here I crossed the main channel to SharC-67R,

where a steep cliff awaited me. I scrambled up the scarp onto a fallen tree branch over an HSW, where the stream disappeared underground to an electric fence with more farmland. The electric probe lit up green.

The stream reappeared on the other side of the fence, so I climbed across a red metal gate. From here I veered to the right.

On a narrow channel with light-brown water, I found an area barely wide enough to qualify as 1.1 meters where it looked like someone had dug a hole. The flow was 1 GPM.

The stream trickled for a long length, nearly diminishing in several areas, but it once again regained strength up to a muddy trickling waterfall. The tips of my fingers touched the edge of the cliff, so I rinsed them off in the dirty water down below.

I stepped onto the grass, weaving my way through thorn bushes while dodging their vines, uphill and onto the stream channel where I noticed, except for drips, that the stream had stopped flowing, so I marked the point as an FOP and identified the proceeding length as a 'No Flow.' I trudged through the dry channel until more thorny vines crowded my way, at which point I went around a longer but clearer way, finally reaching the STP.

Here, too, was an inconsistency: CartoPac indicated the length was 412 FT, but the schedule listed it as 367 ft.

After writing a reminder in my notebook, I turned around ready to head on, but three bulls surrounded me. I left them alone.

I hopped over the red gate and headed downhill through the woods, where I emerged onto a broad field by the main channel which I followed until I reached the upper buffer near SharC-68R, its mouth hidden within a dense clump of rhododendrons.

Around the upper buffer, I proceeded through a grassy dirt path lined with haystacks until I returned to the channel, which I followed until it disappeared underneath an abandoned wooden warehouse. I held my head low so my bump cap wouldn't receive cobwebs, but as I centered my weight the floorboards creaked.

The tributary led to a secondary one, only it was not named SharC-68R-1R, but WKZY6777.

The secondary tributary was over six-hundred feet and had many turns with bushes and brambles over which to cross, and many fallen trees I could use as wide tightropes to cross from one side to the other.

Near the end came a steep, muddy and narrow rise lined with dense clumps of green bushes on either side, and after ripping away parts of them, I picked up a thick staff-like stick, and proceeded like a mountain climber.

With steady support, I rounded a tree and headed down. The STP lay beyond a wall of overhanging vines, so I set my clippers to work.

I crawled through the carved tunnel until I saw the flowing end of the stream, then headed around the way I came, and dropped the stick when I no longer needed it.

A stone staircase descended from a driveway, at the bottom of which a dirt path led to SharC-68R. I backed up and made a running leap across the mouth of the weirdly-named stream and landed on the other bank with ground to spare; my momentum carried me to the warehouse.

CHAPTER 29:

My Amateur Diagnosis

They spoke in tones like windblown willows, their voices raspy, such that comments to one another became whispering yells. I leaned against the wall.

"I told you there was something weird about that guy, but you wanted him here because you thought he was cute and funny. I'm telling you, he's f**ked up *in a way we don't even understand."*

"No *shit,* Sherlock. But *you even said* he did *so well* during the interview that it *would be stupid* not to hire him. And I *told you he could* be a great asset, and *he still can* be."

"But we have to figure out what to do now that he's here, and you even admitted he's a liability."

"He's both *a liability and* an asset."

"Which one?"

Amy paused. "I *don't* know!"

She opened the door, and the handle banged against the wall as she headed for her office.

I snuck to my desk with my head bowed low.

Then I walked down the aisle and over to her office.

Sunshine Lady was seated like a classroom schoolgirl. "So, *how-did-it* go?" she asked with moronic musicality.

"I believe I did very well out there today. I took a picture of a smashed culvert underneath a bridge. An old farmer wanted me to report it because it caused pooling on his property."

"Hmm...." Amy tapped her finger to her lips and looked up to the left. "So *was it* like, a *big tube sticking* out of the ground?" She capped her hands on the top and bottom of an imaginary cylinder.

"Not exactly." I brought a finger down to her eye level. "You'll see the picture in my report."

"Okay. Good for *you for looking out* for that guy. We need *more people like you* in the world."

I showed her the pages of my field notebook. "There are several errors you made in the schedule. First, the downstream buffer of the Sharmin main stem is forty-six-thousand feet from the mouth, *not* forty-seven-thousand feet. Second of all, the STP of SharC-67R is not three-hundred-sixty-seven feet in length, but four-hundred-twelve feet."

Amy took the schedule from me with her fingers and concentrated on it like she was preparing to prove Fermat's Last Theorem, and she brushed the piece of paper with her pen. "Oh, you *don't have* to be so *oh-see-dee* about it." She waved her hand at a forty-five to fifty-degree angle over the horizontal axis.

"What percent error is acceptable for me to ignore these incongruities?" I clenched my fingers in front of her face.

"What?"

"By how much of a difference, or to use the correct mathematical term, *percentage,* must your errors in gauging distances differ from the accepted values given by CartoPac, to justify me confronting you *about* your mistakes, just like I'm doing right now? Fifteen? Twenty? Ten?"

Sunshine Lady swallowed and opened her mouth. "Just *not...too* much."

I ripped out a piece of paper from my field notebook. I divided the absolute-value difference between 46,000 and 47,000 *by* 47,000 and multiplied the quotient by 100%. I did the same for the numbers 367 and 412 respectively. I punched

the values into the calculator on my phone and obtained re-
sults of 2.13% for the buffer and 10.92% for the STP.

I dangled my work in front of her, and her head jiggled with
the paper. "Suppose I use a ten-percent error as the guideline,
which is useful because then all I have to do is move the decimal point one place to the left. In other words, let's say I am
to report any error that is greater than or equal to ten percent.
Assuming this is the case, I would have to tell you about the
STP error because it's above ten percent, but not the buffer
error because it's below ten percent."

She squinted uncertainly, straddling the boundary between understanding and confusion. "So...you're *saying just
the STP* on that *one trib is* wrong then?"

"According to the criteria on which we mutually agree, yes."

"*Okay* then," she said, her face lighting up, "I'll *change it
on the* schedule. What did *you say the* right number was?"

"Four-hundred-twelve."

She brought out an eight-point-five-by-eleven sheet of
paper from her lower drawer and wrote '412' in thick black
Sharpie.

"All done," she said smiling dumbly.

"Thank you."

I left her office and returned to my desk, where I checked
my email and found a message from Dirk Kormisky reading:

Good afternoon Richard,

*We heard you took a picture of pooling by a dam-
aged bridge. We have received this photo and were
wondering what the length of the pooling is?*

Sincerely,

D.K., the "project guy"
Conrad Power, Inc.

I stretched my fingers, then clicked 'Reply' and wrote:

Dear Mr. Kormisky,

I did not provide a length of spread for the AOI in question because the dirty mess your company created, while severely impacting the livelihood of a poor old farmer who has nowhere else to go and nowhere else to live, was in fact located in approximately one spot. As long as the pooling does not grow any more extensively, I am quite sure that you would be able to trace the boundaries of the aforementioned miniature swamp. You would do well to contact the leadership of Murray & Affiliates so that our technicians and scientists can remediate the problem. Thank you very much and have a splendid afternoon!

Sincerely,
R.A., the "public watchdog"

I clicked 'Send.'
Meanwhile, I recorded my hours on Ajera in such a way that I would have no more than nine hours of work each day and no more than forty-two hours of work each week. I minimized my recorded hours, even when I worked for longer than I reported.

CHAPTER 30:

Company Resumes

I remembered my lunch the next day and placed in the back of my truck a box of protein bars and a plastic barrel of pork rinds. I also brought *Physical Geology CliffsQuickReview* as well as the Earth Science Quick Study laminated reference sheets, to try to weave together my formal studies with my professional career. I could have read through the company handbook provided to me in a white three-ringed binder in order to better understand the job itself, but reading it was incredibly monotonous and boring, and through my job performance I desired to express my creative drive. With the progression of autumn, I clothed myself in Under Armour, both top and bottom, and wore a soft gray sweater as well.

"Be *sure you make your* company resume," Amy told me.

I opened the company resumes file in the little manilla Windows Explorer icon and perused the resumes of others. Everybody but Chase had one on file. Many employees wrote they had 'over six years,' 'over three years,' or even 'over a year' of experience here.

Seven weeks is approximately one-point-seven-five months, but when I divided 1.75 by 12, I obtained a repeating decimal.

Therefore, I abandoned this approach and considered how infants and some one-year-olds are referred to, not as zero or one but in terms of months.

I spied on the backgrounds and positions of others. The resumes provided the last names of people whose first names I knew, which gave me the added benefit of forming LinkedIn connections, as well as my favorite pastime of creeping on them on Facebook.

There was a lot to learn. Adam Chiocchi was a geologist with much experience traveling, fishing, and hiking. Brianna Yachin was a more experienced geologist who had worked in the engineering industry. Ronald Giarto was a geologic technician who touted his 'people skills.' Sam Polan was a geoscientist with countless accomplishments, but his writing style made him seem like an absolute idiot, and I could tell from his default scowl that he was an Idiot Scumbag. Kevin Swaney had a background in foreign languages, which may have accounted for his ability to form long sentences off the cuff without really saying anything.

The resumes also gave me a chance to indulge my curiosity about other peoples' college GPAs. With a 3.5, mine hovered over almost everyone else's. I nearly burst out laughing when I saw Alyssa's resume, which listed not her overall GPA, but her major GPA, a 3.1, and seeing that she had majored in environmental studies, which to many minds is easier than environmental *science,* I clenched my fists triumphantly with elbows on the desk.

I considered modeling my resume on Kyle Heshfield's, or perhaps that of Henley Strankop, who made it three years before the bosses got the better of him, but decided to plagiarize the format of Jenna Braubach's with the understanding that imitation is the sincerest form of flattery. Jenna was not an environmental technician like I was, but an environmental scientist, in accordance with her major.

I copy-and-pasted her resume onto a blank Microsoft Word document, and did not need to change much since we had graduated in the same year from the same university, and because her overall GPA was safely above a 3.0, I looked forward to our many reasonably intelligent conversations.

My assignment today was to monitor a weekly section of Sharmin Creek, specifically the secondary tributaries SharC-66R-1R, 2R, 3R, and 3.2R.

After I grabbed my keys, I said hello and waved goodbye to Chase.

"I saw you chasin' those sheep the other day. Sure looked like you were havin' a helluva time."

"Today, I will have an even better time."

I sprinted out the door headfirst with my fists behind my waist like Sonic the Hedgehog, eager to traverse Green Hill Zone and find rings for Jenna, my lovely rose.

CHAPTER 31:

Exploring the Sharmin Tributaries

Reaching the secondary tributaries required me first to pass the blue barrel; I hopscotched on island-like platforms of grass without falling into the muddy lava, leapt to the other side of SharC-66R, then did a double-take as I approached the sleeping bulls.

I darted across the rickety bridge and took out my pocketknife to chase the sheep. After I hopped the first fence, I caught my breath and treaded alongside the streambank until I came to the second fence, over which I swung and kicked the barrel aside as I commando-rolled into the stream.

The main tributary bent to the left, while the secondary tributary ahead was SharC-66R-1R. An HSW appeared past a causeway of brown-and-yellow leafed woods, and I began to measure the flow.

The water's fluctuating height, as well as the difficulty in stabilizing the sensor and meterstick, inspired me to take measurements to only one decimal place, and this technique facilitated my work. I reviewed the data from the flow and saw only the final value, in this case 30 GPM, and there was no way to access the specific measurements.

I proceeded to the upper buffer, but approached an electric fence with thick black insulators surrounding the wires and decided the other side was flowing; then I walked back to the intersection.

SharC-66R-2R emptied from a dark-green rusted pipe into a faded pink plastic basin and spilled out into the primary tributary.

Further upstream, the pipe disintegrated, and water spilled over the remains like a leaking severed garden hose. The streams here were to rivers as wooden Brio train tracks are to railroads. A patch of orange staining appeared after which the flow diminished, and I marked the latter segment as a 'No Flow' all the way to the STP.

Hopping across the meadow to SharC-66R-3R, I continued my trek past a tall metal electric fence with messy orange substance under its wires, gracing the banks like saturated hot sauce on silver-platter eggs.

"Aw yuck!" I exclaimed.

I recorded it as 'Orange Staining With Sheen.'

A region of large ferns on the meadow marked a break in the fence. In its place stood a crooked red gate with bars that appeared to have been smashed by a formidable hammer.

I climbed atop the gate and rode it falling to the ground, and continued to the other side of the fence.

The continuity was demarcated by a fiery offspring of the earth's star. I followed the murky trench on a path leading into a forest of poorly-trimmed evergreens. The stream went dry all the way to the STP.

With burrs on my sweater, I tromped across the metal gate to the mouth of 3R, where I redirected myself alongside the primary tributary toward 3.2R.

I looked ahead like a bounty hunter.

The GPS indicated I had passed it.

My heart palpitations made me wary of a potential wormhole as I proceeded along the secondary stem. The stream coursed across the landscape and disappeared into a thicket of red-leaved oaks upon a hillside, marking a drastic increase in gradient growing into the clouds.

More focused than ever, I turned back and noticed a

sequence of short-grown fading weeds rising between me and 3R.

The plants felt sloshy when I stepped on them in slow-motion, and my muck boot became dirtier. They continued growing along a narrow swampy trellis.

Further upstream, the weeds became more diffuse, until they stopped growing altogether at a thin segment of soggy grass. I followed the stream like Inspector Gadget until it coughed up a clue. I probed my toes and leaned sideways for any subtle change to the lack of vertical boundaries. The entrails of watery grass gave way to a divet a few inches lower. The greatest amount of water appeared in a polluted puddle, and after that the upper-bound buffer crossed a region of No Flow.

I took a deep breath.

Papers with bar charts and technical information lay across her desk like a jumbo deck of cards.

"So, *how-did-it* go?" Sunshine Lady tilted her head side-to-side.

"I had a tough lot." I held my shoulders back as she sat comfortably. "It was rather cumbersome searching for SharC-66R-3.2R."

Her face flattened like a sandwich around the axis of symmetry, while her red pasty lips stuck out like those of a frog about to give a kiss. *"Which* one?"

"'The decimal one with the other secondary – I mean, trib of a trib on the 66R part of Sharmin. I assumed you were not a huge fan of decimals when I showed you my method for calculating percent error."

Her eyes, mouth, and even her cute little nose became Cheerios. "Ooh, *that* one. Aw *yeah, that's* a tuffy! Good for *you for being able* to find it." She smiled with glimmering admiration.

"I was wondering, given your background in biology, if you

understand why there are plants along that stream and nowhere else on the field?"

Amy raised an eyebrow. "I *don't understand* your question."

"Allow me to ask the question this way." I held the tips of my index finger and thumb together. "What *species* of plant is naturally able to grow around sparse dirty water?" My foot tapped inaudibly. "I'm just curious."

She stared into oblivion. "I *have no* idea." Then she looked at the papers.

"Nevermind then." I backed out of her office. "I'll research the matter during my off-hours here so that I am better able to understand my tasks."

Barnyard Boy accosted me. "Sup, dude! You wanna go to Pranti Brothers after work? We're all goin'. Alyssa and Jenna are comin'."

Savvy Socialite and Tender Toucher sprang out of the kitchen.

Alyssa tilted her head seductively. "Richard! Richard! We'd love it if you would *join us*. Won't you *come with us?*"

Jenna folded her hands with her fingertips under her chin. "Please come with us, Richard. Please *come* with us."

"Fine. I'll come. Where can I obtain further information about this rendezvous?"

"Talk to Ron," said Chase. "He's the organizer of it all."

Mister Suckup was sitting in the cubicle behind mine.

"Hey Ron, what are you doing here?"

"Amy let me switch my seat so I could be closer to her and the other higher-ups. What's been going on with you?"

"I heard you were planning a trip with everyone to Pranti Brothers. What's the occasion? And why are we going today instead of tomorrow, a Friday?"

He swiveled around to face me. "I plan a group outing the third Thursday of every month. Pranti Brothers has free beer and two-dollar pizza slices on Thursdays. We're meeting there at five-o'clock today."

I bowed. "I don't mean to be rude and invite myself, but since you said everyone is coming, I suppose that includes me. I would, in fact, like to come. How far away is it from here?"

Ron drew imaginary lines in the air.

"It's actually pretty close, only about ten minutes," he said. "All you do is take South Johnston Road *south* until you make a left onto Meadow Drive, and drive a little ways until you turn left onto Aldio Drive and then you'll see it."

"Thank you very much." I straightened myself to an upright position.

I held the top button of my personal cell phone, typed 'Pranti Brothers' in Waze, and saved the directions.

CHAPTER 32:

Pranti Brothers

T he drive was easy, and I was one of the first to arrive. The crowded restaurant had a high-vaulted ceiling, and bustled with group chatter and televised sports games lining the walls; the collective brightness illuminated the dim wide room.

All nine of us took our seats at a high-stooled eight-person table; Amy pushed a stool to the end of ours. I sat on one side at the other end.

Alyssa was to my left, and to her left Jenna, while Chase sat on the other side of Jenna. Across from Chase was Halley Towser, a hydrologist I had never before met. Next to her was Ron, and to my diagonal left was Level-One technician Brian Garrow. Across from me was a man around my age whom I had seen while leaving the office, an individual who worked at his computer like a DJ, legs spread under his desk; he often wore a blue hat. His baggy clothes covered up his ectomorphic build.

After enjoying a close-up view of Savvy Socialite, I seized my opportunity to size up Halley. She had short blonde hair with radiant blue eyes and pale skin. Her smallish head looked like a deviled egg from afar. Pale Egg was a Seven and would be an Eight once she had longer hair.

What happens at every gathering happened here; we

decided we needed to use the restrooms.

When I returned, Jenna and Alyssa had switched seats.

The man across from me introduced himself. "Norman. Isaac Norman."

"You must be related to James Bond," I quipped with a smile.

"Nice. I've introduced myself that way to other people, but you're the first to catch on."

"Other people may have noticed without saying anything."

"True that." He aimed his finger poorly.

Chatter filled the air around our table. Amy started laughing before anyone had told a joke. Ron's baritone voice dominated the conversation.

Brian introduced himself with a query. He was rather buff. "Guess how old I am."

"Hmm...twenty-eight?"

"I'm actually twenty-two. I just have a rather *seasoned* appearance." Buff Face scratched his spiky light-brown goatee. "I got a job here right out of college."

"How old do you think *I* am?"

"I would've thought you're still in college, so I'm guessing you're the same age as me."

I jabbed my finger upward. "A little higher."

Jenna put her hands on my knees. "Richard, now's our chance to get drunk, isn't that great?"

"Do you enjoy getting drunk?"

She nodded like she was stretching her neck. "I *love* getting drunk!"

"I'll be sure to drink less than you."

In fact, I planned to drink less than everyone else. I didn't always drink, but when I did, my buzz came from feeling cognitively superior to those around me, so in homage to my twenty-first birthday, I ordered a Yuengling because it's the lightest kind of beer.

"I'm guessing you're not a big drinker," said Isaac.

"I tend not to say the right things when I consume alcohol. I'm the good version of Terrence when I don't drink, and the bad version of Ron when I do."

"Why don't you drink much?" Jenna asked earnestly.

"Low body mass?" guessed Brian.

"Not really." I turned to Jenna. "Maybe I just need to find the right type of beer for me."

The discussion of beer reminded me to check football scores on my phone. While browsing the internet, I asked the waitress for one slice of pepperoni pizza and one slice of cheese pizza.

"I see you whenever I leave work each day," I told Isaac. "What's your position?"

"I'm the cartographer."

"You make the maps I use. Do you ever go out in the field?"

He shook his head and sipped beer. "I just stay in the office. Unlike you, I don't get much exercise. You field people are really putting yourself on the line there, going out in the world."

"Because it's unsafe in the wilderness?"

"Lots of reasons, really. Some we're not supposed to talk about."

Isaac reminded me of Deep Throat, especially the Kermit-the-Frog version.

My pizza arrived, and I nibbled on the hot slice.

Jenna's beer was a third gone, whereas I had taken a few sips.

"You better catch up to her," said Brian.

"I'll try to keep my level above hers. Things will be funnier that way."

"But I have a stronger kind than you," said Tender Toucher as her head fell on my left shoulder and her hair covered her face; she had ordered a Corona. "What's your favorite drinking game?" She peered at me with dilated pupils and lay her head on my leg.

"Beer pong."

Jenna coughed into her sleeve and righted herself.

Savvy Socialite gave a vocalized performance of 'Flight of the Bumblebee.'

I continued speaking to Isaac. "What was your major?"

"Geographic information systems."

"Makes sense."

I took a swig of beer.

"How come my indicator jumps around whenever I try to zoom in all the way on a line?"

Isaac placed his glass on the table with a *clink*. "That's because the satellite signal is bouncing off the clouds."

"I see." I put down my beer. "What's the deal with SharC-66R-3.2R? Why is it so weirdly named?"

Deep Throat closed his eyes and grinned. "It's sort of a running joke we share in the back rooms. I agree though, I've seen it. It is a weird stream."

"It could be referred to as 4R. Do you know who named it?"

While bouncing up and down, Deep Throat pointed with both index fingers, hands above his head.

"Why did you name it that way? Just for mischief?"

He dropped his hands and leaned back, chuckling. "Sort of. They actually made me do it. It's a secret."

"Wait, guys – *people!*" Alyssa chirped. Everyone directed their attention to her as remaining bits of conversation petered away; her tongue stuck out of her open mouth. "We forgot to do *cheers.*"

"Oh, that's right."

"Yeah, that's right."

"We should definitely do cheers."

"Let's do it right now."

Everyone held their respective mugs to the center of the table, and only Alyssa spoke. "One, two, *three...*"

"*Cheers!*"

We struck our drinks at a median point above the table, our arms raised like poles of a tent. I jerked my arm away like a pool player using backspin during a critical shot.

Clink clink clink.

All the other glasses clattered together; all the different kinds of beer spilled into the air, and one drop landed on the tip of my hair.

Jenna ordered a second beer as soon as she had finished her first. I took another swig.

"What do you do for fun?" I asked Isaac.

"I sometimes do amateur astronomy on the weekends."

"Same here."

"Do you know much about the history of astronomy?"

"A little bit."

He leaned back. "I have an interesting fact. Guess why arrows shot upward fall back to their exact spot if the earth is rotating?"

"Gravity."

"It's a little more complicated," he said, leaning forward. "Gravity would explain why the arrow comes back down in the first place. Do you know why it returns to the same spot?"

I shook my head.

"It's because the arrow is temporarily in orbit."

"Huhh!" I gasped.

The din grew louder.

"Hey, I was just wondering..." I raised my voice. "I was just wondering, whatever happened to Henley?"

The entire table fell silent in suspense. Amy's face froze; she became a black dwarf. A few murmurs rose to ear-level.

"Shhh!" said Tender Toucher, finger to her mouth.

"What was it that he did −"

"Be quiet!" ordered Savvy Socialite.

The body of Sunshine Lady was still undergoing its episode of rigor mortis.

"He's not here anymore, so what did he do wrong?"

"Shut up!" Buff Face demanded.

I finally shut up. The conversation resumed like an airplane about to set flight.

"Richard, if you need to know what happened, I'll explain it," said Isaac.

"I heard he got laid off. Let me guess: pot."

Isaac sipped his beer and shook his head. "It was actually his right leg. It was an ongoing problem for him. Lasted at least three months, and he was in constant pain. The injury, or whatever it was, eventually became a liability, a safety issue, because they didn't want him to fall and hurt himself further or cause some sort of accident. He was going to doctor after doctor, taking up the company's healthcare stuff – you know how that works – and they didn't want to get into a worker's comp claim, so they got rid of him while he was between diagnoses."

"That's not very nice."

"He didn't think it was very nice either."

The surrounding conversation faded as white noise.

"What's this company's revenue?" I asked.

"Twenty-seven million."

"And how many employees work for Murray?"

"Only one-hundred-thirty-three," he stated. "Amy laid him off by the way."

"*Amy* did?"

Sunshine Lady smiled and chattered like the world was her oyster.

"It was a messy situation. We're not supposed to talk about it. We're not even supposed to call him, but I still do. That night was horrible for him. He barely made it out alive, and he almost got arrested."

"I just thought it was because of pot given his extreme views on the subject. He didn't use it to make his leg feel better?"

"I don't think so. Murray does pot-testing, but they never did it on him. You wouldn't guess it at first, but Henley's a really bright guy. We've had a lot of great conversations together."

I sipped my drink and chomped the cheese slice.

"Many highly intelligent people tend to have extreme views because they base their opinions on personal philosophy instead of the trends of the time," he explained. "It was always tough to beat Henley in chess."

"So what's he doing now?"

Isaac chewed his burger. "He's pretty depressed about everything right now. His leg's getting a little better now that he has a chance to rest it, but he can't find another job. His girlfriend broke up with him, and his rich-ass father doesn't give a shit about him. His mother had pre-existing conditions and is already dead from water contamination, since her jackass divorced husband wouldn't take care of her."

A glimmer appeared in Deep Throat's eyes. He let go of his food and beverage but held his voice low.

"Henley's been suicidal. Keeps saying he wants to f**king kill himself. I've been trying to talk him out of it day after day. Somehow I got through to him, but now he wants to take it out on Amy. He really despises her."

Then I noticed the glass of black tar; Deep Throat had ordered a Guinness. "I never would've imagined that." I started on the pepperoni slice.

"It's always interesting to talk to Henley, even when it's tough. He has some interesting theories about the world. He says there's a war going on between coal miners and farmers, and that we're all in it together, whether we like it or not."

I swallowed and placed my bygone beverage to the side. "How can that be?" I wondered, hands open in front of me. "They both provide essential needs for society, and typically they vote for the same party."

Isaac took another bite. "Henley has a lot of unique ideas. He says Amy is the lynchpin – he keeps using that word – in all this since she talks to both the higher staff like Mike and the lower people like you."

My teeth approached the crust. "But there are other proj-ect managers here too, so why her?"

"Because she gets in bed with the vice president."

"Figuratively or literally?"

"Both."

Isaac almost finished his tar.

"Anyway – now this is just according to Henley, but I sort of agree with it – if Amy is removed from her position, the en-tire organization at Murray will collapse. Then Conrad Power will be in trouble because they won't have an auditor, which means they'll be less exploitative since they won't have as much money, and from there environmental conditions will naturally restore themselves."

I held my head sideways. "Interesting."

"I talked Henley into pursuing his ideas to give him a rea-son to live. Plus, I'd rather see Amy go than him."

"What do you mean?"

"He wants to hire a hitman, just doesn't have the money right now."

"Do you think he'll carry it out?"

"I'm sure he will eventually. He's very determined when he wants to accomplish something, and very clever about it too. Amy's life is dangling by a thread, you better believe it."

The doe-eyed bimbo yammered away living life to the fullest.

"Is he mad at *me* for any reason?"

Isaac waved his hand. "No, not at all. He told me about you, the last decent person he met. Says you were smart and cool and really patient with him."

"Oh."

Deep Throat leaned in towards me. "But don't tell her. I saw you looking at her over there. Henley doesn't want to have to come after you and..." He brought a finger midway up his neck and clenched his teeth.

"I won't tell."

"Ever?"

"Ever."

The noise died down, making our conversation more audible.

"We need to change the subject," I urged. "Pot?"

"Pot. You go first, what do you think should be done?"

"State by state until it's legal throughout the whole country."

"For rec or meds?"

"First meds, then rec."

"So you're a conservative," he stated.

"Why is that?"

"You said one state at a time."

"But some conservatives don't want it to be legal at all," I said.

"Well, which is more important? Medical or recreational?"

"Definitely medical. But then again, it seems as unfair to throw people in jail for ten years as it does ridiculous to legalize it everywhere simultaneously."

"So then what are your thoughts about medical?" Isaac took the last bite of his burger.

"Well, marijuana is like many herbs and vitamins, but it's an anomaly in that it's used recreationally when it should be used only to treat ailments. Medical marijuana, as I've heard, has the potential to save *lives* and bring *happiness* by treating certain diseases. It's a violation of individual *liberty* to arrest someone for curing their ailments. So in that sense, banning medical marijuana is a direct violation of life, liberty, and the pursuit of happiness."

"That sounds like a libertarian argument," he said.

"My grandfather said libertarians are basically liberals who can read, but who lack the motivation to develop a presence on the world stage," I mentioned. "He also said most Republicans are pseudo-Christians. What do you think he meant?"

Isaac shrugged. "I dunno man, I didn't know your grandpa."

I swallowed the pizza crust and peered beyond the sunrays.

Jenna floundered on the ground, giggling with drunken joy. Alyssa stood over her, reaching downward. Everyone else put on their jackets.

"You intellectuals should just stop talking like that and have some fun!" Tender Toucher kicked her legs.

I gestured towards Alyssa. "I remember what *you* said about fun!"

She squinted her well-centered eyes. "I'm glad you *did*. Sometime we can have the kind of fun you were just *talking about*."

"Don't tell me you actually had a *good time,* Richard," said Brian. "You missed out on what these ladies were doing!"

I must have. There were two empty mugs at Jenna's place, both with the same-color beer residue; Bowser had double-lapped Luigi on Yoshi Circuit.

I put on my Bronco's hat. Like the dwindling day, the clock was ticking at her own setting sun; Amy was also a Subtle Serpent. I was neither the first nor the last to leave, but somewhere in the middle.

Part Four

CHAPTER 33:

Bison Creek

"Hey Evan, how do we apply for benefits?"

He leaned over to me. "Just email Candace Meakard."

"Why can't I just go to her office?"

"Because she's in the other location."

"What other location?"

He bore a puzzled expression. "You didn't know we have another location in Meakardville (it's the headquarters)?"

"Does she own the town?"

"I dunno, possibly. It's way up in northern Kentucky (even farther north than where you live)."

Burrs had attached themselves to my gray sweater, so I switched to a green jacket, dark in color but light in weight; the weather had grown chilly.

While working with CartoPac, I prepared my route for the day; I was assigned to Bison Creek, and I had become competent enough in navigation that I could plan a trajectory according to the shortest route.

Upon stopping for gas at the BP station, I considered continuing right to travel a quicker way, but remembered I needed to check the rain gauge before nine-thirty.

I continued driving on Crataft Road and then turned right onto South Sunrise Seashore Road, where no beach was in sight.

When I arrived at my indicated location, BisC-4R, I recognized it as the stream on which Amy had trained me.

From the thinner burgundy canopy fell leaves in every color of autumn.

I parked alongside the road and hopped out, pleased the stream was flowing well for the household.

Near the mouth I found a 1.1 measurement, then followed the stream behind the house and saw the heaving mound sticking out of the streambed.

I crawled under the metal garden fence, then in response to reeling from the cold water that had soaked the front of my clothes and dampened the skin on the front side of my body, ran like a headless chicken across the back garden, trampling on every green plant that was good for food until I warmed up enough for the dampness to evaporate.

Swinging over the second gate, I landed firmly like a pole-vaulter with my hands in the air.

I skipped to the fracturing bedrock further broken apart, and slid across it like a snowboarder.

Around the bend and next to the house, an older teenager carried an Airsoft gun and pointed it at me.

I put my phone in my pocket and held my hands high. "Whoa there, don't shoot!"

He smiled. "I won't shoot you, even though you look like some sort of field bandit."

"Who are you trying to shoot then?"

"My friend."

"I hope Friendly Fire is not on."

He laughed.

"Anyway, good luck finding your friend. Go for a headshot!"

"I'll try, but he's too sneaky. What are you doing in our yard?"

"I work for Murray and Affiliates. They're an environmental consulting company. I'm assigned to make sure the streams are flowing properly for everyone around here."

The boy appeared suspicious. "My mom says not to play in the streams because she doesn't want me to get sick."

I put my palm to my chin. "Huh. Well, tell your mom I'm just doing my best and that I'll look extra hard for anything that comes up."

"That sounds like a cool job. I wanna do that when I grow up!"

"I'm an environmental technician. It is a pretty fun job. You may want to search for colleges that offer degrees in geology or environmental science."

We went along our separate ways.

I ran up the hillside, past the porch swing, over to a flat green pasture near the streambank, and leaned against a tree as I enjoyed my lunch.

The latter half of October beheld a display of fireworks descending from the highest treetops, leaves falling and floating high above, red, orange, yellow, brown, some green, and a few purple.

After consuming a ham sandwich, corn chips, an apple, and carrots, with water from my CamelBak, I proceeded onwards.

Two HSWs lay ahead – the first a 5.6 measurement, and the second a 12.1 near a waterfall, for which I used my extended tape measure.

Surprised by the rapid descent, I raised my bump cap for the brief moment I was underwater and tossed it onto the bank, then doggy-paddled to the shore and hoisted myself up. Water had filled my muck boots, so I emptied them; the sole of the right boot had become withered.

I followed a tributary into the thicket of trees into which Amy and I had ventured. The plastic orange fencing had been slashed. The gradient grew steeper, with coalescing and convalescing secondary tributaries washing the hillsides. I charged up a sharp incline where I grabbed the plastic lining and chopped through it.

At the end of the stream, a long tubular black nozzle spurted out groundwater. A tall iron-rusted stick protruded from the ground onto which a white bucket with a handle rested overtop and upside-down.

I placed the bucket below the nozzle and started the stopwatch on my phone until the bucket overflowed, at which point I pressed 'Stop,' dumped out the water in a mad *swoosh*, and repeated this action twice more. The first time was 28 seconds, the second 31, and the third 30. I averaged the three values and rounded the mean to the whole number of 30. CartoPac calculated a flow rate of 73 GPM.

When I prepared to leave the AUG, I toppled forwards; a hole had seized my left boot, and thick prickly vines of ivy were wound around it. I snapped off my CamelBak, swung it over my shoulder, and unzipped the top pouch for the clippers, which failed to break the vines. I stowed them away and brought out my pocketknife. I sawed through each vine, one after another, and finally broke free.

I emerged from the thicket to continue along the previous channel, where a swampy, algae-ridden pond lay in a steep valley; I raced through the oak trees while crunching the orange and yellow leaves, swinging from every branch and trunk, propelling myself forward, then tumbled with a commando roll.

Underneath the branches of an evergreen pine by the upstream end of the pond lay two Rorschach inkblots; the less severe one spread to the streambank. I recorded these patches as 'Orange Staining' and 'Orange Staining With Sheen.'

Thickets, brambles, and thorns covered the rest of the stream.

I sauntered back the way I had traversed with my project manager and drove to the end of the stream where I hopped out to an electric fence.

When the probe lit up green, I scurried to a silver gate, unlocked it, stepped through, and relocked it. Leaves and shrubs covered the STP; I peeked underneath, saw trickling water, and skidded downhill to a dry segment. A few paces later, the stream came alive again.

CHAPTER 34:

Radical Destruction

The locker room door had been locked at five-o'clock, so I used the main entrance. However, only the lobby door was unlocked, whereas the actual entrance seemed glued to its hinges.

Sitting down while leaning against the wall, I sent an InReach message: STUCK IN LOBBY.

I waited five minutes.

Swoosh.

Fifteen more minutes passed.

When I tapped repeatedly on the door, I received a message from Jocelyn Reical: SORRY AT HOME CAN'T HELP.

I entered through the unlocked door of Waterstone Surveying & Mapping and ascended the wood-metal staircase. The first step creaked, and I heard quite a bit of ruckus. When I reached the top, I beheld the sight before my eyes.

Floorboards were knocked loose; the white-painted walls, in addition to the cubicle walls, were torn apart and damaged. Every tenth computer had been smashed, while bits of scattered hardware lay about the floor like a series of extra-thick crunchy potato chips.

A fifty-something-year-old man wearing a yellow sweatshirt with blue jeans leaned backward, cowering. His balding head suggested the same progression of hair loss as Racecar Dude. *"I'M SORRY! I CAN'T DO ANYTHING TO HELP YOU."* He yammered and stared, weeping and wailing like a dolphin lost at sea or a snail that had lost its concourse.

Racecar Dude wouldn't let go of his baseball bat. It wobbled in both hands like he was about to hit a homerun. "Ya know what – you butthead. Why don't you just scram!" he yelled at the floundering, flustering man.

"You've been chasing me around for *hours,* sir, and I've already told you, and obviously you know this as well, your parents are back together safe and sound in the same house again!"

Bo parsed his lips and shook his head back and forth like the bobble-head doll he could've been, while his face turned redder by the moment. *"Ya just don't get it – do ya!* My parents can NEVER have the relationship they once did unless their water supply is fixed. Make your company talk to ours – ya douchebag! We do the same stuff anyways."

I peered behind the corner.

The man cowered and cowed, covering his head with his arms and looking into them as if searching for treasure in a hole in the ground. He stepped back, trembling, stumbling as he retreated. "WE DO SIMILAR THINGS, BUT NOT THE SAME, as I've already *told* you."

Racecar Dude stepped toward him, his body as vertical as his bat raised above his head, with many a *thunk!* against the ceiling. "Oh yeah – you bastard? Then why don't you just contact the government? Or talk to Jon Wyganti? Or Mike Matthews?"

Clenching his own throat, he set his back against the wall, and like a wiggly worm, cowered on the ground. "Jon can't *speak properly,* and Mike threatened to *chop* my *head off!"* He shook to the concords of his wimbling will.

"I'm gonna crack your f**kin' head open." Bo grabbed him by the shirt collar with his left hand and held the bastard, baseball bat in the other tilted backwards at twenty degrees from the vertical axis.

"Bo! Stop it you punk!" I shouted, my own voice as weak as a hanging cloth on a clothesline drenched by the sun's heat at the beginning of an Indian autumn.

Racecar Dude turned towards me like a deer in the headlights; the victim nibbled and scratched his way out, breaking free and, rushing thence, grabbed the nearest door handle, quarantining himself in the room.

BAM!

Bo swung overhead, toppling a wooden table polished with the finest finish.

SMASH!

Glass from the closed-door room shattered and scattered *everywhere,* the poor man whimpering and *wailing.*

I brandished my pocketknife.

At the same moment, Racecar Dude screamed, "Get outta here, you little sissy – if you know what's good for you!"

He opened the door. "Listen, Thomas. First of all, you're such a *loser* because you go by Thomas and not Tom, or what about *Tommay!* So, here we have it. I can either smack *you* dead – and blame it on my pal Richard from Murray over here – *or* – I can smack *him* dead – and blame it on you. So it's your choice. Do the right thing – and not the wrong thing – but don't do the *stupid* thing either...or else."

The man cried and wailed like a stray dog in the middle of Los Angeles. "Uhh! Uh! Uhhhh! I *don't* know *what* to *do!*"

My head swirled from shoulder to shoulder and back and forth; I didn't know whether the present came before the past or the past after the future. "I...I-I-I I also don't know what to doooo...." I closed my eyes, waiting all the more hurriedly for reality itself to fade away....

I perked up. "Wait, Bo! Can you unlock the door downstairs for me? I really need to get going now."

Racecar Dude's jaw dropped down along the vertical axis,

while the end of his mouth finicked upwards to five-pi-over-six on the unit circle. "You're pretty retarded – Richard! Didja know that – ya douchebag?"

I shimmied my way along, CamelBak against the wall.

To that end, Bo and I circled around the room like two horse-carriages on a merry-go-round. He had sworn, and even used the R-word, yet the Upper Hand was nowhere to be found.

"You're a dickless cretin – *you f**ktard!* Why don't you just go home – to your *MOMMY*. Oh boo hoo! Boo *hoo hoo*.... Alright – you know what you f**khead. It's just me and you – let's do this!"

We circled each other, neither of us daring to strike the first blow. We, as two pinwheels on a pinwheel machine, or two scared rabbits neither knowing either one, had almost reversed ourselves from our previous positions. I grabbed ten stray pens from the toppled desk beside me and threw them straight at Bo's head, but they all missed.

I braced myself against the wall, and Bo's landmine head turned as red as the reddest red giant in outer space. Darkness consumed me, until...

My right hand found a light switch. I struck them on all at once, and Bo's eyes watered and brimmed with water to their surface. "*RRRAAHHH-AHHHH-RAAAAAGHGH!!!!*"

The man behind me fell quiet, yet he screamed. I held my pocketknife, bracing my grip.

"...Uuaaghggghuuaauaghghhah." I babbled like a helpless babbling brook.

I stood on guard, then put my hands up.

"Uuuurrraahhhhh!" Racecar Dude was thunderstruck.

It took him a long time to step forth and come forth and come forward, but when he did, his face was entirely red, including the skin of his balding spot. His spectra-laden eyes, though they swerved up into his head like those of The Undertaker from *WWE*, the whites and even the pupils high above locked on to me like a heatseeking missile. Underneath his valley-shaped eyebrows, his downward-slanted white eyes were brimming with raw malice, and madness was oozing from his face!

I held my pocketknife forward; I had a fifty-fifty chance of survival, but felt the odds were in my favor. We both held our characteristic weapons, yet this was no *Super Smash Brothers*; the character weight was loaded, and the programmers clearly favored him!

I stepped back with my left hand on the door handle, a silvery touch to my bleeding, blistering, red and tired palm, only my palm wasn't bleeding. I opened the door, and stepping backwards, used the dwindling loser's head as higher ground, not reaching for the handle to close it until my other muck boot had stepped off his head.

"RRAAAHHHHHH!!" cried Racecar Dude.

Left arm stiff, I idiotically opened the door. I stepped out of the room on guard.

Bo's bat was in both hands, and he was ready to hit another homerun. I didn't want to let the horse out of the barn just yet, so I held my right arm outstretched.

His bat was above my head.

CHAPTER 35:

It Keeps Going On

"Bo, wait. Kill Mike Matthews."

"*KILL...MIKE...MATTHEWS...?*" He lowered his bat and growled in my face like a demented hungry shark. "Now just *WHY...WOULD I do that?*"

"He's responsible for your parents' water contamination problem – or their lack of water, that is." My pocketknife was underneath his chin. "Yes, I've overheard him, plundering the earth without shame and letting Conrad Power get away with everything they're doing, even urging them on, egging them on.... He even knows the government is blissfully ignorant. I don't really *know* if Amy Lane is the true lynchpin, but...yeah, just keep picking on someone your own gender."

He dropped his bat. "Now that's an *excellent* idea!"

"Just as Mike would say. He needs to be replaced, and it doesn't matter who his successor is, even if it is Amy, I can assure you that she would not be as bad...since she's not as clever or maliciously mischievous and actually pretty flat-out stupid."

Bo stared at me.

"He's downstairs in his office right now," I said. "I saw him through the window. Go after him while you still have the chance."

He picked up his bat and held the top to the ground, with

his right hand around the thinning handle-bottom. "Alright you little funking puckhead," he spat in a daze. "Come with me!"

Racecar Dude charged toward the stairwell, ripping and smashing every last bit of indoor debris.

Holding my pocketknife behind my right thigh, I crept up to him, and he waited for me at the top of the stairwell behind a glass pane.

"Come with me," he said calmly. "But don't do anything stupid!"

"I won't do anything stupider than you."

He grimaced.

Racecar Dude began to descend the staircase, then stepped slowly, step by step with wobbling bat held high.

I pointed the tip of my pocketknife at his back.

Bo sped ahead as he approached the landing.

I threw myself against the wall and caught up to him as we reached the lower floor, creeping behind him with my knees bent as he turned to the Murray & Affiliates door.

He looked at me, and I retreated in a giant backwards leap.

Racecar Dude held the bat in front of me. "So! You have two-and-a-half choices now. You can either call the police – get in a big fight with them – and wait in your stupid Honda *all night long* – tell your special project manager friend Amy that someone like *me* would actually terrorize you and the poor f**k upstairs – *or* I can break us both in."

Bo stood straight, heaving his chest like a diver about to plunge to the bottom of the ocean.

"You saw that chump up in Waterstone. I can smack *him* dead and blame it on you – *or* I can smack *you dead* and blame it...on...him."

He chuckled mercilessly to himself.

"So do the right thing – and not the wrong thing – but don't do the stupid thing either. Or else."

"Just lemme in."

"Don't think this is the first time I've ever done this shit!"
He raised his bat.

"Cover your ears."

I stepped outside and held the door open with my foot and was disturbed by the *CLASH!* even while covering my ears.

Trembling, I approached the doorway and tiptoed around the shattered remains, through the opening with glass like stalactites high above and glass like stalagmites down below.

He had smashed the flower vases into pieces scattered across the floor, while flowers lay across the soaked carpet. Glass shards had flown into the main complex; I watched the floor until the trail diminished.

Bo stood in front of Shadow Guy's office, which seemed darker than all the others. "Where is that bastard?! Mike ain't in *here*." His eyes grew as he shook his open-mouthed head.

"He must have escaped," I replied. "Let me get my keys and we can go out looking for him."

I took off immediately.

CHAPTER 36:

Mindy's Mania

I returned early the next morning having slept little and completely enervated. The front door was locked, so I used my key fob to enter through the side door.

A broom leaning against the far wall accompanied a dustpan holding glass shards, yet the carpet sparkled like ice crystals. The flowers, which could have been saved in watery jars, were crumpled in the wastebasket with their pedals torn and stems bisected.

"Ahh! Aaaahhhh!!" cried Mindy, disheveled with her poorly-combed mouse-brown hair. Total Wreck squealed like a mouse as well. "I can't believe this happened! Oh my god! I can't believe this has happened! I can't *believeeve* this actually ha-a-ppe-ned...."

"I'm so sorry! Let me know what happened to you. I heard on the news this morning some wild kid went around Georgetown County to different businesses and *smashed* the walls and the doors to pieces. But I *know* something like this won't occur again because the police, although they were completely uneasy and guilty about it, shot him *dead* in the middle of the street."

"*Ooohhhhh noooooooooo!!!!!*" she wailed like a dying seagull. "My sixteen-year-old son plays baseball at his high school! It could have been him! It could have been *hiiimm!!*

UAAHHHRRAHHH!"

"Mindy, Mindy, please calm down, I'm sure it wasn't him." I leaned in towards her. "I'm sure a good, kind mother like you wouldn't have raised a child who would do such a thing."

"Yes I would, and yes HE would, too!" She placed her forearm parallel atop the desk and set her forehead near her wrist. "You don't *know* what I can be like as a mother, and you don't *know* how he acts around the kitchen sometimes."

"Look, I must confess – I've been looking through your personal phonebook...because I wanted to know who your son was...because I just thought, 'Wow, what a fantastic woman, I bet she has an incredible son!'"

"Oh, he's incredible alright."

"So I was concerned about him and even called him before I came, early this morning.... So, he gets really angry and irritated that I called him while he was still in bed sleeping, and then, and then he starts swearing at me and cursing me and telling me to f**k off and go to hell and –"

Mindy stopped sobbing, her eyes well above her nose. "So you actually did talk to him then?"

"Of course, why would I lie about it when you're already so upset?"

She straightened up along the vertical axis, and heaved, torso sagging. "Well, what a relief! Look Richard, I need you to stay quiet about several things. First, don't tell anybody that we have a terrible alarm system and that anyone could break in at any time."

"I won't."

"Also, keep me *completely* out of this incident. I could easily be fired on the spot if anyone knows I'm involved in this sort of thing. My kids, including my son need the healthcare from this job. My daughter has strep throat compounded with diabetes, and she's a fat girl, which I don't understand because I didn't start gaining weight until my early forties. And as for my son, he's on drugs so he needs healthcare too, and I really do love him, I just hate his behavior."

"I understand, I won't tell!"

"Good, because my husband is a lazy bum who's out of a job. I just called him, he's in his underpants right now."

"But...anybody could come within an hour." I checked the digital clock on her desk. "We have to think of something!"

Her complexion changed. "Don't worry about that, I've already called the window-and-glass repair company. They'll be here soon, or at least before the head managers show up."

"I'm glad everything's fine then."

I walked to the main complex.

"Also," I said, "it would really help your case if you weren't such a sad sack."

CHAPTER 37:

The Blessing and Curse of Coal

From the picture stand I grabbed a piece of bituminous coal and headed to the kitchen. On my way, I encountered a woman who often wandered around the complex. She was a licensed remediation specialist who was boring to look at but also boring to talk to.

Thirty-two-year-old Lisa Misteak, a curious product of evolution, was excessively tall for a woman, and I had to bend my neck whenever I wanted to inspect her face. Her loose wrinkled white shirt resembled the bowl of rice pudding less bland than her appearance and personality together, and she appeared very weary this morning. Her medium-length brown hair, linear figure, ghostly skin, and wide-focused yet downcast eyes made her an unremarkable Five – neither attractive nor unattractive – in contrast to my upbeat attitude and Eight-out-of-ten looks. Lisa was a horror show; she walked with the slow regularity and indomitable determination of a zombie.

Zombie Woman spoke like a robot and looked like she had risen from the grave when she was extremely tired, but also bore this countenance when she wasn't tired at all. She herself was as dull as her resume and LinkedIn profile combined. One of her steps counted as three of my steps, and if I asked her to a dance, she might perform a three-over-four time-signature waltz with me.

"Hi...Richard...how...are...you...doing...this...morning?"

"I'm quite well, thank you. What are you doing here at this hour?"

"Mindy...told...me...to...come...here...because...there... is...something...we...needed...to...talk...about.... It...is...a... private...issue...between...me...and...her."

Zombie Woman took another step.

"Be sure to keep it a secret between the two of you so nobody finds out."

I inched my toes little by little.

"What...are...you...doing...here...right...now?"

"She also called me, and bade me come, just so there was a man to take care of things."

I took one more step.

"She...said...she...only...called...me.... You...should...not... trust...her...then..." she said, finally beginning to take another step "...since...she...lied...to...me."

"I know what you mean. Mindy really is a wreck. I'm going to get some coffee now if you don't mind getting out of the way."

"Take...your...time.... I...already...had...two...cups...."

"No, take *your* time."

I rushed past her and rested my head in my arms at the high circular kitchen table and placed the piece of coal in front of me.

The FRIENDS OF COAL magnet was still affixed to the refrigerator, only slightly more tilted to the right.

I fell half-asleep and finally had enough energy to make coffee – but at seven-o'clock a recognizable voice said to me:

"Well hey there Richard, you little sleepyhead. Why don't I make us both some coffee?"

"That would be lovely."

Tender Toucher reached her arm around my shoulders and stroked my hair; she looked bright-eyed and bushy-tailed as well. The sound of hot coffee brewing made me feel warmer, and a little less sleepy too.

Soon enough Chase and Alyssa arrived, and they held each other as they walked, but not by their hands. Ron followed in from behind them.

They grabbed their mugs as Jenna poured us our rounds.

Tender Toucher and Barnyard Boy sat next to me, with liquid to the brims of their mugs, while Mister Suckup and Savvy Socialite stood next to us; Ron held his arms to the sides, while Alyssa placed one hand on her jutted-out hip with her phone sticking out of her yoga pants on the same side.

"You know, coal formed from lithified plant debris from ancient swamps," I began, "but in a way, it's also made from human lives."

Jenna nodded but Savvy Socialite rolled her eyes.

"Mining for coal produces acid mine drainage which can seep into waterways and aquifers," I continued, "with consequences to ecological and human health."

"This is your life, dude," Chase proclaimed.

I held up the coal. "But you see...this thing."

"Richard, wait," said Jenna. "What are you doing with that rock?"

"It's not just coal, it's a representation of innocent lives lost. Coal mining poisons innocent poor peoples' water and kills them so the rest of us can live in a modern way. Coal makes a mockery of human life."

"We couldn't live the way we do if we didn't have it," Ron mentioned.

"Don't you think I know that?! Nearly a quarter of our country's energy comes from burning coal."

"Do you *really?*" said Alyssa. "If we just get *rid of coal,* do you think you would even *have this job?*"

"Yeah, I know. Without it we're just a bunch of weak prehistoric humans. We can live like we do because we have coal, I know that. But the coal industry thrives as a result of taking peoples' lives!"

Ron raised his eyebrows. "And? Those people don't want to be victims, but I doubt they would want to have the little money they have thrown away after taxes are raised."

"I actually don't know too much about coal," said Tender Toucher, drinking from her mug, "since I live in a solar-powered apartment, but I believe the government will defeat us if we throw away coal now. And if that happens, many more people will lose their lives due to unemployment and lack of modern conveniences. I don't want that to happen, and I don't want this job to be meaningless."

"You're right, Jen." Mister Suckup took another sip. "We can throw away coal at any time. But right now, we need to carry the economy forward and fight for the rights of miners, as well as our own."

I sat upright with my hands open on the table. "Alright."

Chase chugged the remainder of his coffee like he couldn't feel the burn. "Dude, didn't you say you weren't gonna be such a sourpuss anymore?"

"Alright. Yeah, I hate to say it, but you're right." I brought the piece of coal closer to my face. "It seems as though both our wishes and our regrets dwell in this thing. To prevent creating any more victims in either sphere of society, I'm going to help this company. I will fight for both coal miners and farmers."

Alyssa looked up from her phone, brushed her hair aside, and opened her mouth wide as she bounced on her heels. "Uh, *yeah,* that's what we're *supposed to be doang.*"

Tender Toucher placed her hands on my knees. "Me too. I'm going to do this job as quickly as I can today so we can go to the pumpkin patch. Wanna come with us?"

Savvy Socialite bounced her head sideways. "Pumpkin patch! Pumpkin patch!"

"I'll get back to you on that, Jenna, and I hope I am able to attend that event with you all. But allow me to finish what I was saying before. By nature, people are sinful creatures." I held my pointer finger high while facing her. "Life survives at the cost of another. Then we must continue to bear the burden of our sins for as long as we continue to live."

Barnyard Boy furrowed his brow and set his mug on the table. "Life survives at the cost of another? What the hell are you even talkin' about?"

"I think he means survival of the fittest," clarified Mister Suckup.

"I don't really know how to say this, but I don't think there's a way to justify the lives sacrificed to earn immense profit from mining!" I blurted. "The industry as it exists right now has to be stopped at all costs!"

Ron refilled his mug. "Well yeah, you gotta beat coal to get rid of excessive government oversight."

"Will you...will you show me the way to both peace and prosperity?" I begged. "I can't...I can't pretend like all the environmental destruction isn't going on. This is too cruel!"

Chase offered me a glare. "Well? Whadda ya wanna do about it?"

"You're welcome to join us for flesh football," Tender Toucher chimed with a convex smile.

"Yeah...why don't you go ahead and save everyone like that." I leaned away from her. "I saw an old man with a collapsing bridge near his driveway."

Savvy Socialite rolled her eyes clockwise. "Yeah! Let's fight the government *together!*"

Ron held his palms outward. "Do whatever you want, man. You're smart enough to do the right thing. We all trust you."

I exhaled to my falling shoulders. "Thanks. I've exhausted my reasoning on this matter, but I'm sure I can still be of use."

Tender Toucher patted me on the chest. "Don't forget to have some coffee before it gets cold!"

CHAPTER 38:

Backwards Monitoring

After drinking a cup of microwaved coffee, I felt ready for my next Little Adventure.

Sunshine Lady was looking quite circular and doily today. "Well *you look all* set and *ready to go* there."

"Yes. I went to bed early last night and had a very sound sleep. I am well refreshed and looking forward to the big day ahead."

She smiled. "Well *thaat's* good. Let *me know how* it goes. So *do you know* where you're going?"

"Of course. I am heading off to BisC-5R, very close to where I was yesterday."

"Well *thaat's* good. So *you know* the way. Just *let me know* if anything goes wrong."

She waved and closed the door.

Although both rightward tributaries of Bison Creek were proximate, I parked behind a wooden shed near the STP of BisC-4R. The mouth of the tributary lay in the woods too far from a road for me to make reasonable time in arriving at my assigned area. Therefore, I parked where both STPs conjoined, which meant I would monitor this area not from downstream to upstream, but backwards – upstream to downstream.

I proceeded around the shed and arrived at a tall metal

gate; perpendicular fence lengths intersected it on both sides, and a smaller wooden gate was open far to the right of the shed. I climbed the silver gate like I was climbing a ladder, one bar at a time, then stepped down like a soldier invading a fortress.

A glen stood in between two fields of high hay; I followed the right path, but encountered a donkey. I retreated and followed the less convenient but safer left path, but it galloped around and blocked my way.

Reaching into my CamelBak, I teased the donkey with promises of an early-day snack, and launched the apple to the other side of the glen; the animal followed its instincts, so I continued along the leftward path, darting around hay stalks.

When I stepped over a barbed-wire fence, I realized that part of the stream lay further uphill, within the glen. Squinting into the rising sun, I saw a glimmer of water and concluded the segment was flowing.

I scribbled 'Territorial Donkey' on my JHA and added that 'Stealth' was required.

Upon approaching a rocky waterfall, I sped through the thicket, slinging myself from one branch to another, and continued downhill until I arrived at a flat part of the stream course; water flowed in front of me and behind me.

About half of all the leaves in this area hung on pointy tree branches, and my muck boots crunched on the ones that lay in the banks. The effectual canopy gave an impression of protection, even though it had thinned and browned over the last few months.

To take notes more expediently, I unsnapped the black button of my vest and rushed along the secondary tributaries.

I recorded a 27 GPM flow at a muddy 2.6-meter HSW far downstream and marked it as 'Turbid.'

In carrying out my plan for ultimate efficiency, I realized my notebook was no longer in my vest.

As I sprinted uphill and downhill, my eyes were like

security scanners on every secondary tributary, and I felt an unusual lightness near my right shoulder when I realized my R1 was gone.

For the rest of the day, I raced up and down, screaming and hollering. I plugged in numbers after numbers and descriptions after more descriptions, entering the fakest of fake data.

I retraced my steps and plodded across areas I had already monitored, in addition to random areas I had not monitored at all.

One of the streams, labelled 'NA' for 'No Access' due to 'Landowner Refusal,' I had surveyed not twice, but thrice. Therefore, I studied it a fourth time, going uphill, stopping and digging through every layer of leaves and dirt.

I needed an excuse and a reasonable-sounding one at that. A bear – yes, a bear had chased me.

After catching my breath, I trekked downhill and spotted, underneath a pile of red-and-brown leaves with overlying dark soil, the corner of my R1 unit.

The dark sky enabled me to practice astronomical navigation; I aligned the proper azimuth with the zenith. Guided by the ancient method of charting one's course, I followed each star of Orion's belt while keeping Polaris in sight behind me.

When I climbed into the unlocked truck, I chowed down on a dinner of protein bars and pork rinds while charging my iPhone with the spare battery.

CHAPTER 39:

They're Pretty Expensive

L ight pollution diluted the starlight.
  "Hi Mindy."

She held her head down.

"You know, you're still a wreck, and you'll always be a miserable wreck!"

Mud had caked the sensor of my Hach, so I headed to the kitchen.

"You know."

I developed goosebumps as the statuesque silhouette appeared on the cabinets, rising ever closer with the pointed nose, slinky neck, oblong head, and protruding Adam's apple.

Upon rinsing off my sensor, I squirted a dressing of liquid soap into the sink like cake ornamentation, but the body already rubbed against me.

"You know, that if you were to place the Hach back into your CamelBak there, zip it up with your little jimjam inside, strap it once again to your back, and then walk out of the kitchen, through the cubicle area, down the hallway, and into the locker room, you would then not have to create such an undesirable mess here in this sink, because you would already be washing off your special gear there in a different location."

I had no idea how even Encyclopedia Brown could hold his finger so high.

"*Alternatively,*" he continued, eyes raised then focused on me, "if you were to walk out of the kitchen, go back outside by departing through the main entrance as Mindy had done, and then, walking towards the locker room door, putting your hand on the handle, and opening it, you would also end up in the same location doing the same thing, as long as you still remembered to place your jimjam there, as well as your Hach, inside your CamelBak, and strap it to your torso as you most likely had done when you were monitoring the streams."

I kicked him in the shins. "Get off of me Kevin, you're such a loser. You should be out of here by now and not snooping around, so just mind your damn business for once."

He stepped back, waving his pointed-finger hand. "All I am saying, is that I am simply just trying to help."

"Why don't you help me tomorrow then?" I lowered my voice. "Then we'll both be rested and refreshed so we can help each other out."

Kevin nodded, waving a window-wiper hand. "That sounds like it would be quite wonderful."

After cleaning up the mess, I stowed my CamelBak with my gear underneath my desk. Then I removed my muck boots in the locker room.

I passed Sunshine Lady's empty room.

I glanced over the wall of my cubicle toward Elephant Man's room and saw that he had left as well.

Shadow Guy's desk was positioned away from the door.

The lamp and computer screen illuminated his scornful face. *"How can I help you, Richard?"*

"Hi Mike, I'm glad you're here. I made a bad decision with my field notebook. I placed it in the pocket of my vest and didn't really remember to button it up. But it will definitely not ever happen again, because I will always remember to make sure it's secure from now on. So I was wondering, do you know where the extra field notebooks are?"

"No problem. Come follow me, I'll show you where they

are." Mike rose and motioned with his hand.

I stepped out and let him walk in front.

"I've been working a little late because business is tough right now."

He strode at a below-average pace, blue pantlegs brushing against one another as he stepped soundlessly in his shiny black leather shoes.

"It seems great minds think alike." I tried to meet his gait.

"Why have you been out so late then?"

"Just being really careful and thorough is all. The notebook issue is just a blip in my steady performance."

"Don't worry about it," he said, waving a hand, *"with enough practice it'll be second nature, trust me. So are you having fun out there?"*

"Yeah, I'm having fun." I fell behind him. "The job itself is like another geology field course. Each time I go out it's like a Little Adventure."

He looked back and snickered. *"Well it's good to know you're having fun. And are you being safe?"*

"Perfectly safe." I caught up to him.

CLAP! He smashed his palms together. *"Excellent! I've heard you drive Grandma Style; I can tell based on how nicely you work your way through the parking lot and park. I just received a report of a sighting of something out in the woods that might compromise our image of safety."*

At the very moment he entered the hallway, he began to shuffle forward with feet one in front of the other, making many tiny steps, and the brushing of his pants and shoes became a noisy swish. Shadow Guy stared at the floor as he crept along like he was walking backwards on an airport travelator. I wanted to hop on the gravy train, to ride along with him, but one of my footsteps counted as ten of his own.

Several minutes later, he arrived at a red metal cabinet and placed his palms on the door frame. His shoelace had come loose.

And when he leaned down, his wallet, which was thinner than I expected, slipped out of his pocket, and he grabbed not for his shoe but for the money-holder lying on the ground with his body angled like a trapezoidal camera stand.

"You know what," he said standing upright, *"I forgot the key. I'll go back and get it."*

"Okay. Please do get me another one. I promise to be very careful and not lose it again."

"Alright, I'll put one on your desk. But don't be so careful that you don't have any fun. And don't have so much fun that you're not being safe. On second thought, do be careful with these notebooks, cuz...they're pretty expensive."

Shadow Guy braced his teeth and winked, then walked back and slammed the door.

For the next five minutes, I used the restroom.

FLUSH!!!!

I pulled out my magic marker.

But my desk was clear.

The cheapest ones on amazon.com were five dollars.

CHAPTER 40:

Eleven-Mile Creek

Over the next week, I replaced my dark-green jacket, which I had taped with duct tape because of the pointy branches that punctured it, underneath a firm yet lightweight hunter's coat. I removed ticks from my skin and placed bandages over the affected areas.

I used a small pocket-notebook while awaiting a new proper one. During the day, I often wore my hunter's coat overtop the jacket, only to take it off at midday when the weather had warmed.

"Do you know where the spare notebooks are?" I asked Boiler Brain one morning.

"They're at the stream hub."

"And where's that?"

"Just go right past Amy's office (you'll see it)."

I rushed past her office.

"*Whoa* ho-ho, what *are you doing* running about?"

"Just looking forward to the day is all."

"So, how *have things been going* for you?"

"Just good."

"*Just* good? Did you *see a bear out* in the woods?"

"No, why would I?"

"There was a *bear sighting near* Bison Creek and *we were worried* about you."

"Oh *no!*"

"What's wrong?" Sunshine Lady tilted her head and raised an eyebrow like a concerned nanny.

"I was concerned it might have attacked somebody. I guess I'm lucky that it didn't come after me."

Her tongue was hanging out for no legitimate reason. "So you *didn't see it* and you're *completely safe* then?"

"I'm fine. I'm safe."

"Well *thaat's* good," said Amy, lips about to fall off her face. "Do you know *where you're going* today?"

"Yeah, why wouldn't I? Eleven-Mile Creek."

The stream hub, a small table, displayed many different items: tick-spray, metersticks, snacks, winter clothes, bump caps, and safety glasses. I grabbed an army blanket from a large stack. In a small tray lay two half-filled Rite-in-the-Rain notebooks; I grabbed one and realized I did not possess a writing utensil at the moment.

Heading through the main complex and into the hallway, I reached the red metal cabinet and prepared to bang against it, but the door swung open easily.

I gasped at my true reward: a treasure trove of brand-new field notebooks!

I grabbed one, slipped it under my shirt, and headed to the left side of the complex and back to my cubicle where I placed it in a lower drawer.

Eleven-Mile Creek, abbreviated EleC, was my closest destination yet. On this sunny day, I parked next to a mailbox by a roundabout in a bustling suburban neighborhood.

Brown-trunk trees dotted the hillside and valley; a few tan leaves dangled from their sticky branches.

I descended a modest grassy hillside and walked along the edge of the woods until I found a convenient entrance point.

Then I shoved my way through brush, bramble, and trees, forging a path along a poorly trimmed trail and hopped into the stream, heading downstream to an AUG.

No water flowed from the protruding black pipe barely rising from the surface; I marked the point as 'Dry.'

I hopped along the banks, sometimes landing in the water, and spun across the incised meander. Throwing off my bump cap while jumping and spinning, I screamed 'Ya!' like Mario in *Super Mario Galaxy*, but my cap didn't return to me like a boomerang; it landed near rushing water, so I retrieved it and cleaned it off.

The meandering stream wound from one side of the valley to the other, and I followed it as such, not keeping track of its course entirely, but making sure I saw water at every reasonable point.

Around the bend came EleC-16, a 2.6 measurement with just enough opacity to call it 'Clear.'

Many tributaries were dry from mouth to endpoint, so I marked them as ESD for 'Entire Stream Dry.'

A large fallen tree trunk blocked the stream's course. Bramble and bushes surrounded it, and no standing tree provided swinging branches. I marked this segment as 'No Access – Blocked by Vegetation.'

A small passage opened near ground level, so I proceeded on my hands and knees like Link crawling in search of rupees.

After a small downhill slope, a quick rise led to an area of open sky.

Close to the woods' continuation lay EleC-17, barely a 1.1 in measurement; it carried such a muddy and murky flow regime that I had no choice but to identify it as 'Turbid.'

The steep passage convinced me to climb onto the rising hillside where I found a fresh yard with a hefty man in a red farmer's shirt who spouted:

"Hey you, get off mah property!"

Retreating into the woodsy area, I descended to a well-flowing segment beyond the STP.

From the other side, I hiked along the bank until I

approached the clear area of the previous HSW. By running down the slope I gained enough momentum to glide up a grassy hill with tall brown stalks, huffing and puffing as I propelled myself forward with every ounce of leg strength.

A road appeared on the hillside. I continued walking along the representative hypotenuse across the property of someone who didn't notice my vandalizing muck boots; a woman in a yellow dress greeted me as I marched past her front door.

I treaded along the boundary of the moderately busy road and the unsteady grasslands until I hopped off a short ridge onto the roundabout.

A man in a blue-striped button-down shirt and gray pants awaited me in front of my truck; he appeared to be in his mid-to-late thirties. I prepared myself with the best dialogue options.

"Excuse me, could you please not park here?"

"Why not? This is a good spot for me. What's the big deal?"

"You see," he said as he raised his hand, "the mail truck comes around here at ten-o'clock, and when they see people from a company like yours parking here, they don't deliver the mail."

"That's their fault then; they're just lazy."

"But there's a bigger problem too. Right after your trucks leave from this area – and you're not the first one to park here by the way – a Conrad Power vehicle comes out, and people start dumping toxic waste, not always in the streams necessarily, but around the area where it's usually poorly covered up."

"I won't park here again then."

"No, you can park here, just come by later from now on."

CHAPTER 41:

Natural Causes

The sole of my right muck boot had become torn, wrinkled, and tattered, such that keeping it inside made it uncomfortable for me to walk. In the locker room, I searched for a pair of the same size and style, and the only other Wetland muck boots in size eleven for men – size twelve for women – were those placed in front of a locker with the name *TOWSER* taped to the front.

After glancing around, I replaced Halley's right sole with my right sole and placed *my* new sole in my now soleless boot, and didn't really care because I had always seen a pale yellow head in a cubicle by a white safety helmet with her name attached. The new sole felt comfortable under my right foot.

I began the Field Review when Brian smacked a tattered muddy notebook on the left end of my desk.

"This is yours," said Buff Face.

"Where did you find it?"

"It was in a No Access area lying face down in the stream. I accidentally went into there. You must have too."

"Yeah. It was purely accidental."

My former notebook was smeared, dirt-stained, and downright ugly. I placed it on the shelf.

Chase came around the corner while Shadow Guy held both his shoulders as he followed him. They stood by his cubicle, down the aisle from mine.

"What was the cause of your grandfather's death?"

"Natural causes."

"Louder."

"Natural causes!"

"Good."

Shadow Guy walked to the front entrance.

Chase sat in his cubicle, staring blankly.

I signed a card on Mindy's desk, and when I returned both Alyssa and Jenna stood around him.

"We'll do whatever you *want*," Alyssa reassured him in a soft tone, stroking his shoulder.

"I'll share my Chick-fil-A with you anytime," offered Jenna, hand on his head.

"I'm sorry to hear about your grandpa," I said to Chase. "I hope he found peace in his last days."

Tears welled in his eyes as he clutched a black pen. "He didn't."

"I can't believe it," I began. "The people who suffer most from fracking are those who live downhill. We have to find a way to help them."

"You'll only make things *worse for us*," warned Savvy Socialite. "We should just be glad we have our *own lives*."

"But if we don't do something, things will continue to get worse for them. We can't just abandon them."

"That's just the way the world is," Tender Toucher stated. "Some people are just more fortunate than others."

Chase fell silent, yet his eyes indicated he was listening.

My fist clenched of its own accord, but I held my hand low. "And I'm *sure* all the people who depend on the earth more directly than we do are *not* content with that reality. And yet, they provide sustenance for everyone else, including people like us."

He looked up at me, eyes pink and face pale. "Dude, you have a good point, keep goin' on. I wanna hear what *you* have to say."

"The elderly..." I continued, raising a finger while lowering my voice "...are dismissed by mining companies because they can always use old age as an excuse for their deaths, at the time in their lives when their immune systems are weakest. But they still deserve our protection just as much as everyone else."

Tender Toucher placed her hand on my shoulder. "It's good to know you're concerned about Chase's grandfather, but business doesn't work that way, so you're wrong."

"No, *you're wrong!*" I clenched my other hand as well.

She and Alyssa walked away, chatting to each other under their breaths.

Barnyard Boy seethed like a steaming kettle.

"I'm sorry," I said.

He sighed loudly. "This just makes me so *MAD!*"

Chase started trembling out of his seat, and when I tried to hold him still, he hurled the pen into the corner of his cubicle where it splintered into ten or so long sharp pieces.

"I just wanna explode!" he exclaimed, and smashed his fists on his desk, jiggling the computer mouse.

"Is there any way I can help?"

He faced me but did not look at me. "Let's just say I've sworn revenge against this company. The deal with my grampa was so awful it just makes me wanna *burn stuff down* sometimes!"

"No, not Murray and Affiliates, that's us."

"Then I've sworn *complete revenge* against Conrad Power."

"That's...better."

"My life has been *so* frustrating. I been helpin' him day after day and night after night, but people all around here just don't give one flying shit about it and they even try to make it worse."

Chase placed his forehead on his arm alongside the desk. "I lost my scholarship after two years from helpin' him because he was in so much pain and sickness. I came here hopin' to make a difference for people like him, but it was all for noth-ing. Dammit!!"

The eraser he threw against the far wall made a dull *thud* as it bounced to the floor rather inconspicuously.

I walked back to my cubicle. "You have the right to do whatever you want."

CHAPTER 42:

Mineral Rights

It was the third Thursday in November, and in the week before Thanksgiving break, Ron prepared a gathering at Pranti Brothers.

The mostly empty building beheld a few restaurant-goers in the main room, and Ron sat on a stool by himself at the bar.

Based on the color and texture, he had ordered a Yuengling.

Seeking the Upper Hand, I ordered a glass of water while I waited for my pizza.

"Hey Ron."

"Good to see you dude," he replied, eyebrows raised.

"I guess no one else wanted to show up."

"Well, at least you did."

The waitress delivered his hot spicy chicken wings which looked delicious and resembled the surface of the planet Venus, just as she placed ice-water in front of me, which I sipped as though I were drinking up Neptune.

"It's good you could come," said Ron, seated at my left.

"Yeah, I'm glad to be here."

The brunette waitress caught my eye; she was rather attractive, and so was the other waitress overseeing the other side of the bar, a visually appealing blonde.

Meanwhile, I kept an eye on the sports scores.

"So, what have you been up to lately?" I asked Ron.

"Well, you see..." He raised his arms and stretched his hefty back. "Ever since I moved into the cubicle right behind yours, I've been working as a negotiator."

"So you just talk to random people on the phone? You don't get to go outside like I do?"

He gave an off-kilter thumbs-up. "I enjoy it for the most part. I like working with people, talking to them. But sometimes they get annoying, you know what I mean?"

I nodded. "Do you have a background in business or public relations by chance?"

He shook his head. "I'm actually trained as a geologist. But I do have experience working as a bouncer, so I know how to manage people, keep them in line, especially when there's about to be a fight."

I leaned in closer so I could hear him under the din.

"And I started out doing what you're doing for this company, only I lost about twenty pounds before I started going out in the field. What's your background?"

"I was actually looking to go into education. I was an academic tutor last summer and considered obtaining a teaching certificate in earth and space science, so I could teach young people about our place in the universe, only the education courses seemed really ridiculous and boring. I like science itself better."

Ron sipped his beverage, and my pizza arrived, delivered by the same attractive brunette waitress. "Yeah, I know what you mean. Public education isn't for everyone."

"But maybe those who don't like the public school system but still want to teach should consider private schools?"

He shrugged. "Maybe."

"So who exactly have you been talking to?"

"Landowners." He turned to me and set down his drink. "We're in the middle of a mineral rights dispute."

My pizza was still too hot to fully chew.

"I just contact people and convince them to let

businesspeople, managers, and technicians go on their property."

"And they let you do it?"

He looked to the ceiling and opened his right palm slightly upwards. "Well, not *me* particularly, I'm just advocating on behalf of Murray and Affiliates, everyone who works here, so we can get things done in a timely fashion."

I chowed down on my pizza. "So what's the thing about mineral rights then?"

"Mineral rights." He took another bite of his chicken wings. "Those are what *we* have access to, everything underground and below property level."

"But isn't everything below their land also *part* of their land?"

"Some states interpret things that way," replied Mister Suckup, chewing a mouthful, "but in other states, like here in Kentucky, *we* actually have rights to everything below ground zero – it's called eminent domain."

"So how do you obtain the minerals you need without digging up their precious soil?" My quizzical expression must have seemed embarrassing to him.

He shook his head and waved his paw gently as he swallowed. "I just have to phrase things the right way to avoid legal issues. It's usually not a big problem once the excavator comes in."

"But don't people get mad when they see you tearing up their property?"

"Huh huh huh," he chuckled while grabbing another wing with his fingers. "First of all, we don't say it like that. Second of all, it's actually not as typical as you might expect. They usually just occur when we need to use explosives. And when disputes do arise, there's nothing they can do about it after we've gotten what we needed. But if anything out of line happens, I come over to their location to help stop the chaos."

"And do you ever report those issues to Amy?"

AT ODDS WITH EACH OTHER

His head vibrated. "No, she never notices those things — you know what she's like — and I don't ever want to get in trouble with our authority figures."

"I didn't know you'd get in trouble for simply reporting that."

He shrugged. "You never know."

I started on the pepperoni slice. "Interesting how these things work sometimes."

"Yeah, it definitely is." Ron glanced at his phone and texted. "I have a friend coming to meet us any minute or so."

"Would I know him?"

"You probably wouldn't know *her* unless you've really dug deep into issues at Murray," he explained, arms outward. "But she's a long-gone product of spite, not for everyone here, but for some of us."

"Yet you still keep in touch with her," I stated, enjoying the heartwarming food.

Ron chewed in rhythm with his nodding head while squinting his eyes. "It's good to know what she's up to. But when she comes — and you'll know who she is just by the way she looks and acts — don't ask any complicated questions or make weird comments like you usually do. I'm serious, just stick to simple questions."

I leaned in towards him. "Is she *special* then?"

His head fell to the side. "Oh, she's special alright. Just not exactly in the way you're thinking."

"I'll act perfectly normal and respectful, I promise."

"Good."

CHAPTER 43:

Revolution Girl

The door swung open, and in came a prancing figure with long silky-smooth white-blonde hair, which flopped to and fro as she skipped like a majestic horse. Her mouth was open in perpetual excitement with her tongue hanging out a bit.

Everyone turned to her; all the men looked eager and all the women looked envious.

Time slowed down with every leap of love and laughter.

She turned and came to us, still skipping like a pony.

The up-close view was positively captivating, and I wished so badly for a panoramic view. She was not so much hot as she was beautiful, a Ten-out-of-ten to the maximum, or even higher, as she appeared to be an angel descended from on high and made the waitresses look like ghosts.

Her facial structure screamed with gorgeousness, and she wore no obvious makeup yet didn't need any; she was about five-foot-five, and her figure was perfect, for she was neither fat nor skinny on either side of the continuum.

The skin on this creation of magnificence was smooth, tender, and light yet not at all pale, graced and well-sautéed by the sunshine of heaven to which she smiled, and though most people had already turned around, some men were still captivated, and time continued to slow down further....

She carried a glory about her unsurpassed by any understanding of time or reason, and she bore an extremely light countenance, with kindness radiating from her well-spaced emerald eyes which beheld a fiery green passion the world had never known.

This woman's light-green sneakers with wide loopy laces, dark-blue form-fitting jeans, and light-yellow sweater, the end of which rested just above a pink leather belt, altogether made her resemble a succulent piece of Nonni's limone biscotti, or perhaps a light-breaded cupcake with green, blue, and yellow sprinkles atop vanilla icing, or even a vanilla milkshake from Dairy Queen, also with green, blue, and yellow sprinkles atop whipped cream.

Beauty was no longer in the eye of the beholder, for this woman was beauty itself. I had never understood the phrase 'drop dead gorgeous' until now. *She was absolutely stunning!*

The chatter in the room picked up.

"Dude! Stop staring at her you creep!" Mister Suckup bonked me on the head with his fist.

"What the hell are you talking about?" I turned to his ruddy rusted face. "I was looking at the sports scores on the TV behind her. Apparently *you're* not interested in the end of the Packers' game, and you're supposed to be the tough one. Jeez!"

Then I seized my opportunity to turn back to the lady. "I'm sorry, I didn't mean to offend you with my language. Are you alright?"

She nodded and blinked, a single blink communicating all the peace, rest, benevolence, and beauty sleep throughout the world.

"Would you be bothered if I watch sports while you're here?" I asked.

The woman shook her head gradually and blinked twice, which enchanted me; her lashes waved away any concerns.

Ron eyed me with his teeth clenched. "Why don't you ask

her some questions about herself – *simple* questions."

"What's your name?"

Her smiling mouth opened, and her pink tongue was the last thing to move out of the way. "Emily," she replied with smooth and upper-register pitch that made her voice soothing to my eardrums and music to my ears.

"What's your favorite color?"

Her mouth now opened with the laughter of a child. "White."

Ron gave me a single thumbs-up and leaned in towards us. "Good, just keep going." Mister Suckup looked incredibly nervous.

"How old are you?"

"Thirty-three," she stated; she could have easily been ten years younger.

"Keep up the good work," said Ron; he relaxed and turned around in his seat.

"Who are you as a person?"

He reached an extended hand, fingers spread in every direction. "Richard...noooo!!!"

It was too late. The woman stood back, propped her hands on her hips, shoulders down and level, her lymphatic posture absolutely perfect.

She started to perform the macarena before she uttered another syllable, and the dance continued into her monologue in a valley-girl American accent. Emily didn't use the Common Speech, but went perhaps too far in the other direction.

And as she explained herself, her voice was smooth, melodious, and flowing, gushing forth with grace and glee, yet the rapidity of the legato heart-melting sound should have required a sportscaster to announce, 'Drumroll, please!'

"Greetings to both of you fine young gentlemen who are enjoying a meal together on this wonderful evening of this glorious day; *hello to you* Ronald with whom I am very well acquainted, *and hello to you* Richard as well, *whose name I have*

just recently learned and assumed simply by applying context clues, *so please graciously* forgive me and kindly correct me if that is not in fact your real or given name. *Every* name is a gift, *and I wish* to identify you correctly and properly.

"*As I have already* stated for the purpose of introducing myself, *my* name is Emily. *I am* thirty-three-and-a-half years old, *my* favorite color is white, *and I love* jewels in equal measure to the passion which I possess for environmental issues and related causes. *To* me, *life* itself is a gift, *and I value* my own life as much as that of anyone else, *for on the day* I was born I rejoiced as much as did my own beloved and irreplaceable parents. *Now* at your sincere request, *let me tell you a little bit* about myself so that you might familiarize yourself with me as an individual."

My eyes themselves were dizzied by her continual dance, her platinum hair flowing along in synchronization.

"*My* personal history is as follows, *so might* I ask that you please listen closely, Richard, *for the sole sake* of learning about me as a human being, *as I am quite* certain you would desire that I might pay close attention to you as the wonderful human person you are if you so wished to introduce yourself. *Now* then, *shall* I begin properly? *Thank* you very much.

"*I taught myself* to read at age one, *taught myself* to write at age two, *mathematics* at age three, *calculus* at four, *classical literature* and physics at five, *completed an IQ test* at age seven on which I received a score of two-hundred-eight, *at age eight* finished writing a six-hundred page novel entitled *Everything We Share*, skipped a good many number of grade levels which enabled me to finish high school at ten, *graduated* from Princeton University *summa cum laude* at age twelve, *master's* from Yale University at thirteen, *Ph.D. in political science* from Harvard University at sixteen, *having completed* a well-written and well-rehearsed thesis on the cultural dynamics of ancient civilizations. *Subsequently I obtained* an additional doctorate degree in macro-scale geophysics. *Currently I hold* employment at Wooddew as a Level-Two environmental scientist; however, *I find myself* utterly bored with my assigned tasks, *for I am never presented with much* of a challenge or opportunity for advancement and seldom receive assignments which require me to explore the outdoors, *the wilderness* and surrounding world. Therefore, *in my plentiful free time* I initiate telephone conversations with private landowners in an attempt to inspire them to revolt against ongoing projects which require geological utilization of their private property.

"*Furthermore, in an attempt* to quell misery and rage afflicting terminated employees by these deceitful and greedy corporations, *I also frequently* initiate undisclosed phone conversations with such individuals as well. *I believe my role* in society is to stir matters up a bit, *to convolute* them for their proper purposes, *to inspire rebellion* and revolution against the economic elites of society, *for our* current system of business relations and enterprises thereof, *that* is, *our* current system of capitalism, *the ever-burgeoning demand* of economic growth along with the ongoing mutual animosity between agriculturalists and industrialists, *is incompatible* with our duty as a society to care for the least fortunate among us and –"

"Hold up," I interrupted, catching my breath.

Everyone else in the room had resumed their conversations, and I could not keep track of everything Revolution Girl was saying because she spoke so naturally at a million words a minute.

I tapped the shoulder of Ron, who had almost finished devouring his chicken wings, and I consumed a mouthful of pizza, downing it with water, much of which had melted from the ice cubes.

Emily righted herself and stood back. "*I will* most certainly do as you say and 'hold...up' if you so insist."

"What are her political views?" I whispered to Ron.

"She's just weird."

"Well, what do you think of her? As a person, I mean."

"I dunno man, there are a few good people on one side... and a bunch of communists on the other." He hunched and added discreetly, "I told you not to ask the kind of questions you usually do, but you pretty much blew it, and this is what it's come to now. You were totally wrong not to follow my advice."

"No, *you're* wrong. It's going perfectly well."

"I'm *Ron.*" Blinking rapidly, he said, "I mean, I'm right. Right about what would happen if you asked an inappropriate question."

Removing my hand, I replied, "Look, I'm sorry. I just want to see what she's like, that's all."

"It's all on you man."

I bade Emily continue. I had never seen anyone stand so straight yet with such dignity, and presumed an invisible string tying the top of her head to the ceiling, or a metal rope rather, yet her athletically voluptuous form was not the least bit uptight.

"Capitalism..." I began.

"*Yes,* continue your sentence," she said, waving her hand.

"Capitalism is necessary in society because it is the economic engine which provides goods and services to the most people in the most efficient manner," I stated, holding a finger in front of me, "and therefore it's the best option."

Revolution Girl rolled her eyes round and round, over and over again while puckering her glossy pink lips and tapping her fingers and thumb together in imitation of a chickadee.

"*Oh* you silly goose, *you have no* idea what it is that you are trying to say, *nor in* the manner which you are trying to say it. *You might as well* be a blathering head on Fox News. *A revolution* is coming very soon, *and* it is quite obvious, *at least* to a person like myself, *that traditional energy companies* will become an artifact of humanity sooner than anyone would presume."

She made my head spin, and I wanted to get rid of her if at all possible, but not yet, not until I put forth the best callous right-wing argument I could possibly imagine.

"Actually, if you think about it —" I started. "If you think about it…"

Emily leapt forward with pomposity in her steps.

Ron mumbled on his phone.

"History *actually* shows that, well, when, communism — socialism — hasn't worked when it's tried in places which means —"

Revolution Girl bounced forward again and stood pompously right in front of me, invading my personal space. My jaw froze, and I both loved her and hated her at the same time.

She shoved her palm in my face and covered my mouth so firmly I could not even move my lips to speak.

With a grin of one-upsmanship, she opened up her lips and spoke forth, *"Quite* clearly, *you simply neither know nor understand* the topic about which you are communicating with someone light-years beyond your clumsy level of intellectual understanding. *It is with* manifest obviousness that nobody, *especially* myself, *cares* about what you have to say, *as you yourself* are unable to speak properly in order to convey your ideas in a coherent fashion."

As she grinned with glee, Emily's lilac-scented breath was a cool whispering willow among rolling fields of soft green grass, and I enjoyed the physical sensations of her being even as she put me through mental anguish. She got in my face as she held my mouth closed, with less than an inch of space between our foreheads, while every beat of her voice was the drumroll to her speech.

"For what reason do you speak with such monotony, *uttering small words* and simple phrases ever so slowly, *rather* than educated, *smooth and sophisticated* vocabulary in the likeness of myself? *Your* university education, *which should have* been free by the way, *failed* to teach you anything important,

or perhaps you mumbo-jumboed your way through like everybody else. *Are you* really that dull-minded? *Your thoughts* must be a blank slate with crooked words for borders."

"Mmm!" I tried to make my voice heard, but did not want to slather on or bite the skin of her hand which felt like Haagen-Dazs vanilla ice cream on my lips.

"*Now* say something!"

Revolution Girl removed her hand and tapped her foot and snapped her fingers like a musical score in *presto*.

"*The train is boarding* at the station of your sluggish brain, *and here I wait* moment after moment for your dimwitted reply."

"You're just...*wrong.*"

An earthquake trembled around me because I could not hold my ground.

"'*Wrong,*' to use your uncultured silly-goose vocabulary, *about which* of my previous statements?" She held a fist high, her light arched eyebrows centralizing on the point of facial symmetry.

"That's just not how the world works."

The palm was back on my mouth.

"*I was rather quite* interested in communicating with you upon my arrival since you are, *to* be totally honest, *rather* quite handsome, *but now* find myself completely uninterested, *in that* you are evidently indistinguishable from a rainbow-colored cardboard box. *Your* turn!"

The hand was off.

"But why..."

The hand was on.

"*Do you* understand what I mean? *You are* slow and stupid."

She winked and bounced her head from side to side on the invisible miniature trampolines on either side of her ears.

"*You* are very unintelligent."

My gaze remained fixed on hers, and even though both her

physique and facial complexion were spectacular, her words flowing like a waterfall from her tender-cheeked baby-faced mouth – with dimples on both curved cheeks of her babyface – were what grabbed my attention most of all.

Even as she spoke down to me in the air with hair waving, her greatest feature was her unstoppable argumentation.

"Why do you have to be such an idiot?"

And even as she leaned in to talk down to me, her posture remained balanced and stable –

"You are very mentally slow, *indicating the embarrassing* reality that your imagination is dark dull-gray matter."

– with her shoulders well-positioned and her back still straight with her gait evermore forward.

Revolution Girl licked her dandy lips as her entire bodily expression defied gravity in sheer physicality of the super-genius geophysicist she was, while relishing the delight of pounding me into the ground with cutthroat-style debate.

"Colonial policy and imperialism existed before the latest stage of capitalism, *and* even before capitalism. Rome, *founded* on slavery, *pursued a* colonial policy and practiced imperialism."

Not a glimmer or trace of any staining substance marked her pearly whites shining forth as much as her cognitive brilliance.

"But – well – why – comnism – bad – humnum nature..."

CHAPTER 44:

More of Revolution Girl

"**Y**ou, *Richard, are most likely* the dumbest person on Planet Earth, *both in a* literal and in a figurative sense."

I had not seen her eat anything and could only imagine what brand of toothpaste she used, or the nature of her diet, on account of her smile which shone so brightly I squinted, as well as her exercise regimen and diet together on account of her body which she shimmied in all its curvaceousness so elegantly it made my –

"There has never been more of a dullard throughout the whole history of the world than you."

She removed her hand from my mouth and yammered away because she knew she had already defeated me speechless.

Revolution Girl stepped back several lengths of her swanky shoes, raised both fists in the air above her head, spread her feet apart with knees bent while smiling with unlimited happiness from ear to ear.

"To the degree that corn is sold above its value, *other* commodities are, *to* the same degree, *sold* below their value, *such that* the sum of values remains the same. *The social movement* as a process of natural history, *governed by* laws not only independent of human will, *consciousness and* intelligence itself per se, *on* the contrary, *determining* that will, *consciousness* and intelligence.

"*If, as* historical materialism charges, *the characteristics* of both people and society are determined by objective economic factors, *then society* will move in a certain direction, *driven* by these factors, *regardless* of whatever else happens. Therefore, *to put matters* in perspective for someone of your caliber, *alternative* energy will replace coal, *oil and natural gas* practically overnight. Hahahahahahaha!"

It took her a few seconds to say all of that.

"But that's not even how revolutions work! The automobile replaced the horse-and-buggy over a matter of years, for example."

Revolution Girl marched forward, lifting her feet off the ground one at a time, knees nearly to her chest, while her tongue smacked against her upper lip and her eyes rolled around and about endlessly.

"*Listen Richard,* you silly goose! *You do* resemble a goose somewhat by the way."

"You look like a swan."

She straightened her hair and raised her chin.

"*I shall interpret* your blithe comment as a compliment, *for swans as animals* are often associated with grace and beauty, *both* of which I certainly strive to hold in abundance."

With great efficacy, Emily pressed her palms on the sides of my head, and straightened her legs while leaning forwards at a forty-degree angle from the horizontal axis, almost making my nose touch her own small nose. I enjoyed the whiff of cool-mint blueberry as her face consumed my entire field of view.

"*Sometime you ought* to record yourself speaking, *for the following* would be a recorded audio message of your vocal expressions: 'The...*automobile*...replaced – the – horse *and buggy*...over a...*matter* of – years.'"

I had to admit that was an excellent imitation.

"*For what reason* can you not connect your words properly as I do? *Enunciate* and speak more fluidly! *There must exist* a broken noose between your brain and your mouth."

Emily must have been of purebred Irish heritage, and she was both classically and ethnically attractive.

"In your simple realm of emotions you are angry because you are quite well aware of the reality that I am many-fold times smarter than you, *and in accordance* with refusing to admit this truth to yourself, *you justify* your feelings of inferiority by telling yourself you are more talented in certain endeavors than I, *or that* you are cooler than I, *but in actuality* those comforting and reassuring beliefs you hold are baseless and utterly false, *and deep down* you know it."

My eyes wandered downward to the spectacular sight even as her words enchanted me, and her back stiffened as she placed a palm across my eyes, and everything went dark.

"Similar to most men, *you are an* atrocious pig with listless wandering eyes. *I shall speak no further* with you until you agree to respect my dignity as a woman and abolish your perverted gaze, *even though you well know* I am by far the most delectable-looking specimen of the fairer sex on which you have ever laid your unintelligent glare."

The other palm felt soothing to the upper half of my face, and having temporarily lost two of my senses because my tongue remained inside my mouth, I could breathe only through my nose.

"Now speak forth the following phrase if you wish to resume your conversation with me: 'Dear Emily, you are the most beautiful and respectable woman I have ever seen.'"

Both hands were off, and the world had returned.

"Dear Emily, you are the tss-hee-hee-tssk, the most beautiful *and* the most respectable woman I've ever seen."

Revolution Girl crossed her delicate yet sturdy arms and lowered her nicely-rounded chin. She pivoted on one foot, leaned backwards, and turned her head while eyeing me with tender love and mercy.

"Very well then. *Though it bothers me* quite a bit that

you speak with contractions, *I understand* that someone like you might need to hasten your speech, *for* as I have said, *you speak* almost unbearably slowly; *you also ought to read* more widely to improve and expand your vocabulary so that you might be able to communicate more eloquently with someone of my culture and upbringing."

In a flash, the palm was pressed to my lips.

"Now when I remove my hand once again, *you* must say, *'Yes,* Madame!'"

She *stomped* and removed her hand.

"You're a bitch."

"And think before you speak!"

The exchange proceeded as such: Revolution Girl placed her hand on my mouth whenever she wanted to say something and removed it during the moments in which she granted me opportunity to prove my communicative capacity.

"Yes, Madame."

Emily pulled her shoulders all the way back in terrific style and faced me directly, just as she had before, only this time she was even closer.

"I would have appreciated a little more enthusiasm, *but your* grumbling growls shall suffice."

She wrapped her other hand around the back of my head.

"Ask me an intelligent question."

"Why do you talk so fast?"

"Excuse me? *Do you* really believe I 'talk...fast' to use your terminology? *First* of all, *you have* used an adjective, 'fast,' *when the proper* word for the given context of your question is 'quickly,' *an* adverb. Nonetheless, *I shall interpret* the question as you seem to have intended it, *only I do not* believe I am SPEAKING to you quickly, *for I speak* at a normal steady rate with my colleagues from all three of my Ivy League alma maters. Therefore, *from my educated perspective* you are the individual who prefers to use language reminiscent of a confused, hungry and ignorant raccoon."

Her face sparkled with prettiness, her smile radiant with joy. I was transfixed and tried to look away, but she held my head steady so she would remain in view.

"*Would you,* an extremely dumb person, *care to hear* my commonplace benevolent eloquence?"

"Sure."

"*Very* well then!" she spat cheerfully, nearly kissing me. "*If* that be so, *I expect* a fully coherent and timely response from your monotonous mouth. *Shall we* proceed along these terms of agreement?"

"Agreed," I said weakly, peering into her eyes. I was covered in a raincloud by her hair which carried not a single wrinkle or crease, much like her dauntingly smooth complexion.

"*You* enounced a two-syllable word for a sentence, *rather quite pathetic* even for an individual of your blockheadedness!"

I nearly became high with fantasy on the unending breath of roses and daylilies.

"*Henceforth, I shall speak to you* as though you were a sophisticate of my caliber. *Here* we go!"

Her nose touched mine as she wiggled her hips distractingly, though I remained focused on the succession of smooth-scented pink lips rapidly in motion.

"*Let the ruling classes* tremble at a communistic revolution *and the proletarians* have nothing to lose but their chains *for they have* a world to win; *working men* of all countries unite!"

Her grin awaited my reply, yet I could not back away to think for a moment or even please her spunky green eyes with any coherency in my feedback.

"I'm sorry, I didn't catch any of that."

"*I* knew it all along." She bonked her forehead lightly against mine. "*Your exquisite* dumbness is as dismal as your physical appearance is fantastic!"

"Are you a communist?" I asked as she held my shoulders in place.

"*Shut up* and listen, Richard! *One can make* politics as

complex or as simplistic as one desires, *so in understanding* the efficiency and expediency of your thought process, *allow me to convey* political issues as simply as my refined intellect allows. *One side* is correct in the coherency and veracity of their worldview, *while the other* side is downright foolish."

"Is it really that simple?"

My mouth was covered again, while Emily marched in place with her feet gracing the floor like an overly-curvy buoyant ballerina. Her facial countenance never ceased to sparkle with angelic delight, while she rolled her shoulders forwards, then backwards at the same rate.

"For instance, *the most pressing* matter today is climate change."

"Not everyone agrees."

Emily hugged me, then swung with all the efficacious grace of a swan onto my lap.

"The dramatic and unstable rise in temperatures as a result of the Industrial Revolution affects living beings and especially humans, *whether* the moronic ones like you know it or not. Additionally, *guns must be banned* everywhere at all times, *for they are far* too dangerous for anyone to keep in a modern civilized society. Furthermore, *as a nation* we must provide open borders to all refugees from everywhere across the globe, *otherwise our leaders* and especially our president are a bunch of cold-hearted ignorant fascists."

"So what do you think of him?"

"I shall run for president as an Independent when nobody expects it and defeat him single-handedly in all three debates, *in logic* as well as in dominance, *spectacularly winning* the final showdown in a stellar victory of both the popular vote as well as the electoral college, *which* is racist." The eyes of Revolution Girl locked on to mine. She was definitely huggable with her soft yet firm physicality and amiable high-class demeanor.

"How are we going to switch from traditional to alternative

energy so quickly then?"

Emily bounced on my lap without a single loss of rhythmic jiggle, and my legs did not hurt at all.

"You are uniquely adorable, *and when I look more closely* I see that your appearance actually resembles that of a baby beagle, *as* does your bark. *Unenlightened people like you* are unaware of the fact that the government is hiding advanced technology that can produce energy for the entire nation many times over, *because the conservative* energy enterprises are providing hedge funds for politicians on the dumb side of the aisle so they can stay in business perpetually. *But* the matter is quite urgent, *for people are suffering* illness and death all across the land due to these traditional measures. Henceforth, *we must fight* ardently for the health of our planet and its people!"

It peeved me that politics was more a matter of one's facts than one's viewpoints, and I was therefore at a loss for words.

"Are you slow to provide another response?" She tickled my neck.

"How can we provide food for so many immigrants on limited resources?"

"The federal government holds twenty-six tons of emergency food in secret storage."

"Why didn't they prevent starvation during the Great Depression?"

"Do you really believe Herbert Hoover was a compassionate president?"

"Certainly not all natural disasters are a direct result of climate change."

I spread my hands outward which she grabbed onto with cat-like reflexes, holding both of us steady.

"To your point, *perhaps* not, *but a hidden tectonic fault* exists in the crust of the earth which only I have discovered and of which every other geologist is completely unaware, *and a high-magnitude* earthquake will occur there in the near

future. *And* as you are probably well aware, *I am a consider-ably* sensual and touchy-feely individual, *though sometimes* I punch people. Mmwah!"

She kissed me on the forehead and gave me a noogie, and with a bountiful backwards leap, assumed a gymnast-style landing with hardly a sound as her feet made contact with the floor, arms in the air.

A few glares came our way, and Ron grinned.

He pulled me by the shoulder. "Why don't you stick with simple questions, just for the sake of decency?" he suggested with deep undertones.

I turned back to Emily jogging in place. "What's your favorite food?"

Revolution Girl stepped forward, though not too close this time, set her palms squat on the upper part of her hips, and puffed out her large upper torso with such pomposity that her posture rose beyond the pinnacle of perfection, such that she seemed to gain an extra inch of height, while bouncing on her toes and giggling with wonder and awe.

"Personally, the food which I enjoy consuming most is bananas because they contain high amounts of potassium which helps regulate my fluid balance, *muscle* contractions and nerve signals. However, *I consider* food as proper nourishment for my body, *so my daily* consumption is based on nutritional rather than pleasurable criteria, *and although* I am neither a vegan nor a vegetarian, *I always eat* as healthfully as possible given the circumstances, *as you* can probably tell just by looking at me. *I always have* different styles of eggs for breakfast after brushing my teeth with Crest, *and I eat only* organic food to avoid ingesting cancer-causing pesticides so that my perpetual youth carries well into triple-digit age."

"So are you going to live forever then? And are you going to have anything to eat or drink here?"

Her hands plopped to the lower part of her hips and she tilted her chin upwards with blossomed lower body protruding outwards while jumping with joy and alternately crisscrossing her legs.

"*In response* to your first question, *I shall live* as long as I possibly can, *to accumulate as many beneficent deeds* of societal goodwill before I gaze upon the face of God, *beholding the Bible's promise* of unlimited everlasting free socialism for every true believer. *In response* to your second question, *Pranti Brothers* serves no organic food, *so I have prepared my own* healthfully delicious dinner as a supplement to meeting new and interesting people like yourself."

"Please tell me you're not on crack!"

"Hahahahaha," she laughed, patting her midriff on the sides while jumping in a squat. "*Of* course not, *you* silly goose. *I neither* drink nor smoke nor use recreational or prescription drugs, *even though they all* ought to be legalized at once throughout the entire country as the Constitution guarantees. *I drink* plenty of water each and every day, *at least* eight large full glasses, *and consume whole grains only* while eating mostly fruits and vegetables and severely limiting my sugar and caffeine intake, *but I do* tend to eat quite a great deal so I have enough energy for my multifaceted workout routine six days a week with rest on the Sabbath, *though most* of my boundless and abundant energy is a simple result of being high on my zest for life!"

I bowed my head forward. "And you wouldn't have a zest for life if we had communism in this country!"

"Just ask her what she does for fun, that'll get her off the hook," whispered Ron.

"What do you like to do for fun?" I called out in the midst of the crowd cheering her on as she hopped around, spinning clockwise while lurching her legs into the air about three feet off the ground, tapping her toes in midair, then bouncing off the ground again as though the entire earth were a trampoline, doing the same stunt round and round.

Emily seemed to have heard my question in the midst of

the applause, even in the continuation of her dance moves.

"*I sleep* for eight hours every night with my special stuffed giraffe so that I am awake and alert enough during the day to accomplish all that I intend. *I am the leader* of an amateur debate squad; *I have* achieved extensive victory in Lincoln-Douglass debates, *for I have* won fifteen gold medals, *one* silver, *and* two bronze. *I read* classical literature extensively, *and* finished *The Lord of the Rings* trilogy in five days and *Les Misérables* in eight days, *for* example. *I have written* most of the contemporary Broadway plays under various pseud-onyms, *and in my off hours* I invent new designs for lunch-boxes while developing an ongoing mathematical model of the relationship between the earth and the universe, *as well as* one intended to describe the entire universe itself."

She pumped her fist while spinning around on her heels, and I thoroughly enjoyed the panoramic view.

"Whoo hoooo!" the crowd cheered.

"Aren't women crazy?" Ron asked me kindly.

"Some women are." I nibbled on my pizza crust.

Mister Suckup lowered his forehead. "But she definitely is, though...wouldn't you say?"

I turned back to Revolution Girl, who uttered phrases when she landed on her hands for each backwards cartwheel in succession across the walkway, sweater and hair flying about with glamorous glory and grace.

"*If we have chosen* the position in life in which we can most of all work for mankind, *no* burdens can bow us down, *because they are* sacrifices for the benefit of all; *then* we shall experience no petty, limited, *selfish* joy, *but our* happiness will belong to millions, *our deeds* will live on quietly but per-petually at work, *and over our ashes* will be shed the hot tears of noble people!"

Near the end of the aisle, she finished with a backflip, land-ing on her feet with arms to the sky. Revolution Girl giggled with delight.

"*Ta* da! *Thank* you all, *thank you all* so very very much!"

"Yeah, she's definitely crazy," I said to Ron, who smirked smugly. "But not all women are crazy, so you're still wrong."

"I'm *Ron.*" He paused, counting the words I had just spoken. "I mean, Alyssa is crazy too."

Moving my empty dish to the side, I rested my elbows on the table. "Yeah...I guess so."

"So then maybe I'm right." Ron raised his pointer finger at a twenty-degree angle from the horizontal axis.

Emily breakdanced in the middle of the floor, seemingly weightless, swinging her legs in counterclockwise and then in clockwise circles faster than Mario *or* Luigi would if the player were to repeatedly press 'B' while holding 'Z', with absolutely no deceleration in angular momentum!

Everyone else was at their seats again, though a few men still looked on astonished.

"*Hack* the entire system! *Karl Marx* will have his payday! *It is time* for an energy and environmental REVOLUTION! *Karl Marx* will have his heyday! *Bomb* the coal factories at night if we must! *Use* psyops if necessary!"

Her jeans must have been made from the finest fabric for legs with such agility, strength, and mobility.

"Does anyone ever try to chase her?" I asked.

"Uugghh!" burped Mister Suckup as he set his next beer to the side. "Many do, many. But she outsmarts all of them."

"Well it's good she's smart," I added sarcastically.

"She's fluent in fourteen foreign languages. But she also knows advanced gymnastics, kickboxing, regular boxing, kung fu, du jitsu, karate, taekwondo, and martial arts...as backup options."

"Good for her for knowing techniques to defend herself. But have any aggressive men ever tried to *go after her?*"

He nodded sullenly, taking another sip of his yellow-orange beverage. "It's happened on several different occasions, but I keep telling her she doesn't need to know all that self-defense and attacking stuff since she's already faster *and* stronger than pretty much all the guys out there, which I don't understand. Emily is the most athletic and physically fit woman I've ever met."

I downed the remainder of my water, all melted ice at this point. "Wow...."

"That's why I didn't want you to get in a fight with her."

Ron rested a paw on my shoulder.

"You screwed up at the beginning, but handled the conversation the best of anyone yet. Some guys have gotten really mad and gone after her. I actually think she likes you."

I finished the rest of my pizza. "Really?"

"And she's given a few bloody mouths. Her fists are like rocks, so don't ever mess with her."

Mister Suckup read a missed text and put the phone in his pocket.

The din grew quieter.

"Can you give me her number?"

He stared downwards. "Nope. Too risky."

"What's her last name?"

"Can't tell you that either."

I observed Ron, somewhat bothered. "Nice talking to you today," I said, rising to my feet after paying the tab, "see you later, Ron."

"You too," he replied, paying his own tab.

I waited by the front door until Emily finished the dubstep song she was performing through karaoke:

"Rippin' my heart was so easy...*so EASY*. Launch your assault now...*take it EASY*. Raise your *weapon*.... Raise your *WEAPON*. One word...and it's *O-VE-ER*."

CHAPTER 45:

Introduction to the High Life

At the end of the following day, Amy communicated to me my Sunday assignment.

She led me to the locker room door, where affixed to the wall was a panel with buttons, mostly digits from 0 to 9.

"This *is the security* panel. When *you come* in, you *need to* lock it, and if *you mess up* the police will come. Has *anyone taught you* how to use it?"

I shook my head.

"Then *allow me* to explain. First, *you press* 'Enter.' Then you press *one*, then *eight*, then *nine*, and then *two*. Last, *you press* 'Enter' again. Make sure *you do this* before *going out on* your Little Adventure. Do *you need me* to write *down these* instructions?"

"No, I can remember."

She bowed her head. "Well *thaat's* good. Now *this one's* a tuffy. Do you know *why the passcode* is 1892?"

"Obviously because it's the year in which the company was founded."

"Good!"

"Now supposing I mess up, someone could obviously set the thing right, correct?"

Sunshine Lady smiled. "Brian will be the *only other person* here tomorrow, so *he can help you* out."

"Thanks for showing me."

Chase greeted me as I walked to the main complex.

"Sup, *dude!*"

My reflexes responded to the high-five just in time.

"We're goin' gambling at Riverside Casino tonight, wanna come?"

Alyssa and Jenna jumped out from behind the cubicle wall.

"Richard, we'd really love it if you'd join us," pleaded Tender Toucher, hands together and head sideways as if resting on a pillow.

"Casino time! Casino time!" said Savvy Socialite, palms in a V-shape under her chin. "Please come with *us!* Please *come with us.*"

"Sure. I'll come. I must warn you, however, I plan on going to bed early tonight to maintain my sleep schedule since I am assigned to work on Sunday. What time do you plan to meet there?"

"I'll let you know, prolly at eleven," answered Barnyard Boy coolly. "I'll give you my number and we'll be all set. Do you know where it's at?"

I nodded confidently. "It's right near the University of Prestonsburg. Now...my Sunday schedule indicates a second rain gauge. Do any of you know of its location?"

"It's on Stockman *School Drive,*" said Alyssa.

Isaac saw me leaving.

"Where are you going?"

Standing straighter than an arrow, I crossed my arms. "I'm going out to live the High Life tonight."

"I've got a theory that might interest you."

"Yes?"

Deep Throat raised his finger and pointed to the farthest reaches of the ceiling while tilting his head at a twenty-three-point-five degree angle.

"You know how current cosmological models suggest the

universe is infinite and infinitely expanding? I actually figure it's a closed loop rather than flat space, so if you traveled faster than the speed of dark energy, you'd wrap around to the earth. From this perspective, the prevailing theory of cosmology contradicts that of the Big Bang, that the universe began as an infinitesimally small and dense point."

I furrowed my brow. "Wow, I wish you could show me the mathematics that suggests that."

"I wish I had the proper training in physics to demonstrate that," he added, hands apart. "It's just something I've been thinking about. But I do know one lady who might be able to help us."

"You should try gambling sometime."

The front door of a nearby Wendy's was locked.

Waiting in the drive-thru, I texted Barnyard Boy: 'Hey Chase this is Richard (personal cell). I've decided to meet you at Riverside Casino at 11p.'

At the ordering-board I requested a Double Stack with french-fries and water, and paid extra for it because they did not consider it a proper meal.

Waiting at the automatic swivel-window, I received the following: 'Hey what's up man. I think we're gonna end up going later cuz everyone has plans for early night.'

I pulled into a parking space, and since several people were leaving, reached for the door.

When I found an empty seat, I texted him: 'Alright see you Monday then. Can't stay up that long sorry.'

I chowed down on the quasi-delicious heart-attack meal.

'If we go out earlier I'll definitely text you,' he informed me.

I burped in well-deserved satisfaction as I left the fast-food restaurant.

My phone dinged as I drove to the University of Prestonsburg campus, where I spent five dollars on a ticket for the parking garage.

Per personal policy, I never examined the screen of my phone while driving, so I waited until I was inside the underground garage, where I read: 'Could you do like 11:30/12?'

Because of poor reception, I rode the elevator upward four floors and stepped onto the sidewalk, where I people-watched students going for an evening stroll.

'Let's try for next week but earlier,' I texted.

As I drove home, my cell phone *dinged*, and I read the text in my bedroom: 'We can prob do 11 if you need. Also don't think we're going next week.'

CHAPTER 46:

Working on Sunday

The schedule was nearly twice as long as that of a weekday. Using my key fob I entered through the locker room door, then gave an upward flick to every switch of the main complex, making the room much brighter than the dim morning. Then I turned off half of them.

Brian was nowhere in sight, not even in either restroom.

A few papers were strewn across his desk.

I acknowledged the lack of security cameras and my supervisors' unique interpretation of the open-door policy.

A picture of Mike rested on Amy's desk, the same one he used for his LinkedIn profile and the only photograph of him I had ever seen. Inside her drawers I found vegetarian paraphernalia and a box of Nutri-Grain bars.

It tasted better because I had stolen it, and as I enjoyed the healthful snack, I wondered how someone who was a vegetarian had ever become so fat.

In a cubby of Shadow Guy's desk was a book entitled *Astral Traveling for the Advanced Practitioner*.

To the left of the bookcase stood a structure larger than a trophy but smaller than a statue.

The firm foundation of gray marble bore two dark-blue upward struts with golden vertical ledges, the tops of which were connected by a stone platform, upward from which stood a silver rod holding a golden bowl with a same-color figurine on top. Its scaly, spiky wings resembled those of a bat-dragon hybrid, and its torso was like that of a trilobite, while its claws were as sharp as its teeth comprising about half the area of its twisted mongrel face, with seven horns atop its head, though one was broken.

I turned it aside and read the plaque on the lower gray marble: 'Michael E. Matthews,' and below his name was the phrase, '33rd Degree Freemason.'

After that experience, I entered Jon's office, even smaller and more cramped than it appeared from the outside.

A single white coffee mug rested in front of the computer.

Large brown patches stained the carpet.

Bottles of medication lined the upper shelf of his desk, none of which I could properly pronounce.

Resting on the end of his desk was a copy of *Tom Clancy's Power Plays* with a bookmark placed at the midpoint of the page range.

The upper cardboard box behind his seat was labeled BOOKS HOLDER in thick black magic marker. Inside the box was an abundance of Tom Clancy novels, everything from *Red Rising Storm* to *Command Authority*.

Then I peeked behind the door.

The black-and-red crisscrossed hilt was approximately a third the length of the entire silvery blade rusted near the bellguard, and the tip was as sharp as a shark's tooth. It hung from a loose rope over a protruding nail. The saber looked like it had been used on an African safari, perhaps in Cameroon.

I closed the door.

A blaring alarm sounded when I entered the code. The brownish screen read 4:50 and counted down by the second.

"AAAAAAHHHHHHH!!!"

With my ears covered, I raced throughout the lower floor until I returned to the locker room at 4:17 and held the 'Enter' button.

The noise ceased.

The door was locked from the outside, and my CamelBak was inside.

I tugged on every door, then wandered to the back, searching for an open window.

On the far end I found metal trashcans, which I placed by the lowest rise and stood on top of them, seeking an opening to Waterstone Surveying and Mapping.

I searched the perimeter one last time, then contacted Jocelyn via InReach: HELP LOCKED OUT.

She responded: AT HOME NOW, CONTACT BRIAN.

I selected 'Brian Garrow' and sent the same phrase.

A buzz accompanied the message: SORRY OUT AND ABOUT.

On this partly-cloudy day, I made my usual rounds, rushing through the brown leafless woods, fudging measurements even for the rain gauges.

An hour after sunset, Buff Face returned and found me waiting in my vehicle. I told him I needed to grab extra snacks for my Little Adventure.

My name was listed on neither the Eblen schedule nor on the ones for the Harvon or Baylor mines. I emailed Sunshine Lady:

Hello Amy,

I am pleased to let you know I have finished today's schedule completely and thoroughly, but cannot find my name on any of the stream monitoring schedules for this week. What is my upcoming assignment?

Thank you,
Richard A.

Minutes later I received:

Hi there sweetie,

We have a very special visitor coming tomorrow. He'll be giving you and some other folks a 24-hour training course in MSHA. It will be really Neato Frito!

Take care,
Amy

Part Five

CHAPTER 47:

Spirit of a Black Train

Some people emphasize certain words when they speak, while other people emphasize other words. Dan was someone who emphasized every single word he spoke, and when he opened his mouth, the fabric of the universe coalesced around him.

Here he was, standing behind a small rectangular plastic table with a white binder and papers spread across it. I could tell he was at least six feet tall, even though I was sitting down. He was broad but not fat, and he had large heavy shoulders. He wore an unzipped black jacket over a dark-gray long-sleeve shirt, which puffed out with every muscle in his torso, as well as black jeans with silver linings with all the pizzazz of an amateur guitar hipster. Brown tightly-laced cowboy boots adorned his feet with jean cuffs tucked into dark wool socks.

Dan's head was covered by a gray cowboy hat, which only served to cover up the fact that he was bald. Indeed, there was more hair in his graying goatee than on his scalp. Right below his indistinct eyebrows were his beady eyes, and it was hard to tell in what direction he was looking, while tan leather skin had hardened his mouth into a concave frown under his pug-like nose. In his right hand he held an expensive-looking smooth wooden cane, but by its shaft and not its handle.

Fifty-three was the age that came to mind, and his

self-presentation smelt of burnt coal. I was afraid to get run over, because Daniel Verny carried the spirit of a black train.

"Attention!"

Fear gripped me. I was not the only one to cover my ears, though I had not yet taken account of everyone in the Instruction Room. All I knew was that I was one of the first people to arrive, and that Jenna had clung to my right side. Alyssa waved at him.

"Attention!"

All eyes were on him and only his hairy non-existent lips moved, yet smiling would crack his face apart. As people scrambled for their sanity, my eyes darted about, taking stock of everyone here. At the double-L-shaped table configuration, five people sat on each side, fifteen in total.

Jenna was at the end of the row, and out of all of us Tender Toucher sat closest to the door, which meant I could take credit for protecting her if she needed to escape. At the same corner was bestie Alyssa, who would have been little help, and at Savvy Socialite's right was Barnyard Boy, who would've made things even worse.

Chase's companion Mister Suckup was on his other side, who would be just fine here if he kept up his natural tendencies.

Next to Ron was also Buff Face, resting his muscles on the table like gold to be polished, and at Brian's right side I noticed the mouse-brown hair of Mindy, who had no reason to be here.

On the other side of the room and near Total Wreck was Sam, looking like a complete loser today because he was wearing red pants with a blue shirt and white shoes, making his dirty-blonde hair darker than his footwear.

Next to Idiot Scumbag was Adam, his hair flatter than an airport rampway, and on Fly Fisher's right side – my left side – was Halley, who had been upgraded to a Seven-point-five because her blonder hair had grown out slightly.

Left of Pale Egg sat Brianna, no longer a happy bunny, for

she leaned with chin resting on an extended palm and elbow on the table.

And at the far left corner was Silent Soldier; Terrence had the discipline not to engage Brianna in idle chatter, yet could not resist the temptation to surf the internet on his phone.

On my left side were three people I had never before seen at Murray, all of them unmistakably men. Two had dark hair, and one may have, but he had an ugly buzzcut that diminished the color saturation on top of his head.

The one next to me was a big chunky guy whom I would not mess with because he wore the same style jacket as Black Train.

Next to him was a tall skinny guy whose Adam's apple was visible in profile view, which bobbed up and down the few times he spoke in his roughneck accent and whose long neck, long nose, and filthy hair made him a real-life version of Cletus from *The Simpsons*.

The buzzcut guy was short, and if he stood beside me, I could rest my fist on his prickly hair, which did not help the fact that he was vertically challenged.

Chunky, Cletus, and Buzzcut *all* looked like poorly-educated rural thugs, and I never bothered to learn their real names, because by the time they had told me, they already would have forgotten that they had revealed their true identities. The phrase 'dumb as three rocks' was well and alive with them; their combined IQ was most likely lower than Black Train's weight, and the onus was on them to prove otherwise.

The people-analysis was Matrix-style; I sized up everyone in a few moments.

Dan cleared his throat, which sounded like grinding in a train engine, and he began to speak in what some might consider plain English.

"I. Am. Your. Instructor. For. Mine Safety and Health Administration. You all will. Listen to me and obey me. I was surprised. That. I got this job. Teaching. All of you."

He pointed around the room, head following finger.

"One of the supervisors here. Amy. Wanted to hire. Someone like me. I was emailing her. The other day. She seems to have a pretty decent sense. Of humor."

"Decent doesn't even begin to describe it," I muttered.

Tender Toucher started laughing.

She stopped of her own accord, but Savvy Socialite moved her shoulders back and forth as if running a marathon, and after every ten seconds, she would stretch backwards and high into the air with her nice flat back at an eighty-degree angle from the horizontal axis, joyously reaching for stars that shine in the night and cannot be seen by day.

I tried closing my eyes and covering my ears in a pseudo-imitation of Helen Keller, but I was too transfixed. Her shirt should have been lower than it was, and I wondered why this particular piercing was not on her ears today.

I didn't know who deserved my attention more: her or the instructor. My focus was averaged out, and I looked straight ahead at Adam, the least remarkable of us all!

My head shimmied left and right; I couldn't focus on the safety information coming from the steaming anger of Black Train, for I was distracted by the coquettish mannerisms of Savvy Socialite.

Somehow, I regained self-control and focused in on what Dan was saying, but only because I might never meet someone like him again.

"I don't actually have to teach you. Anything while I'm here. I work for the state government. I just have to stay in this room for twenty four hours. Which I could do. If I really wanted. But you people."

His finger shimmied across the room, bouncing from every crest and trough like a furious ocean wave.

"Have decided to split that time into three days. Which is fine with me. Because I still get paid the same amount."

I exhaled; nobody else looked nervous.

"Let me tell you a little bit. About myself. I quit school after third grade. Because I had to leave for the military. Now. You may have noticed that I just did a little bit of math. I divided twenty four by eight. And got three. Pretty good for a third grade education. Isn't it."

Remembering to look for redeeming qualities, I recognized that his voice sounded similar to that of Foghorn Leghorn from *Looney Tunes*.

"I am an adjunct. In the geoscience department. Of Kentucky State University. It doesn't go *real smooth* for some people. When I'm there."

Black Train's voice obscured my cough.

"Cuz I ain't real politically correct. The people there want me to talk all fancy talk. But that's just not who I am. I got hired part time. Because I've had some experience mining. And in the military. And I know some stuff. Same reason I got hired here. My experience with not being *safe*. Pretty good for a third grade education. Isn't it."

Actually, it was excellent for a third-grade education!

"Now. Let me tell you what happened to me. With not being safe. About ten years ago. I was the foreman. I was in a mining accident. We were doing *blasting*. The pole shot across my head. Ripped off the left side of my face. Impacted my brain a little. Took me a little while to recover. But by the time I was all better. They wouldn't let me back. Now right after the accident. The government thought the whole thing was cool. So they hired me. It's been a well paying job. I didn't have to do anything at first. Used that time to get all patched up. Even as they were paying me."

He dropped his cane and raised his hands just below shoulder-level.

"All that money from good old Uncle Sam. Helped me get my life back on track. Just gotta write down everything I'm gonna do each day. Otherwise I forget. The docs did a pretty good job with me. The government has really good health care. I didn't believe that at first. All of this."

He covered the left side of his face with his left hand.

"Is fake. Fake skin. Fake eye. But I can still see out of both. *Aalll* of that hard earned money you and your friends and your family pay in taxes. Went to me so I could have a decent life. Money's been good to me. Heck. Money makes the world go round. That's what I tell my kids."

I cared about America's youth and enjoyed the company of children, but whoever his kids were, I didn't want to meet them.

"I get paid at my job no matter *what* I do. But I still work hard. And you think I've had a bad life. You people have to work hard else you don't get paid. Anyway. It took my wife some time to get used to the new me. We stayed together. Cuz the government gave us more money for being married."

He swiped his cane across the room.

"Now are any of you married? Or soon to be married?"

Chunky looked up from his sullen stare and raised a fore-arm, elbow on the table. His lower lip hung down, which made him look like a tired frog.

Dan invaded his space. "Tell me your situation."

His jaw dropped further. "Warr gitn marrd in two wecks."

"And how many kids will you have?" Black Train got in his face.

"Raht naho, I've a gurl, she 'as a boi."

He smashed his cane between Chunky and Cletus. *"No!!!"*

Chunky looked to me, but I was not going to help him with his problems; I wanted to see if he could solve them using his own wit and wisdom.

"They're *both* yours. Now how old are you?" Dan stood back and pointed at him.

"Thahrty fahv."

"A thirty five year old man. Who has a kid from a previous marriage. Should know better than that!" he spat, pounding his cane on the floor.

He walked slowly to the front of the room.

"You young people get divorced and remarried. Remarried and divorced. And the government doesn't even pay you to do it. You hop from one company to the next. Expecting more and more benefits with less and less work. You want everything for free. Your education system. Has brain washed you to become socialists. There is only one word to describe you millennials. *Entitlement!*"

Alyssa thrust her arm in the air, fist trembling. "*We* are the generation that will solve the *world's problems!*"

It was her turn to get run over.

Black Train stomped toward her slowly, yet was already halfway across the room, and when he approached her, he stopped short.

"You are the generation. That. Is. The. *Source* of the world's problems today!"

I held my hands out in balance-scale mode. "Maybe we're both the source of *and* the solution to the world's problems."

"We are the *solution,* always *believe that,*" Alyssa whispered earnestly.

Dan huffed and puffed. Then he looked towards me and pointed at me. "Heh. I like the way this here guy thinks. He should be your new boss."

Poorly-suppressed snickers traveled around the room like *the wave* at a baseball stadium.

The steam from his red ears cooled. He returned to his usual spot.

"It seems we've entered a discussion of something. I'm not allowed to talk about. So let me come clean. I am not allowed to discuss with you people. Religion *or* politics."

I wasn't quite sure what we were supposed to be learning from him at this point.

"Now I don't know too much about religion. But let me be clear on politics. One side's right and the other side's wrong."

He flipped his hand over and back.

"For example. Immigration is the biggest issue right now. Some people think we should let folks who entered without permission stay. But guess what. The best thing to do is just steamroll 'em outta here. And kick the bums off welfare to work the fields. Then we'll put a buncha welcome mats along the border. With *landmines* underneath!"

Black Train looked like he had just built a wall along the southern border of Antarctica.

"Also. Some people think we need to find peace in the Middle East. But guess what. We should really just start *carpet bombin' shithole countries!* Also. Some schools have anti gun policies to prevent school shootings. But guess what. The states with the highest amount of school shootings have the strictest gun laws! Also. Some people today think the earth's getting hotter than it ever was. But guess what. During the Cretaceous there was more carbon dioxide in the air than there is today! Also."

Even as my eyes were fixed on him, I knew where the heavy breathing was coming from.

"New York says there are now thirty one different genders. But guess what. Biology says there are only two! That's another science thing the other side gets wrong. And they call people like me anti science. But to be fair."

He motioned in circles with his hand.

"There are such things as hermaphrodites. When the chromosomes get mixed up. Although they are relatively rare."

Savvy Socialite opened her mouth and stretched her hands. "But those are *genders,* not *sexes!*"

Black Train grimaced. "It seems as though there is a need. For audience participation. Fine then. I need a volunteer."

"Me, me-me-me-me-me-me, pick *meee.*" Alyssa's hand flailed like fireworks on the Fourth of July.

No one else raised a hand, yet Black Train still looked around the room.

Her manner was overeager, and her face was like flint,

though not Flint, Michigan, for it was clean, clear, and radiant with the desire to change the world.

His crooked eyes landed on her. "Well it seems like we have a total of one. Okay girl. What is your name?"

"Lissie!"

Dan stomped toward her, stopping halfway across the room.

"Lissie. Huh. That was my second ex wife's name. I guess you do remind me of her. Though not too much. Alright then. What is the book right outside this room? I may have seen it before."

"It's the SDS book," piped in Tender Toucher.

"Well. Why don't you go and get it then."

As soon as he said this, Alyssa scurried out, and as soon as she scurried out, she scurried back in holding the manual.

"Here it *is!*"

"Good." Dan grabbed it from her.

He reached into his pocket for his reading-glasses and flipped the pages back and forth until his finger landed half-way to the end. "This book is only about. One third complete."

"What does SDS stand for?" I whispered to Jenna.

"Safety Data Sheets," she replied aloud.

"Now. There could be something really bad that could happen. If. Say. Someone were to choke on something. But that's one of the things that's been filled in right. With the Heimlich maneuver. You also ought to add here. That one way to tell if someone can't breathe. Is if their face is flushed. But for people of a certain *ethnic background.* It's hard to tell!"

Black Train stepped back as subtle guffaws arose.

"See I did good there right. Like I said. I ain't real politically correct." Dan groaned. "Now. I am pointing right here in the book."

He peered over his reading-glasses at Alyssa.

"Because there is something that could be very unsafe. If it did happen. I am pointing to a place where there is no explanation. For what to do if someone gets something stuck in their eye."

He dropped it *smack* in front of Savvy Socialite.

Black Train looked around, chin and finger tied together in an invisible knot. "Now does anybody here. Know what to do if a speck. Or a piece of dirt gets in someone's eye?"

I raised my hand. "I do!"

"Yes. Young man." He stared at me.

"You go to the bathroom and wash it out with water."

"That is cor-*rect*. I can already tell this young man. Is the smartest one in the room."

Terrence glanced up from his phone.

"Now the problem is. If the government agents come in and see *any* section incomplete. Especially with something like this. They could shut this place down. Just. Like. *That*." He snapped his fingers, and Jenna gasped.

Spreading my hands apart, I stated, "And they would be *completely* justified in doing so."

"Ex-*actly!*" said Dan.

"Richard!" Tender Toucher slapped my neck.

I turned to her. "All I'm saying is that it would be the right *thing* for them to do, *if* they were here, which fortunately for us they're not."

"*Richard!*" Jenna slapped me again.

The crowd mumbled as I received a round of angry glares. Even Halley looked peeved.

I raised my voice. "Look!"

Dan was smiling, and his face was fully cracked apart.

"The fact is, although we as people possess individual rights, the government would be completely within *its* rights if we are out of compliance to tear us down as Mister Verny here said, 'just like that.'"

Brian placed his hand to his forehead. "Oh my god!"

"Dude, are you seriously that f**ked up?" asked Chase.

Jenna looked away from me, and her face was red.

Brianna glared at me with downturned eyebrows. "You're *such* a *dick!*"

"Not as much of a dick as Dick Cheney," I retorted.

"SO YOU'RE SAYING YOU DON'T FREAKING HATE RAND PAUL?" inquired Idiot Scumbag.

"Do you?"

CHAPTER 48:

Hitting on Alyssa

"How did your time gambling go?" I asked the High Life protégés.

"I won! I won!" Alyssa grasped for straws in the air. "I'm so *happy*. I got a hundred *dollars!*"

Jenna had a modest smile. "I won ten dollars. How did your time here go?"

"Let's just say I should have done the socialist version of stream monitoring, where we're *outraged* that one percent of the streams contain ninety percent of the stream water."

Jenna laughed, slapped her thigh, and lost her balance.

Barnyard Boy shook his drooped head. "I can't believe it. I lost five hundred dollars at the casino."

Chunky turned to me. "Ah wanna show ya somethin' that'll rilly make yer heart spin."

"No! Don't corrupt his innocent eyes." Tender Toucher reached over me, waving.

"I have innocent eyes?"

By her effervescent expression, she seemed to think so.

"Why do my eyes look innocent?"

"I dunno...just cuz."

I turned back to Chunky. His eyes definitely looked guilty.

"I guess innocence is relative," I said to Jenna. "No one is completely innocent."

The company provided free Subway, so in honor of Black Train I grabbed as many helpings of Italian hoagie as I could eat.

Jenna had taken leftover Halloween candy from the stream hub, and she soon became high on sugar just like she had become drunk on alcohol.

I seized a Kit Kat bar from her and dangled it in front of her eyes. "Ooh, *chocolate.* You know you love it."

"I *do* love chocolate."

I felt relieved that the giddy version of Jenna had returned. Still, I needed to hold my tongue to ensure that nobody could read my thoughts like they were written in a black-outlined cloud-bubble above my head, so I immersed my mind in nothingness by imagining a mysterious black orb.

"Richard, you look really bored." Tender Toucher held my hand. "Why are you staring at the ceiling?"

"Just thinking about how I can be a more effective communicator, that's all."

"Don't worry about it. Let's just enjoy lunch together."

I nudged her on the shoulder. *"You* need to entertain me."

Barnyard Boy and Savvy Socialite held an even more delicate conversation.

"My body already fits perfectly into yours."

"Don't call me Kissie Lissie while *we're here.*"

"Tonight, we're gonna have a *good-good*...niiiight."

"F**k...*you.*"

"We can do *what-what,* whatever we want, YEAH."

"Look, I just don't want anything growing *inside of me.* Ohh...*bingo!"*

Meanwhile, I was thoroughly enjoying my meal; I complemented my sandwich with Doritos in a cool-blue bag, a snickerdoodle cookie, and fizzy carbonated Fanta.

"The Italian subs are really good," I commented to a general audience. "You should try them."

Mister Suckup's bulbous head emerged from behind

Barnyard Boy gesticulating passionately. "You think *those* are good? I'm a full-blooded Italian and I can make the *best* pasta sauce of anyone here."

"But these don't *have* pasta sauce. I even took out the tomatoes; I don't like tomatoes."

His face reddened by the second. "You did *that?* That's an insult to my family, to my heritage."

"Hey, I actually *am* part Italian." I jiggled my hands and arms.

"But you're not a *full-blooded* Italian. I can tell that just by looking at you."

"I'll tell you what. I've made spaghetti before and boiled my own marinara sauce. Let's just leave it at that."

He shook his fist, his face redder than Mississippi every fourth November. "Don't use that phrase *marinara* with me! I bet you *burn* the pasta sauce when you try to boil it too high. I never burn the sauce. I can boil it so high and still make it taste so good that Mount Vesuvius would erupt inside your mouth!"

Mister Suckup's face reached its maximum redness.

"I have to go to the bathroom." Jenna pushed the seat behind her.

With only Chunky as a next-seat neighbor, I prepared in my notebook a bullet-point list of everything I knew about farming, fishing, and hunting, recalling my father's advice: *Fake it 'til you make it.*

Chunky tapped me on the shoulder with his stumpy finger before I had finished assembling my facts. "He lahks her."

I furrowed my brow. "I'm sorry, I didn't catch that."

"Ah said, he...*lahks* her."

Cletus stuck his bony face into view. "Urrrh hurrhhh."

"Whom does he like?" I asked Chunky.

"Dat gurl ho jus' left."

I leaned over and wagged my finger. "Hey you, down at the end."

Buzzcut turned towards me.

"Does your buddy there 'like,' as this man put it," I said, tapping Chunky on his noggin, "the fine young woman who was just seated next to me?"

He stared at me for a few moments. "Yuh."

"Ses he wans ta slip wit her," Chunky added.

"Urrhh *huurrrrhhh.*" Cletus slung his head up and down with his wiry neck.

Savvy Socialite strutted around the corner, adjusted her pants, folded down her shirt, and with phone in hand, extended her arm in front of him. "Here's...her...*number.*"

Cletus smashed his thumbs one after the other into his phone, glancing up and down until he had recorded all ten digits.

She pranced to her seat, thrusting her shoulders back and forth. "I am *such*...an awesome *wing-girl.*"

Then she resumed her intimate conversation with Chase. Alyssa did most of the talking.

"...and I didn't really like it *that much,* and I started seeing really *weird things,* but at least it wasn't as bad as *being on crack.*"

"Being on crack?" I piped in forcefully.

Savvy Socialite's face froze, stiff as a board. She opened her mouth and clenched her jaw without smiling. "Did you just accuse me of being on *crack?*"

The room fell silent.

"That's what I heard you say."

Alyssa bared her teeth with eyes fierce, and clenched her delicate fist. "Do you know what you could do to someone's reputation if you accuse them of being on *crack?* Did you know that you could really hurt someone's career by *saying that?*"

"My apologies."

Her shoulders fell as blood rushed into her complexion.

She turned to face the front of the room and moved her shoulders back and forth as if swimming in freestyle. Savvy

Socialite bounced in her seat and never forgot to display her preening stretch.

Poor Alyssa. She was reaching for an invisible branch that wasn't there, yet I knew she was much too suave for imaginary friends, even though she began to talk to herself.

"Conrad *Power...*" Her shoulders sped up to twice their normal speed "...is why I *have this job.*" Alyssa's shoulders never stopped moving. "I wanna marry a rich coal miner and live at the top of a New York City *skyrise.*"

"You'd be an urban sophisticate," I commented.

"Huh?" She looked at me. "I'm an *Aquarius.*"

"That's all well and good. I mean, you'd be a high-class lady living in a big city."

"Oh." Savvy Socialite stopped, finger to her lips with eyes upward. "That's *right I would!"* She bounced her head back and forth with luscious hair flopping. "But can you puh-*leeze* stop being such a *nerd?"*

Ouch. "You know, lots of guys played video games when they were young, and some still do. Even Bo plays video games, and you wouldn't call him a nerd."

Alyssa brushed her hair and opened her mouth with jaw angled diagonally, holding this position. *"No,* I mean the thing you just said *before,* herb and – *whatever.* And, *anyway...*Bo only plays the *sports games,* and not the *weird ones,* like *you probably do."* She was looking pretty dumb with her finger and her thumb in the shape of an L on her forehead.

She pulled out her phone and started texting. "Jesus *Christ."*

"Isn't that a bad word?" Chase wondered.

"God *dammit,"* she added.

"You sure no one here is going to put a bar of soap in your mouth?" I warned playfully.

Savvy Socialite leaned in toward me, brushing her hair aside, bouncing her head with the tips of her earlobes almost touching her respective shoulders. "Good thing I'm... *twenty-four!"*

CHAPTER 49:

Fashion Show

Jenna exhaled with hands on her hips. "I'm back."
Dan stomped into the room and drew down the projector screen. With hat in his armpit, he rubbed lotion on his bright red head, and before he placed it back on he looked like an industrial Doctor Eggman. With cane in one hand, he held a remote in the other.

"Now. Let's get to the part where I start to teach you some stuff. I am going to show you. A series of pictures that will. Show you what can happen to you. If you are not safe near a mining site. Now."

He pointed around the room with his cane.

"Most of you here. Are from Murray and Affiliates. But a few of you. As I've been told. Are from somewhere else. Raise your hand. If you are *not* from Murray."

The three buttheads raised their claws.

Black Train approached Chunky. "Tell me. What organization you are a part of."

His throat gurgled before words emerged. "Kinmug."

Dan's posture shot upright. "Alright then." He turned to address everyone, palm still glued to the table. "We have a few people here. Who are from Kenn Mag."

He stepped backward to his place like a train with its wheels in reverse. "Now. The safety protocols. Are taught differently.

At different companies."

With a flick of the remote, the screen turned a bright blue.

"That is why I. Am going to show you some images. Of people who were not properly prepared. Or who were not thinking before they acted. And all the deaths and all the injuries they received. As a result of not being careful. They are bandaged up and stitched up. In ways that will shock you and horrify you. But that's the point."

Alyssa bounced in her seat. "Fashion show! Fashion show!" she exclaimed, framing her face with her fingers and thumbs.

"Dammit!" Dan thrusted the cane against the floor by its ferrule and stomped toward her.

It was her turn to get run over again.

"This is no fashion show. Girl."

"No, no, no, *nuh-nuh-nuh-nuh-nuh-no,* this is just the thing we were used to doing at the Prestonsburg *Dance Marathon,* whenever there was an exciting new *presentation coming up,*" she explained, legs kicking under the seat.

He placed his hands on the table, running her over for good.

"Whenever they would all come up to the *stage,* and we were all like, '*Who's that?*'"

She held up her hands, opening and closing them repeatedly like flashing lights in a railroad tunnel.

"And then they were *all like,* 'We're the *fashion show!*' And then we would all say, '*Fashion show! Fashion show!*'"

Alyssa's fingers and thumbs danced around the frame of her face. She was the real fashion show, and her demeanor helped her survive the accident; she had obtained a Power Star and shimmered with temporary invincibility.

"So I'm just used to *saying that,* whenever there's a new *announcement coming up.*"

"Whatever!"

Her defense inspired Black Train to roll back into his shed.

"Now. The show will begin. But one thing first. The

government says. That if you are ever out anywhere near a mine. During your professional working hours. You are automatically classified. As a miner."

"Fashion show! Fashion show!"

Every slide revealed diligent people making small errors in mine safety etiquette, causing otherwise uneventful partnerships with imperfection to go so wrong that they risked life and limb and had one, or sometimes both, taken away from them. The ones who survived could no longer lead normal lives, and the ones who did not survive were soon forgotten by everyone around them.

Savvy Socialite played on her phone, distracting Tender Toucher and Barnyard Boy in the world of hip-hop culture, gossip, and fashionable friends.

"Now. Were any of these accidents. That I just showed you. Acts of god. That is. Could they have been prevented if people just took time. To make sure they knew what they were doing. Is there anything here. That resembles a lightning bolt. Starting up from high above. And striking someone *dead.*"

We shook our heads.

The misfits behind me immersed themselves in a world of their own, not a fantasy world, but a different part of reality, a more cultured, wholesome, sophisticated and urbane side to life – the High Life.

"Are there. Any questions so far."

I raised my hand.

"Yes. Young man. The wise one."

"I was wondering if there was going to be any sort of test or exam by which we could assess our knowledge of these important concepts in safety you've articulated?"

Black Train focused on me and stomped toward me, but very slowly; I had time to roll out of the way in case this locomotive had a loose wheel.

It was my turn to get run over.

"Do you really. Want. To take. A test. There is more to life than just taking tests. Young man. I thought you of all people. Would be smart enough to know that."

"So how will you assess our knowledge?"

The entire room groaned.

"Fashion show! Fashion show!"

"I can show you reality. So you don't have to take. A test. Which is what I'm doing. Right now. You think I of all people. Nothing more than a third grade graduate. Would ever be giving out *tests?*"

I shook my head.

"I've given this same presentation. Many times. But only in English. Because if English is good enough for me. It's good enough for the rest of the world. And *all* the people I've taught. Have learned from it. Pretty good for a third grade education. Isn't it."

The words spilled out of my mouth like water from an overflowing bucket. "Yes sir, it's absolutely excellent for a third-grade education, and I couldn't bear to ask for anything more."

He backed up and continued speaking.

"Now. You may have just noticed. That I mentioned *god* in this room. As I've told you. I am not allowed to talk about politics *or* religion. But we've already had something. Resembling a political discussion. And I know who won *that* debate."

He nodded at me, and I smirked while folding my arms.

"So we might as well do the same for religion. I will tell you up front. Well you may have already guessed it from what I've said. I am not particularly religious. I believe once you're in the grave. That's it. And there's not much you can do once you're there. So I'm trying to save you all. From that fate. The grave is for the elderly. Life is for the living. But we'll all get there some day. And there's no reason to speed it up. I should have been more careful the other day. I was climbing a telephone pole with a ladder. Don't ask me why. But when I got to the top. There was this real *pious guy* who came along. Real nice guy. But he told me to go to church. And to be fair. It was on a Sunday. But you know what I said to him. I said this. I'm closer to my god up here than you are to yours down there! He didn't expect that kind of response from me. Pretty good for a third grade education. Isn't it."

Alyssa drew chemistry diagrams on notebook paper, and Chase created an acronym, while Jenna tried to get their attention. Dan droned on, expressing the same warning with the same shock-factor in different scenarios in all manner of rhyme and rhythm, like an extended round of Tetris.

"What animal does Alyssa remind you of?" Chase asked me.

I pointed at Barnyard Boy. "A kangaroo."

He looked like he had just been struck by a lightning bolt. "Holy crap, I was just writin' down random letters and they ended up spellin' KAGAROO. We must have some sort of special connection between our minds, dude!"

"I'm pretty sure those are called *soul ties.*" She crossed her arms over her lower torso and closed her eyes halfway. "They form when there's an *unhealthy friendship.*"

"Don't you think she's just a little bit weird?" I extended my hand carelessly towards Savvy Socialite.

Jenna examined her chemistry drawings as well as the screen of Alyssa's phone.

"Oh, you have no idea just how *weird* she can be!" said Barnyard Boy.

Alyssa rolled her eyes and slapped him efficaciously on his arm.

"I can imagine..." I put in subtly. "Why do you think you started writing KAGAROO?"

"Well, I started with the letters K-A-G, and then wanted to make it...fancier. You know what KAG means, right?"

"Keep America Great."

"So I'm just drawin' a possible symbol for that, and wanted

to make sure you agreed with me on Alyssa since I don't have a kangaroo here."

"How about this: Keep America Great Always Running On Oil."

"Nice, dude!"

I squinted. "Are you well-connected in some important way I don't know about?"

"Compared to you I prolly am."

"Whenever I type in 'far left' in a Word document, the computer wants to capitalize the 'F' and the 'L'. Do you suppose there's some sort of conspiracy?"

"I dunno man. Bill Gates is an evil maniac who kills regular people."

I paused. "No he's *not*. He's the founder of Microsoft. We're talking about *that* Bill Gates, right?"

He clenched his teeth and eyed me suspiciously. "There's only one I know of."

Black Train was speaking fluidly, yet still in incomplete sentences.

"Do you know if there are any Amish people in the countryside around here?" I asked casually.

Alyssa's head perked up from her designs. "My cousins are *Amish*."

"Are you Amish?"

There was a sour taste on her face. "Are you *joking?* Hello! I *work* for a *living*."

"But Amish women work for a living – around the house. They just don't get paid. But they *do* work, of course. They work very hard."

She scoffed with eyes rolling. "What I *mean is,* they don't actually go out and *have a career*. Like *I do*."

"So you're saying you work harder than they do? Right now?"

"*Yeah*."

Jenna put down Alyssa's phone and looked at her own.

"Let me show you something interesting." On my own phone I showed Jenna a series of memes on imgflip.com, and she giggled at all of them. I scrolled through them page by page, her eyes transfixed on the images as much as on me.

"Draw me a picture," she requested, her voice a soft ocean wave. She tore out a piece of paper from her notebook.

"Hmm...okay."

I googled for images of celebrities; on one side I drew the face of Kim Kardashian, and on the other side that of Justin Bieber. I signed my name on both sides, and Tender Toucher reached for it with her soft hands.

"Whoa that's really good!"

"You can keep it."

"I'll keep it somewhere special." She held it against her chest.

The double-sided drawing remained at her place thereafter showing Justin Bieber.

"Now let's take a picture together," said Jenna.

"Picture time! Picture time!" Alyssa nearly broke the barrier of our undertone conversation.

Jenna held up my phone before us; Alyssa and I leaned in on either side of her, our heads tilted diagonally so that our faces would appear on the sides of the final picture.

But when Tender Toucher recorded the image, our faces were chopped off and only our foreheads appeared, while she remained front and center.

"You should change me to your background picture," she advised.

I kept her as the background on my phone, and as my save-screen a picture of the earth from outer space.

"You know, Alyssa gave the guy over there your phone number while you were gone." I pointed at Cletus, holding my fist steady as I jabbed my finger like an automatic door-knocker.

She leaned over the table, bearing a positive impression.

"He really likes you, apparently. So be on guard, or don't

be on guard. Your choice."

Jenna nodded. "Thanks for telling me."

Alyssa looked up from her phone. "F**k *you!*" she spouted. "Chase has a degree in electrical engineering you know."

"Richard, stop makin' stuff up," said Chase.

I wrote my phone number on the paper in front of Jenna, above Justin Bieber's head. "I'm competing with *Cletus* over there."

She looked back at him, her face brilliant, and as she laughed, the decibel level rose to the point at which it might distract Black Train. "You're really good with nicknames."

I smugly upturned one end of my mouth. "You think so?"

Kevin started to watch our learning session, wobbling and holding a glass bottle.

Ron noticed him. "Hey Kevin, looks like you've been drinking lately."

"Heh heh," he responded, dazed.

"Watch this," I said to Jenna.

I faced the straggling figure and pointed at him. "Looks like *Encyclopedia Brown* here finally learned to loosen up a little!"

The whole room gasped – then fell silent.

Kevin dropped the bottle. *"What* did you just call me?"

"I'm just messing with you, dude. Let's both get back to work now."

"Don't call me Encyclopedia Brown *ever* again," said Encyclopedia Brown as he walked away.

Savvy Socialite looked up at me. "Richard, did you take that one course at *Prestonsburg,* 'The Oceans, Atmosphere and *Climate'?*"

"Yeah, why?"

"I was just thinking of what Dan said about *climate change.*"

"Oh. Yeah, global warming."

"It's actually called *climate change.* What grade did you

get in that class?"

"An 'A'. A pretty high 'A', to be frank with you. What did you get?"

She gazed in awe. "I passed it *too*. But I thought Kayla was a *bitch*."

"Oh yeah, Doctor Worthington. I know what you mean."

"Attention! There is something very important. That we need to discuss here. We need to talk a little bit. About manga."

CHAPTER 50:

Guardians of the Earth

"**N**ow does anyone at all. Have any familiarity with manga." A discussion about Japanese comic books brewed among the constituents.

"I remember reading the first book of *Fullmetal Alchemist*." Dan heard me and responded with positive body language.

"The first thing I had to realize is that you're supposed to read the pages backwards. The story was about one brother who didn't turn into a robot and one brother who did."

"Ex-*actly*." He waved a pointed-finger hand as if hitting a forehand in a game of tennis. "Edward loses his leg. But Alphonse loses his entire body. You just hit the nail on the head. That is my *favorite* manga series. Because it shows the type of injuries that can occur. If you're not safe while mining. And it's very important to all you people. Because one miner at Conrad Power. Got his whole body smashed like a pancake. And lost his life of course. While doing longwall mining. At Eblen Fork Mine. Only twenty five years old."

"How do you know so much about manga?" asked Jenna with head tilted.

"I don't really, just that one book. And *Tales of Symphonia*, which was originally a video game about renewing the earth, just with a bunch of religious and philosophical themes. It's analogous to what *we're* doing, sharing the flow of water, only it's about sharing the flow of mana."

Her eyes grew like hard-boiled eggs. "Jeez, Richard, grow up. Real life isn't a video game."

"That's just what *you* think." I placed my finger by my open mouth. "I'm fully convinced we can all find a way to keep the earth completely clean, while providing goods and services to all of humanity, without sacrificing a single life."

Jenna furrowed her brow. "So...what do you plan to do about it?"

"I've been thinking about that for a long time. Someone asked me why I work at Murray and Affiliates...what it is that I want to do. I want a world where everyone can have a normal life. I'm tired of business and government sacrificing people's well-being to the whim of their desires. I'm tired of discrimination against the poor and vulnerable. I'm tired of people becoming victims. I'm tired of it all."

"Okay, but that's way too idealistic. Business and government can only succeed by victimizing people. That's just the way the world works, and anything you say doesn't matter."

"Then we need to change that structure. This world...was, after all, made by God. Right...?"

She stared blankly.

"Regardless of how the earth came into being, man has undeniably altered the planet – which means, for better or for worse, *we* can utilize our roles here to change it for the good of everyone in Georgetown County."

"Hahahaha," laughed Tender Toucher, closing her eyes and falling back with arms across her body. "You talk like you're such a hero, Richard."

"I'm trying to illustrate for you what the *ideal* situation would be," I urged with my hand stiff like a car entrance gate. "The ideal situation is to have every stream flowing freely with fresh, clear water. Every drop of water, every breath of air, every ray of sunshine, is part of what we share. We can end the war between coal miners and farmers, as well as the collusion between government and business, by insisting that there must be a way for everyone to coexist in peace."

"Are you saying you can become the next Erin Brockovich?"

"Look, I'm not Erin Brockovich. While we're here, I want to save not the whole world – because no one can do that – but save the local environment from destruction, in my own unique way, with the help of my friends...like you."

I opened my hands to her.

"That's nice and all," she replied with a modest smile, "but there's a certain way we do things here. You sure you wanna turn your coworkers *and* employers against you like that?" She raised an eyebrow.

"How about if I ask *you,* given a choice between those who wish to sacrifice the environment, and those who wish to preserve it, who would you side with?"

"The side that's likely to win," Jenna answered, fingers spread apart. "But we should preserve both the economy and nature."

"Exactly." I thrust my pointed-finger fist downward like a hammer. "So the first thing we must do is devote all our resources to caring for the least among us. Fortunately, it appears our roles are suited to being guardians of the earth, so we should be able to make a difference in a short period of time."

She nodded and gazed upward. "Okay. I get what you're saying."

"In any case, even if you don't agree, thanks for listening to me."

"Is he for *real?*" asked Savvy Socialite under her breath, leaning in towards Tender Toucher. "Sheesh!"

Dan summoned our attention. "This is the part where I. Can weave in my own experience a bit."

"Story time! Story time!"

The screen displayed an underground mine full of trucks, ladders, and heavy equipment.

"This is the part. Where I'm gonna talk about my time. Doing *blasting*. It's where you break open the earth with *EXPLOSIVES*. So you can get the coal underneath! Now you may have thought I was no friend of blasting. Because of what happened to me. But guess what. I've also had great fun with it. Especially when it affects other people. There's just a joyful satisfaction in knowing you done a real good job. Cuz some mutherf**ker complains about getting hit. Well *boo hoo* to those people. I enjoy unleashing the *flyrock*. That's the rock that goes through the air as a result of blasting. It can travel up to half a mile in any direction. And it goes so fast it *kills* people. Pretty cool huh. So there was this one time. When we shot it through the air. It was a huge chunk of granite. Ended up smashing through the living room window while they were there. Of one guy living around the mining site. He was frightened as hell. Didn't know what to do about it."

He tapped his cane and foot together in rhythmic excitement of his own memory.

"His kids really got the shit scared outta them. Kept havin' awful nightmares. The bitch wife suffered a heart attack. Even though she was pretty young. But she was a fat f**k. So guess what this poor bastard does next. He was pretty damn poor by the way. He calls the mine. So I get assigned to go to his house. And I find something I didn't expect. He's got a marble driveway. And I go into his house. To his living room where the flyrock landed. Glass *everywhere*. Pretty horrible situation. For him and his c**tbag wife and their bitch kids. The guy doesn't know how to fix it. Doesn't have the money to get it fixed. So he gives me permission to take a piece of the flyrock. And we find out it's not granite but marble. So guess what we do next."

Black Train slammed his cane on the ground and his fist on the table, both creating magnitudinous earthquakes.

"We sue *him* for taking a rock from *his own driveway!* Breaking through *his own window pane!* And then *blaming it on us!!!*"

He pumped his fist in the air as an explosion of laughter and applause filled the room.

"Sure gave that sucker a run for his money! All the money he had that is! But he didn't have enough. To pay for all the liabilities and costs and other damages. So guess what. The government gave us more money! Money that *he* probably paid in taxes to support his *own* family. Boy. I sure *love* how government and business can work together for the people. And help each other out. See what I mean. Money makes the world go round. I tell my kids that all the time."

Alyssa and Jenna giggled together in wicked glee while doing the pattycake, and I only wanted to acknowledge the pattycake.

"Now we wanted to get rid of that mutherf**ker for good. So he couldn't complain no more. So guess what we did next. I took a bottle of this liquid. It was labeled *ee arr ell*. ERL!"

"What does erl mean?" Jenna leaned over so I could see her naturally well-constructed face.

I googled the letters, and the first link took me to urbandictionary.com – 'erl: redneck term for oil.' I showed her the definition.

"I guess we're all just a bunch of rednecks then," she said.

"It's not a good term to use."

"But *other* races have *other* words to describe themselves," she argued, palms apart and eyebrows raised. "So why can't we?"

"Look, it's just not good to use any of those words."

"So I get to go to his house again. I bring the bottle of erl with me. Take a match and a lighter as well. The family's all together there in the living room again. Buncha tape across their broken windows. Watching their tiny tee vee. So then I light it and get out right away. Fry 'em like bacon is what I say. But they escape too. Felt like Dallas in the middle of the summer that day. Now the government didn't notice. Cuz he wasn't paying taxes no more. And by that point. We convinced the judge he was trying to burn down his own home. And guess what. The government gives us more money so we could help pay for all the damages! They lowered our taxes as well. While raising those of everyone in the community. Pretty sweet ain't it."

"HAHAHAHAHAHAHAHAHAHA!!"

Everyone wanted to get the last clap. The vocal cords of the chumps next to me were more active than they had ever been, yee-hawing and hee-hawing. Dan chuckled heartily, dropping his cane with hand on his stomach, drowning in guffaws.

"So now the government gives us even *more* money! To help find out where the sucker's at. So they could record his whereabouts. Me and my partners figure that family's all off dead somewhere. Last I heard. Only they don't get their own graves. Might makes right. It's a dog eat dog world. Eat or be eaten. But lemme ask you something. Who has the real right? Did he and his funny folks have the right to be there? Or lemme put it to you this way. Who was there first? Were they there first? No! The mine's been active for well over a hundred years. Late eighteen sixties is when Conrad Power first started. Yet the family moved in ten years prior. Couldn't find anywhere else to live. Actually. If you think about it. Mother Nature was there first. She's been here before *all* of us. Survival of the fittest they call it. You didn't think I knew that. Pretty good for a third grade education. Isn't it."

CHAPTER 51:

Smoke Break

I sent out an SOS-style query: "Was anyone in this room in the *gifted* program when they were in high school?"

Glares and smirks filled the Instruction Room. Terrence and Sam gave me the stink-eye. The crowd grumbled and rose out of their seats, shoving each other out of the way.

"Man, I really need to chow down on a good ol' fashioned cigarette," said Barnyard Boy.

"You know, the British people call them 'fags,'" I said, "which is what you shouldn't have called me if you actually thought I wasn't quite like you."

"Oh yeah, it's about time I got some nicotine in my system," agreed Tender Toucher.

The hustle and bustle ensued.

The dopes to my side lurched out of their chairs with giddy anticipation, sounding like donkeys as they girdled to one another, with hardly enough space behind me for them to get out and suck on their sophisticated pacifiers.

Even Dan scoured the corners of the room and headed for the door.

"Smoke break! Smoke break!" She hopped up and down bringing her knees in the air.

"Do you smoke too, Mindy?" I asked.

"Yeah kid, you got a problem with that?"

"No, not at all. Go ahead and *burn yourself out* for all you're worth."

She too gave me the stink-eye, framing it with her finger and thumb as a necessary slipshod makeshift monocle.

Fly Fisher still sat there, a dull and tired expression drawn over his round face.

"So you don't smoke either?" I pronounced the first syllable of the last word as *eye* instead of *ee*.

"No man, I gotta maintain my lungs so I can go hiking, biking, and fishing."

"Me too. I also don't smoke for other reasons. Lots of reasons, really. Current research suggests all the smoke inside one's body might creep up into their brain. But most of all, it's because I believe my body is a gift – a temple as it were."

A smooth grin crept along Adam's face. His mouth drooped to five-pi-over-four on the unit circle, and his voice played the same C below Middle-C at an *allegretto* tempo. "Alright, well that's pretty slick there dude."

We shared a moment of stillness.

"So how's fly-fishing with your girlfriend coming along?"

"We just broke up man. About two weeks ago."

"Oh. I'm sorry to hear that."

"So you got anything *cool* to talk about?"

"What was the main plot of *A River Runs Through It*? I don't quite remember."

He shrugged. "I don't really know man. I'm just sorta into it cuz o' the kicks and giggles and shit."

I peered at him. "And that's why it's your favorite movie."

"Yeah, I guess." He looked upwards. "Or at least one of them."

"That's pretty cool."

"If you say so."

The landscape was visible through the window behind him. "I'm heading outside now to catch some fresh air."

I stretched my legs with cramped knees cracking, and kicked

the beer bottle, which rolled across the carpet to the other side of the hallway like a bowling pin with too much freedom.

Dan, wearing his reading-glasses, perused the SDS manual beside its stand, leaning against the wall with his legs crossed, brown pipe-weed cigar between his teeth, sullying the hallway like a burning coal engine. His tobacco sure smelled nice.

"Hey. There. Kid. You some sort of altar boy. Or what."

"Never was an altar boy. But I'll take it as a compliment, for what it's worth."

I headed through the locker room and out to the surrounding driveway area, a courtyard with sunshine, merry chatter, and lots of activity, with clouds rising from the ground.

Everyone was smoking, and I enjoyed the second-hand experience. I joined the familiar threesome chatting, and suppressed a cough as spittle hung from my mouth.

"Sup, *dude!*"

"Well hey there."

"Richard time! Richard time!"

I pointed to Savvy Socialite with my eyes fixed on her. "Now Alyssa. I noticed during our lecture that you and Daniel had a little dispute about the veracity of climate change. What was your take on it?"

"I don't wanna *talk about it right now.*"

She turned to Chase and blew a series of smoke-rings. He caught her breath as a rising tide, while Tender Toucher touched me, then continued their debate.

I turned away pondering my identity and industry, and switched the difficulty level to Hard Mode. Gazing into the soon-setting sun, I didn't realize the door was closing.

"*Keee*-ree-aay...*elaay*-ee-soolll," I sang under my breath.

From in between the lockers, a bass-guitar growl accompanied a whimpering noise. As I crept forward, I pinpointed the source as my own.

Racecar Dude was holding Encyclopedia Brown in a headlock.

CHAPTER 52:

The Fight

The fight is on!

As they grunted and groaned, I shimmied to the side of the brawl. I tried shoving them aside, but when I had almost finished the combination, my fingers were jammed between Racecar Dude's thick elbow and the crevice of my locker.

"Have either one of you done anything with my belongings?"

He eyed me, teeth as tight as a clamp. "Not *yet*. But your *friend* here...Uncle Brown – or whatever you called him when you were in there – is trying to break into your locker and get into your stuff."

Bo choked Kevin as squealing cries escaped from his mouth.

"Richard!" he coughed. "Help!"

"You really shouldn't have opened your locker there kid! Cuz now you made it just a little easier for this snoop to get inside."

I stood back with my teeth clenched and my fists clenched as well. "Then close the damn door for me, will you!"

Bo tucked his hand underneath Encyclopedia Brown's chin, and with a wrestling move reminiscent of ancient Greek fighters, shoved him headfirst into the metal frame of the locker. I heard the click and took a deep breath.

"*Aaahhhhh!!!!*" Kevin tried to rub his head, but Racecar

Dude held both wrists together and began to twist his arms in a pretzel-knot.

"Bo, come on, just stop it." I raised my fists, even as he spun Kevin sideways and pinned him against the wall of lockers, pressing into the lowest pressure point on his back.

"I'm telling you – this little punk wants to know what you have inside."

"Why? I'm not hiding anything. And all of the stuff inside is mine – not his."

He shook his head as he twisted Kevin's neck. "You just don't get it – do ya? Kevin thinks you're hiding something in here that could really hurt the company."

As Encyclopedia Brown choked, Bo's eyes rose out of position, and madness was still oozing from his face.

"I'm gonna *kill* this motherf**ker if he tries to get away with any more of his investigations – you hear me!"

The redness on Kevin's face was turning to blue.

"What could I possibly have that could *hurt this company?*" My heart raced, my blood boiled, my knees quivered, and my body trembled.

"*Heelllppp...meee...*" he groaned with all the torment of a corpse rising from the grave. Yet his body floundered as he kicked, spat, and squealed, and his knees dropped to the floor. He wriggled like a snake caught in a mousetrap, while Racecar Dude's left arm wrapped, as though in a vice grip, around the circumference of his neck across his Adam's apple.

"It doesn't matter right now!"

Bo's eyes returned into focus as though emerging from a thicket of clouds, and the development of color saturation in his face was only a few seconds behind that of Kevin.

"He does this shit to *everyone* whenever he thinks they're hiding something or they've been out of line at all!"

The scream bounced off the walls of the room like a ricocheting pinball.

I stepped forward, my hands deadlocked into unbreakable

rocks. "And I haven't been *out of line,* so he has no reason to be near my locker *at all!*"

Racecar Dude bared his teeth as though worms could wiggle through each and every crack and crevice.

"It's either now or never ya douchebag. Listen – Richard. Here's what I'm gonna do now that you've come around."

His guttural utterances were like fumes from a burnt-out racecar, and I didn't know why I took another small step forward, and didn't expect to smell his putrid breath from a few meters away as I stared into the trenches of his complexion.

"I really didn't want to have to do this – but now that you're here..." he said, trembling "...this is it – and you better decide. I've got my baseball bat right back around the corner. So this is it. I'm gonna kill him and blame it on *you* – or I'm gonna let him go – smack *you* dead – and blame it on him."

Kevin's face was blue, and the rest of his body was white; words were ripped out of my mouth as much as breath was gone from his lungs, and I wobbled.

"So do the right thing – and not the wrong thing – but don't do the stupid thing either. Or else."

I felt the physiology of the fight in my bones; Bo was short and stocky, Kevin was tall and skinny, and I was medium and medium. I stood back, clenched my teeth tighter than ever before, my head vibrating to the tension in my knees, which buckled underneath me.

Racecar Dude shook his head in rhythm to my gesticulations. Kevin's eyes were silver platters.

"It's *now or never* – Richard!"

Backing up for a running start, I charged headlong into the mess while hearing Kevin's hopeless chokes.

I leapt in the air, kicked him in the jewels, and punched Racecar Dude's blood-red head from side-to-side with the only simple boxing moves I knew, screaming and crying.

"Get off him, you bastard!"

My vocal cords strained and vibrated more than my thoughtless mind.

Kevin fell to the floor, heaving and panting, while color returned swiftly to his face.

I continued punching Bo. My fists were jackhammers, and I pounded into Racecar Dude's face until the world would explode!

Racecar Dude fell over, but I kept kicking him.

With my left hand I grabbed him by his shirt collar, and with all the strength I had, dragged him up against my own locker where he could see me, and with my right hand smacked him silly like a bobble-head doll.

"....aaaarrrhhhgggg!!!" I shouted.

Elephant Man came by; the room fell silent.

I turned to look at Jon. He stopped. He was carrying a mop with a bristled brush in one hand and a dark-blue bucket of opaque water in the other. He looked at me as much as I at him.

I smiled and opened my mouth. "Heh heh heh. Well, uh... well, we're just a couple o' dudes messin' around is all."

His jaw hung low, and his eyes fell flat. "Huh."

Jon walked along, but Racecar Dude picked me up with all his baseball-player strength, and in the moment I was airborne felt I should've been on a rollercoaster, and hit my head *smack* on the locker behind me, thinking I might've blacked out until I opened my eyes when I landed on top of Encyclopedia Brown's thin, weak frame.

Bo walked away, shaking his head in disgrace.

I summoned the resolve to rise to my feet.

Kevin lay on the ground, weeping and whimpering, so I kicked him on the head. "You're such a f**king *loser,* Kevin."

Then I headed back to the Instruction Room.

CHAPTER 53:

MSHA Wrap-Up

These shenanigans persisted for three days, at the end of which came a commonsense lecture on mine etiquette and safety so brief yet so tiresome it resembled a thirty-second commercial.

Black Train held pens in one hand and pink rectangular slips of paper in the other.

He rolled up to me and bobbed his head. "Now. This is a part that you son. Will really like. Since you're the one. Who wanted. To take. A test."

"That's right, I most certainly did." I held my head high and shoulders low.

"I am going to hand out. Pens and papers to you all."

From his binder he pulled out a series of manuals smaller in area than an eight-point-five-by-eleven sheet of white paper.

"This is a test. To see if you can follow instructions. For filling out. Your certificate of training. To show that you have already completed. Your twenty four hour emmsha course."

After he passed out these materials, I examined the manual from the Department of Labor of the United States of America, entitled *A Guide to Miners' Rights and Responsibilities Under the Federal Mine Safety and Health Act of 1977.*

Featured on the cover, a blonde lady with safety frames

wore a green helmet, and smaller photographs of male miners surrounded her.

Dan directed our attention to the pink papers titled 'U.S. Department of Labor Mine Safety and Health Administration.'

"First of all. We're gonna do the easy part. That's the serial number. I can help you do this part. If you really need help. Write down. Zero zero zero zero. For your serial number. Because it just don't matter that much."

I quickly wrote four zeros in a row with perfect penmanship.

"See. The schools all teach you to count from one to ten. But they never tell you about *zero*. Zero is an important number. Because it just doesn't matter. Next. You are going to print. Not write in cursive but print. The full name of the person trained. That's you. First. And last. Now. Be careful. Because if you make just *one* spelling mistake. The government will consider it. A lie. And they'll sue you for falsely identifying yourself. For who you really are."

"And they would be *completely* – nevermind."

"So be careful. You *can* however. Use your middle initial. But as long as you put a period after it."

I signed *Richard M. Armadale*, then grabbed a spare piece of pink paper from the shelf, wrote four *zeros,* and printed my name like a laborer.

"*My* handwriting is really *rounded and feminine,* so it shows who *I am,*" said Savvy Socialite.

"Next. You need to *check*. The type of approved training you received. But don't put a check. You want to put an *ex*. As in. My three ex wives. Because otherwise you might *swoosh* it too big. And the government will mark the whole thing as invalid."

"Where do we put the 'X'?" I asked impatiently.

He faced me like a soldier and saluted. "You sir. Will put an ex next to New. Miner. And so will all the rest of you. Because you are. New miners of course."

I placed a double-swathed checkmark next to 'New Miner.'

"Next. You want to mark the type of operation and related industry. So check. I mean mark. Surface. And Coal. Next. Mark today's date. But if you don't know what today is. Well that's too bad for you. So just ask someone beside you."

Guided by my iPhone calendar, I wrote *11/21/2018*.

"Next. You will *skip*. Section Six. Because that is where I will sign. Next. You will write. The mine name. *Eye dee*. And location. So write. Murray *vee bee eff.* And don't ask me what that stands for cuz I don't know. And under that. You will write. Austin *kay why*. Because that is where we're at. Next. You will write where I'm from. And don't ask me where I'm from cuz I don't know. Just kidding. On the right side of Section Seven. Write. Kentucky State University. And under that. Write. Frankfurt *kay why*. And under that. Write. *Dee* Verny. But be sure to put a period next to the letter. *Dee*. Otherwise the government will think I only have one letter to my first name."

Alyssa groaned. She looked up and yelled, "Can we puh-*leeze* have another *smoke break soon?"*

Black Train pointed at her, hunting her down with his eyes. "I can smoke you down *real good* girl. If you want. But I work for the government. So I won't."

"Sheesh!"

"Next. You will write today's date. If you don't remember what today is. Just look at what you just wrote."

Dan surveyed the room.

"Next. I will need a volunteer. Anyone at all this time. To demonstrate for us. How. To write. Their signature."

"Ooh! I wanna go! I wanna go!"

She pulled down her shirt and hippity-hopped to the front of the room, where he drew up the projector screen by its string to reveal the whiteboard.

Savvy Socialite, with perfect posture and perfect prose, spread her feet apart and with great efficacy, signed in large loopy handwriting, *Alyssa "Lissie" Cale.*

"That's very beautiful. There. Girl."

She skipped back like a smiling puppy.

He faced us. "Now I need all of you. To sign your own name. On the right side. Of Section Eight. And if you don't know what your own name is."

Black Train stepped towards all participants, running over everyone at once.

"Well hell hell now. You're just about as stupid as they come. Ain't ya."

Dan made a frowny face on his already frowning face.

I snickered louder than everyone else.

"Actually. If you really don't know your own name. I can help you out with that. Just look back at Section One where you wrote down your own name. Read it. And write it in cursive. This is the one time when you *will*. Actually. Have to write. In cursive."

Terrence had fallen asleep.

I scribbled my name in quixotic, masculine handwriting.

"My signature is all curvy and feminine *and loopy!"*

I held up my pen and pointed at her. "I'll write all over your pathetic signature with my name attached to and intermingled with yours! How would you like that!"

Giggling and smiling she said, "Hmmm..." while raising a finger to her chin with eyes to the ceiling. "Not *yet.*"

"That was actually a really good comeback," I replied.

The entire class roared in guffaws. Dan chuckled over and over again like a whistleblower with red paint in the sky.

"You'll be the human female Jar Jar Binks."

"Hel-*lo!*" She spread her arms and faced me with her mouth half-open. "Aren't I *already?*"

Dan summoned us with a motion of his hand. *"Attention!* There is one last thing I need you all to do. I need you all. To wait. For me. To come around and sign *my name.* On your page in Section Six."

His scrawl, *DanielVerny,* looked rather cool. He added

'KSU' on the side and 'K483' underneath.

Terrence sprang awake, while Brianna and Sam threw a stuffed football across the heads of Halley and Adam, which Total Wreck watched like a cat about to pounce for its toy.

"I also request. That you fill out these review sheets. Where you will rank me. On various items. As your instructor."

The review sheets listed ten categories of proper teaching style, including Teacher Preparedness, Communication Ability, and Content Assimilation. The five rankings were Terrible, Poor, Average, Good, and Excellent.

Everyone else marked all categories as Excellent, but I spread my checkmarks all over the map, and I was the last to finish.

"Now that concludes your introduction. To. Mine Safety and Health Administration. I was glad to be your boss for these three days. You are all now miners. Wouldn't ya know it! Heh heh heh."

I gazed at the miner's guide in front of me, flipping through pages of dumbed-down legal text.

"Lissie is hands down class clown," I said aloud.

CHAPTER 54:

Cletus and Jenna

Black Train rested an elbow on the SDS stand. "You've got a bright future ahead of you kid. With this company."

"It's good to know you see potential in me," I said.

He fumbled in his pocket for the cigar. "You don't have to do too much. To succeed at a place like this."

"It's actually a pretty easy job to be honest with you. I'm looking forward to training others in the way I feel I should have been trained, just to let them see how straightforward it is and to help them enjoy the work they're doing. Sort of like writing a book in the *For Dummies* series."

"See. I just *love* the way you connect the dots there," he responded, chuckling. "Well good luck to ya. My life hasn't been easy you know. I wish I could somehow change myself. And fix who I am. But I've just been through so much shit in life. That it's impossible. I wish I could know if there's an afterlife or not. But I just can't. Maybe this is *all there is*. Sometimes even when I write stuff down. I forget to look at my notepad. Oh well. I guess some people are just meant to have a rough life. It always *cheers me up* when I can teach a fun filled room. With people like you."

"Well I'm glad to hear it."

Cletus approached Jenna more closely than I ever had; he was using cheat codes.

Chunky and Buzzcut held their own discussion off to the side.

I hoped to break up the conversation. "Hey hey hey now, how did you all like the instruction from Dan?"

"We thought he was really nice and cool but felt bad for him," said Jenna.

The punks nodded.

"Yeah, me too." I converged to make all five of us one group. "What are we discussing here?"

"Just work-related stuff," said Jenna. "And plays."

"Plays?"

"Uh huh," answered Cletus. "Shakespeare."

"Shakespeare," I repeated.

"Oh, Richard, this is my friend Bartholomew." She introduced him with an open gesture.

I shook his held-out hand. "Nice to meet you."

"I met Jenna at the play last night," he said. "I was going to give her my number, but then forgot. You seemed rather concerned about it."

"Just interested in what was going on, that's all. Maybe it was just the noise in that room, but you sound different out here."

Chunky extended his large palm. "We were just trying to act cool is all."

"So we could get along with the teacher there," added Buzzcut as I shook Chunky's hand.

"So you said your name is Bartholomew."

"I'm Bart, but I go by Bartholomew," said Cletus.

"And I'm Vick, but I go by Victor," said Buzzcut.

"And I'm Tony, but I go by Antonio," said Chunky.

I squinted and developed a piercing headache. "Right...."

Tender Toucher looked at me, then looked at the others.

"We saw *Hamlet* last night," said Bartholomew whom I still thought of as Cletus. "Do you know much about Shakespearean plays?"

"A bit," I replied, my mouth very dry.

"What's your favorite part of *Hamlet*?"

"The whole thing, really."

"My favorite part is when Hamlet says, 'O God, O God! How weary, stale, flat and unprofitable...Seem to me all the uses of this world!'"

"Yeah, that's one of my favorite parts too."

Tender Toucher stared at me, her lips tight.

"So...*why is that your favorite part?*"

"It's all our favorite parts," said Chunky-Antonio.

"Because it describes how we're keeping an eye on the energy companies," Buzzcut-Victor explained. "And how eventually, all their hard-earned profit will come to nil once they break up into smaller independent energy companies that don't share federal dollars. But we're in conflict right now because they want to stay big and powerful so they don't have to divest. The public might be able to help us out, once we convince them that large enterprises that abuse natural resources inevitably destroy their land, poison their water, and pollute their air. We're trying to prevent riots."

The warmth flowed back into my face. "Interesting."

Jenna's smile returned.

"So you're all from Kenn Mag then. How did you get started working there?"

"If we earned a score of one-hundred-ten on an IQ test we could hold any position in the company," said Bartholomew. "I got 125."

"And I got 129," said Antonio.

"And I got 133," said Victor.

"Oh. Where did you all go to school?"

"We all went to Kentucky State," Antonio answered. "We all have master's degrees in geology."

Victor nudged him. "Mine's in environmental science, remember?"

"Oh, that's right," he said, nodding.

"And I'm working on my Ph.D. in environmental engineering," added Bartholomew.

I sighed deeply. "Right...."

"So...Antonio! How did you say your relationship is coming along?" inquired Jenna.

"Well, my fiancée was a professor of linguistics at Harvard, and now she's seeking employment around here, and doing research on the development of Tolkien's mythological languages." He bore a sorrowful expression. "We both got divorced and sued by our former spouses for reasons that weren't our fault, so that gives us a similar background and something we can relate to."

"Hang on a second," I said, "I'll be right back."

I held back mild nausea and dizziness as I ran to Black Train sucking his cigar.

"Mister Verny."

"Yes. What is it."

"Well, uh, my new *friend* over there – Antonio, says he weighs more than you. But I don't know what he meant."

"Naw! Not more than me. I'll *pound* his fat ass to the *ground!*" he exclaimed with the proper accompanying motion.

"No, no sir. You definitely do not have to do that."

Antonio eyed me as the three men began to leave.

"I'm between two sixty. And two sixty five. There's *no way* he's bigger. Or tougher. Or stronger. Than me."

Scratching the back of my head I said, "Maybe that's not what he meant."

Dan took off with the binder under one arm and a small black suitcase in the opposite hand. "Take care now."

"Mister Verny," I called out quietly, running up to him. "Thanks for teaching us."

He nodded, smiled, and departed.

Jenna stood alone outside the Instruction Room.

Alyssa leaned into an open cabinet while holding the SDS book in her left arm. "This is gonna take a really...*long time.*"

Savvy Socialite was wearing black yoga pants and a short gray shirt; she had dressed for a summer stretch to prepare for an approaching winter. "I need to get started *right away,* because tonight I wanna go *shoppang.*"

"Good luck with finishing the SDS manual," I said, wondering if she would ever be any less of a miserable pathetic attention-seeking slut.

"Tha-*anks.*" She swiveled her hips in rhythm with the fluctuating cadence of her voice.

"Well hey there Richard. I filled up my notebook and was wondering if you know where any extras are?"

"You'll *never guess.*" With finger placed to my lips I said, "Ssshhhh!"

I opened both unlocked red metal doors.

"Oh...my...god!" Jenna put her arms in the air.

I handed her a fresh, brand new, yellow Rite-in-the-Rain notebook and immediately closed the doors.

Tender Toucher held it to her chest. "Thank you so much."

Shadow Guy stood in our way and stared us down, crossing his arms with key in hand while tapping his right foot, looking very, very displeased.

Part Six

CHAPTER 55:

Amy Follows Me Around

In the morning after Thanksgiving break, Sunshine Lady jiggled in front of me, holding her hands on her hips.

"I'm *coming with you* today."

"How come? What's the occasion?"

She shrugged and protruded her lower lip. *"Just* cuz."

I rose to my feet. "Okay. When do you want to leave?"

"Let's *take separate* cars. You can *leave whenever* you're ready."

Bringing a finger down to her level I said, "I must warn you though, it may take me longer than you expect to get to BisC-5R, as I tend to drive sixty miles per hour in the right lane, Grandma Style."

She waved her hand. "Ooh *ho-ho, I* doubt that. I bet *you'll get there* before me. It always *takes me really long* to get ready, and I'm *by far the slowest person* of anyone here."

"I'll take your word for it." I grabbed a shoulder strap of my CamelBak. "I'll be leaving as soon as I get ready."

"Okay, but *don't do anything before* I meet up with you."

Waiting by the wooden shed, nearly forty-five minutes had passed before a Murray & Affiliates car pulled up behind me. I had turned the heat halfway between neutral and full blast, and even started listening to NPR.

Sunshine Lady had dressed herself in a bright purple winter coat, blue mittens, black snowpants, and pink furry earmuffs with a smooth brown scarf. *"I'm* reeeady! You *lead the* way."

I locked the door of my truck, which flashed as we headed behind the shed, where I hopped the fence while she went through the gate.

"Wait, is *this the place* where you wrote that *there was a donkey* somewhere?"

"Yes. I specified that it was a territorial donkey. Be on guard."

We strode ahead; she slipped and nearly fell.

"I don't *see him* anywhere." Amy stopped and held her fingers to her forehead like a visor, turning her head from side to side. "Where *is the li'l* fella?"

I moved onward. "It's colder out than it was before. Maybe he's hiding somewhere, or hibernating."

"Yeah, he must be *in his special li'l shed* back there."

The moisture of her breath filled the air as she caught up to me.

"Buurrrr." She held her torso. "It's *cold outside* today. I wish *I was in my* office, drinking *a hot cup* of tea."

I strode forward. "Don't we all. Yet you chose to follow me."

"How come *you parked down* here and *not at the other* end?"

"There is no convenient parking spot near the mouth, whereas here there is."

She tapped her hair. "Ah, *good* thinking. So you're *just doing it* backwards?"

"Exactly."

We approached the end of a narrow passage of bare trees.

I hiked up the slope through the woods, grabbing tree trunks and tree branches, pressing my boots to the slippery ground.

Scaling my way downwards, I descended to the end of

the stream. "Alright, I'm at the STP, and I'm recording it as 'Flowing.'"

"Okay, *be* careful!"

I trekked along the thin bed.

Her mittens lay at her feet, and she had started braiding her sleek hair while humming sweetly in a major key.

The donkey stampeded down the hill.

"Aahhh!"

"Time to go on."

I stepped nimbly over the barbed-wire fence.

The fence got the better of her snowpants and she tumbled, lying face up and giggling.

The donkey trotted away.

I crossed my arms. "Need a hand up?"

Her body rose as she inhaled. *"Sure."*

The stream descended from a ten-foot waterfall and continued into a ravine.

I grabbed each tree trunk and proceeded athletically down the hill, sometimes sliding like a snowboarder, and slowed myself as my momentum decreased with my muck boots pitter-pattering in the stream.

"Whoa, *hold up* there." Sunshine Lady waved her hand; her mitten was a useful blue indicator, but only because a cloud hovered in the background.

She scaled the downhill slope taking the longest path.

"Wait up," she called.

With her muck boots against the base of a tree, she clutched the trunk. "Ugh."

Amy was directly in my line of sight, so I stepped aside.

She arrived at my standing spot while I wrote in my notebook.

"Are you *already writing down* the flow?"

"No. I'm creating an SCM table right now because I forgot to when we began." I put away my pen and notebook. "In any case, the HSW is up ahead – I mean, *downstream* and ahead of our path."

I hurried ahead and stepped nimbly here and there on a series of fallen branches, some thick and some thin, crossing over them like it was no big deal, my feet moving at the rate of those of an amateur athlete training with stepping aerobics.

Sunshine Lady tumbled over them and fell to the ground. She barely made it through the underside of the branches, and when she emerged, she was soaking wet.

I offered a hand which she accepted.

"Sorry *about* that. I'm *just really* slow. I'm *probably the slowest* and the *laziest person* here."

"You've proven that quite well. Anyway, we're at the HSW now. I'll take the flow."

Amy shook her head. "The *stake is actually* up there."

She couldn't point properly because she was wearing mittens instead of gloves, but I still saw it.

I lined up the meterstick with the stake. "I'll drop a one-point-one here."

"Richard!" exclaimed Subtle Serpent. "You can't just *eyeball* a stream and guess the width without measuring it."

"Of course not. I was just kidding, you knew that."

The 1.3-meter cross-section required an ungodly number of measurements. This time, I added in the second decimal place, measuring aloud, and brushed aside the leaves.

"Make sure the *leaves* are out of the way."

"I just did."

"Make sure *all* the leaves are out of the way."

I grabbed the leaves up to the fallen branches and threw them in piles on one side of the stream.

Then I resumed my activity.

"You need to make *sure* all the leaves are out of the way before beginning to take your flow."

A single leaf floated out of bounds; I grabbed it, crumpled it, put it in my pocket, and performed the recordings with near-perfect efficiency.

"Let me *see* your work."

I handed my phone to her, unconcerned that my thumb had slipped twice and tapped a '2' instead of a '1' both times.

"Good."

Subtle Serpent inspected my hands. "Are those *gloves* waterproof?"

The water into which I had submerged my hands soaked the fabric and dampened my skin. "Yeah, I'm pretty sure they are."

Sunshine Lady returned my phone. "So *just as helpful* feedback, make *sure the leaves* are out of the *way before taking* the flow, and that you *measure the width* before deciding *what it* is."

"Of course. I wouldn't have done it any differently."

"Okay then."

She stepped away and held her shoulders back.

"That's *all for* today. I'm gonna *go check on Jenna* and Brianna now. They're *working together* on the *other side of* the hill."

"I see what you're doing. You're going around helping people with their stream monitoring techniques today. Thanks for your help. I'm a better technician for it."

Amy waved goodbye and turned around. "Have a *wonderful rest of* your day, sweetie!"

I sped through the rest of the schedule, dropping one-point-ones and ignoring all the leaves.

My picture hung on her wall with Kim Kardashian showing.

Jenna rose from her cubicle. "Well hey there Richard, it's good to see you. How have you been? Isaac told me you were concerned about Henley. He did find another job and abandoned his plan for world domination – which included assassinating Amy – just because he didn't want to get arrested."

"That's good to know."

"How did your time with Amy go?"

"Reasonably okay," I said. "She followed me around today, but she wouldn't tell me why. Did she follow you?"

"You mean in the office?"

"No, out in the field."

"I was all on my own today. She came back just before noon."

"Were you anywhere near Bison Creek?"

Jenna brought her finger to her mouth and looked upwards. "Well no, not even close. I was in Harvon, not Eblen."

"And Brianna wasn't with you?"

She looked at me like I was a fantasy creature. "Brianna told me she was here the whole time."

"Why do you think Amy followed me around today?"

Tender Toucher rubbed my head. "She was probably just trying to help you out, that's all."

"It all seems very strange to me, but you're probably right," I agreed snickering.

"So don't worry about it, everything is okay and everything will be okay."

I hunched at my desk.

CHAPTER 56:

Racecar Dude's Turnabout

Later that day, Bo arrived at my cubicle. His face was red, and his valley-shaped eyebrows had become mountains. He held his head down, but glanced at others when they were looking away from him. The baseball bat was in his hands as he sauntered towards me as though he were his own benevolent twin.

I gazed at the far wall, then turned to face him.

He knelt before me displaying the baseball bat in his hands with arms outstretched. "I want you to have this."

I stared at him. "What are you here for?"

"I have a lot of respect for you, man. After what happened. I can't do this anymore...it's tearing me *apa-a-a-rrrrrt.*"

Bo bowed his head as he held the bat further towards me; he took one hand off the bat to wipe a tear from his eye, then put it back on the handle-bottom. He looked up at me.

My voice was sterner than his; I now held the Upper Hand. "Why did you come to me today...right now...at this time?"

"I want you to take this...from me. I can't live like this anymore.... I'm such a terrible person...and I didn't even realize it."

Taking a deep breath, I hid it under my desk.

Racecar Dude sniffled and sobbed. "The way you stood up to me back there...the other day...*uahh hahhha-*

uahhhahhahaaa...just made me realize...that I'm not who I should be. I'm not the man I...*aahahhuuaahhhhh*...I-I I ever really wanted to be."

"So what's been going on?"

With my left hand I grabbed the bat, then took it off.

He sniffled. "The water problems...from what Conrad is doing, it's, it's, it's *so, so so...terrribblle*. They're soaking up the streams...they're killing all these innocent people...all the fracking...there's no water in my parents' house. And it's all *myy faaauult*."

"How is it your fault?"

"B-b-because they wanted me to become a professional baseball player."

Bo swallowed, inhaled, and exhaled.

"They wanted me...to become rich...so I could help give them a better life. And I almost made it. But I didn't. And every time I go out and drive I just...I just, I just feel like I always need to go just a little bit faster all the time, just...just to get to the next base, and somehow make it, make it big. Earn the big bucks. My parents are stuck downhill near a valley with no water, and their relationship has never been the same."

He took a deep breath and sat down, crossed his legs pretzel-fashion and leaned against the backside of Evan's cubicle.

Boiler Brain looked at him, then stared at his computer screen.

"I wanted to make it big so I could support them. Help them have the life they dreamed. All the fresh water they could want. *High up on a hill somewhere*.... But I let them down, and they're disappointed in me. They won't ever show it. But they are, it's so easy to tell. I bet your parents are proud of you for all you've done, and only because it's obvious that someone like you would never become a professional athlete."

I held my hands apart. "Look, this is obviously about you right now. And as it concerns me, what is it that you want me to do for you?"

"Just to forgive me, maannn...."

"Okay fine, I forgive you. But don't go back to the way you were – you know what I mean – or I might just unforgive you."

"I'm *never* going back to the way I was." He widened his eyes as he shook his head. "Mike Matthews, man. I *really* f**kin'-f**kin'-f**kin' *HATE* that guy."

Bo sighed; his face was unflushing itself, and the tears therein were drying away.

"Conrad Power *has* to be brought down at all costs," he said adamantly. "But it's really Mike who's the problem. He's driving the whole operation. He just keeps letting 'em go, getting away with anything at any cost, you know. Even encouraging them to do what they're doing. He's so destructive, and he just doesn't care. He even loves it. We gotta get rid of him, someway, somehow, but he's just too clever and sneaky and – and shifty and all, you know what I mean? Man, justice is what is justice, man."

I nodded slowly. "So again, what should I – or you – *do* about it?"

"Just stay in the game man, just stay in the game, it's all we really can do."

He shrugged and, still frowning, sat upright and cleared away the remaining tears, and his face softened to a pale pink.

"Does not making the major leagues really justify your criminalistic behavior? You could easily end up in jail you know."

Bo's voice stopped at a firm key. "Okay, no. Just by asking that, I can tell you have no idea what it's like to come so close and then fail at something."

"Fine, I admit it. I have no idea. But how come you came to me?"

Leaning in, he opened his face and inclined his head. "Cuz...you're the only one I can trust, why else? That's why I'm saying sorry to *you*. I've seen the shit you've been through and the way you handle it."

"What about the handicapped kid? What about the man you crashed into? What about your *outrageous* driving habits? What about Thomas from Waterstone? What about – what about *Kevin?*"

Racecar Dude held up a hand. "Dude. Let's just keep this between me and you, alright?"

I stuck out my lower lip. "Sure, that's alright. So what do you want me to do with the baseball bat?"

"Just take it. And keep it away from me."

"Won't someone want to know what I'm doing with it?"

He smirked and raised an eyebrow. "Ya really believe anyone is gonna think someone like you will act out?"

I shook my head. "I'll take it then. And I'll stow it away for good. Forever. And even if you asked, I wouldn't give it back.

"Good. So keep it. Do the right thing...and not the wrong thing...but don't do the stupid thing...either. Or else."

I leaned in and opened my arms. "Or else what?"

Bo walked to the kitchen where he grabbed a black leather jacket and opened the back door.

CHAPTER 57:

Conrad Power

With the coming of winter, I dressed in Under Armour both top and bottom, wool socks, and winter coat, which I wore overtop of my ripped green jacket. To my head I strapped a warm hat made of real rabbit fur and put on large insulated gloves overtop thinner gloves for phone use.

My assigned region around Sharmin Creek had grown more extensive.

Driving along the country roads, I observed the streams periodically.

I drove past a golf course through which the Sharmin main stem flowed, and onto a paved golf-cart pathway just wide enough for my truck, noticed water at the lower buffer, and continued throughout the park like I was on early-December lookout duty, until I wound my way around and came through the parking lot of One Pine Country Club and back onto the road, traveling on Route 17 in the opposite direction from which I had come.

A steep embankment rose on my left, while the only safe-looking area to park was directly in front of a light-green single-floor rectangular house; I left two wheels on their land.

A peasant came out; he appeared to be about fifty years old, with graying dark-brown hair. The thin man had a long neck and wore a thin jacket, no gloves and no hat, and held his arms around his chest as he stepped toward me.

"Esscuse me. Yer on mah...*properdy.*"

"Sorry, I'll move it."

He returned inside his home.

I tried to drive deftly in reverse, but the hill was slippery, and the uneven snowy ground where the woods began was about half a foot lower than the road. The left wheels buckled, and I held the brake just as I was about to crash into the trees behind me. I activated the parking brake and got out at once.

The truck was no longer on the road, but at least that rube could no longer see it. Embarking to the HSW, I found orange discoloration by the streambanks before I arrived at the cross-section.

This was my first time on SharC-66R-1L, so I checked the record on CartoPac to see if it had ever been reported. Orange staining had not been recognized on the point at which I stood, but over a period of several months it had been recorded in different locations along the stream progressively.

I looked back at the orange mistake, observing the foreign specimen. One edge flopped in the stream current, and it seemed to have a mind of its own.

With one more recording of 'Orange Staining,' I contributed to its trail on the map.

The 2.6-meter HSW to which I descended yielded a flow rate of 43 GPM.

The staining distracted me as I hiked to my displaced truck.

It sank backwards when I floored the gas pedal. I changed the setting from H2 to H4 and pounded the pedal, sending flames of mud onto my windows and windshield. I drenched the windshield with fluid while letting the mud on the windows coalesce. Once again, I pressed my foot down; the vehicle roared as it lurched forward about a foot, but then slid back. I switched to the L4 setting, and tried to get out, but the truck vibrated as it sank deeper.

Mud covered the front tires about halfway up, and the rear tires about three-quarters of the way. Underneath that thin layer of snow was a wide mud pit unfathomably deep. Through the InReach I sent: TRAPPED IN MUD.

A large silver truck carrying a spare tire attached to a rope came around the bend that marked the summit of the hill. The side of the vehicle read: 'Conrad Power, Inc.'

Two men stepped out; both appeared to be in their mid-forties. As they walked toward me, I observed that the man on the right was taller by a few inches than the one on the left. The one to my right had dark brown hair, while the one to my left had either graying blonde or light brown hair. They came up to me, smiling. The taller one wore a gray Conrad Power sweatshirt, while the shorter one had on a blue Tintech Plumbing hoodie.

"Looks like you had a little accident here," said the gray-sweatshirt man.

"I didn't park well and got stuck in the mud."

"We can tow you out," said the other.

"That would be great. You both must be from Conrad Power, of course."

"Well, not really, I'm just a temp for hire there," said the one with the company apparel.

I turned to his companion. "And I see you might be?"

"No, I just work for a plumbing company and I'm going along for the ride with him."

"Oh. Okay, I'll get back in my truck then and let you tow me out. Thanks for coming along."

With the ignition turned on, I rode my truck gradually ascending out of the mud pit.

I closed my eyes and imagined our companies as two arrows on a physics-based force vector diagram, pointing in opposite directions along the same line of repose. The encounter reminded me of how the number six looks like the number nine upside-down, they the nine and I the six. I bared my knuckles together.

Finally, my truck was back on the road safely, but their vehicle remained facing me. They were both standing in front of their truck, and I in front of mine.

"Thanks for getting me out of there. It was much easier this way than having my own people come get me."

"Sure," said the taller one.

"No problem," said the other.

I took a breath and lowered my shoulders. "You know...apparently we're supposed to be at odds with each other," I said lightheartedly, punching the air boxing-style. "But I'm glad we can help each other out as individuals in these small ways." I held my arms out to the sides. "So once again, thank you."

A thundercloud hovered over me, while music in a minor key played in my head. A sour moldy taste wetted their palettes; before they even looked at one another, both bore the same clenched grimace. Neither sound nor time existed as we stared at each other in those silent everlasting moments....

I gazed at the dirt road, pondering whatever they could be thinking. The ball was in their court.

The man on the left started to chuckle lightly and slowly, and then at a faster rate, closing his eyes. The other one stepped towards me, waving aside the discomfort. "Don't worry," he said, "we won't tell Kevin."

"Oh yeah, I know Kevin. He's a good guy."

I winked and returned to my truck, at which point they drove onto a road I hadn't seen until I approached the summit.

There was a road sign: 'Conrad Power Drive.' A sign for a Conrad equipment building stood right next to it. I redirected my truck using their large parking lot which beheld a vast domed structure.

From the hilltop, I saw all the land of my daily trek, the formerly green but now brown landscape, pastures with interlocking streams, all the way across the valley. Dense clouds hung high above, but patches of blue remained. The whole terrain was a map, just like how real life is a video game.

When I approached the precipice, with my right turn signal on, I noticed, scrawled in faded magic marker on a yellow diamond-shaped DEER-XING sign, the phrase: 'Stop Hillary.'

I kept the parking brake activated. My InReach buzzed as I held the footbrake.

CHAPTER 58:

At Odds with Each Other

Chase and Alyssa opened the front doors of a yellow buggy. "Wo-ho what happened there?" asked Chase. "Did you go through a swamp?"

"Almost. Some Conrad Power people saved me from myself."

"Well, we're glad you're *okay,*" said Alyssa.

I found Encyclopedia Brown outside by the locker room door, sitting with his large goofy shoes flat against the pavement and his back against the wall. He slumped his head and scratched his scalp with the long fingernail of his long pointer finger.

"Nice to see you're getting some fresh air, Kevin."

He stepped in front of the door, holding up his finger, and at that moment I noticed that the bend in the upper knuckle made his finger replicate his entire body on a smaller scale. "Did you say – did you say to Conrad Power that we are at odds with each other?"

"Yeah, why?"

I brushed by him and opened the door.

When I turned around to close it, he was back in his former position.

Adam was in the locker room. "So Jocelyn, can you make sure the data on my spreadsheets matches that on my...hey

Richard, we were worried about you. We heard you got your truck stuck in the mud."

"It was a humbling experience."

Fly Fisher patted me on the back. "Don't worry about it man. It happens to pretty much everyone at some point."

I held my breath. "Did you just call her 'Jocelyn'?"

"That's me," she said off-key, waving weakly.

"Jocelyn...Reical?"

"That's my name, don't wear it out," she quipped insipidly.

I was thoroughly disappointed in Lazy Loafer's appearance. She was too short to issue any authoritative commands in person, and there was barely enough space between the edge of her short frizzy dull-yellow hair and puke-green fuzzy sweatshirt to avoid sparking a fire on the back of her stumpy reddened neck. There was a fifteen-degree hunch between her upper body and the vertical axis, and her torso was *manifestly* square.

She couldn't keep her shoulders stationary when she moved, and although she walked slowly, she swiveled her elbows back and forth as she took one step at a time like she was wearing metal boots, hustling and bustling. Her legs grew drastically thinner down from her hips, such that her feet were smaller than her shoulders.

Jocelyn may have had a beautiful heart, and certainly had an attractive first name, but her face was a bowl of frozen chicken-noodle soup, and she was just flat-out ugly, a Two.

"Ah, so you're the mysterious lady inside the control room," I commented poignantly. "Wonderful to finally meet you."

"Haha, that's me," she said in the same pitch as she straggled to the laboratory. "Usually I just work in my office, sometimes at home."

I strode up the small ramp into the main hallway and held on to my JHA as I went around to my desk the long way, where I wrote brief euphemistic comments about the submerging vehicle.

"Richard, may *I speak with you* for a moment?"

Slowly but surely, I walked over to her office.

Amy was smiling.

"Hi *there,* sweetie. I just *wanted to make sure* you were okay *after getting stuck* in the mud."

"I'm okay. All in one piece, as you can see."

"Well *thaat's* good. Just so *that doesn't happen* next time, always *make sure you have two tires* firmly on the *road so that when* you stop..." She pressed her palms on the desk "... oh, you *probably already know* about traction."

"From now on, that's how I will always park."

"When *you slid into the mud* pit, were *you on anyone's* property?"

"I was *not* on anyone's front or back yard."

"Good," she said softly, "otherwise *we might have to pay* for property damage."

"So I'm okay, you're okay, and everyone's okay. I'll get back to work then."

I turned to walk out at once.

"But *one more* thing," she said. "The *president and the vice president* of Conrad Power said that *you told them in person* that we *were at odds with* each other. Jim Conrad *thought that was a* very strange comment."

Subtle Serpent wrinkled her brow and lightly smashed her small fist on the desk. "Richard, you *must* remember professionalism!"

"But-but I *was* being professional," I maintained as my skin crawled off my bones.

"We're not at *odds* with each other."

"We're not?"

"No! They *pay* us." She eyed me ominously.

"They pay us," I murmured. "Why don't we just consolidate?"

"That's *not* how this works," she said with fiery ice-bombs shooting from her eyes.

"Do they really pay us?"

"Of course," she said, opening her palms. "How did you *think* we got our money?"

I shrugged. "I dunno. Some government agency?"

Subtle Serpent stared at me with sealed lips.

"The Department of Environmental Protection, maybe? Yeah, I bet they pay us too."

She scoffed and rolled her eyes. "Goddammit, Richard! *Get* your act together."

"Is what I said really so much worse than *you people* who take the Lord's name in vain and destroy his creation?" I yelled with my trembling fist held high.

Sunshine Lady straightened up, swallowed, and folded her hands on the desk. "Let's just *forget this whole thing* ever happened. Just *keep up the* good work. You're *doing a good job* with everything."

The music wasn't finished. "And *you're* doing a good job being an environmental *pseudoscientist,*" I sneered.

Buff Face was working on his computer at a relaxed pace.

"Hey Brian, there's something I need to understand."

He took his hand off the mouse and swiveled around to face me. "Sure."

"How would you describe our relationship with Conrad Power?"

"What do you mean? I wouldn't really know, since I'm not active in the higher-up stuff."

I hesitated. "Let me phrase it this way: What *is* our relationship *to* Conrad Power?"

"Well...they're our client." He held his hands to the sides. "But you knew that, right?"

My mouth was parched, so I headed for the kitchen, where Jenna refilled a water bottle at the sink. She was wearing corduroys.

"Hi Jenna."

She spilled her water in the sink.

"Well hey there Richard, how has your day been?"

"It was...*okay*. Well, actually now that you mention it there was a funny little thing that happened between me and some people from Conrad Power."

Jenna smiled and nodded. "Uh huh...."

"I just sort of said, in an offhand way, that we were at odds with each other, and now everyone here seems to be giving me a hard time about it." I smiled.

Tender Toucher's eyes sank into her face, and her mouth was ajar. "You said *what* to them?"

"But you know how it goes. Think about it this way: *They* destroy the environment, *we* restore the environment."

I held my fingers to her face.

She turned around and tilted her head upward while crossing her arms. "Jeez Richard, grow up! The DEP is the bad guy."

"The *DEP* is the bad guy...."

With elbows on the desk, I rested my chin in my palms.

CHAPTER 59:

Limited Oversight

With December well underway, year's end came as gradually and still yet as charmingly as the fallen snowflakes that floated down from the heavens and watered the earth never to remember their former ways in the sky.

I returned again to my former route that wove through the many tributaries of Sharmin Creek. All the trees were bare, their leaves long gone. It was a gray day, and the wonder and awe I beheld at first gradually yet greatly diminished from the exquisite summer environment in which I first began. The sense of exploration begotten by vast swaths of leaves, plants, and shrubbery had died under the weight of the fallen season. The birds no longer sang me songs, and the woodland creatures no longer greeted me.

I examined the dying streams carefully. Most of them looked absolutely terrible; some were brown, some were gray, and some were completely dry. Nothing had been remediated since I last monitored this area, and if rivers themselves had emotions, then these brooks would be home sick with a case of the winter blues. Clearly, I had not done an adequate job the first time around, and although I put forth a reasonable effort, all of my reporting seemed to vanish away into the snow under my boots, melting as the very things I had tried to prevent became one with the streams, as though I had not even been here in the first place or had not done my job well enough.

At least now came a fun part, as I headed back from the intersection of two streams similar in width and depth near the stone staircase.

I prepared to leap across the steep bank as I had several months ago and shout 'Yahoo!' like Super Mario as I hurdled myself from one side to the other, with everything below unmistakably lava.

Only when I did start running, I failed to achieve enough traction with the snowy ground, and gained too little momentum, so that when I propelled myself from the ledge, my boot slipped, and while airborne I said not 'yahoo' but a shortened form of the word 'firetruck,' and when I landed seven to eight feet in the lava, my right leg buckled and bent under the rest of my body, and I cried out using a sophisticated variant of the word 'darnit.'

I hobbled back to the stream mouth and made my way across the broad snowy field to a low-lying area of an elongated valley.

Brushing off the snow on the drooping trees, I discovered a long bench on which to rest my leg, and being ahead of schedule today, I had the spare time to benefit from this leisure.

I hadn't recognized my proximity to New Scales Road until I noticed a patch of gray underneath the white blanket that covered the whole dell, save brown and dark-green footprints on the farmer's land.

In a cottage on the same side of the road, Old Man came hurrying, scrambling in my direction. I climbed off the bench.

He huffed and puffed trying to maintain all the stamina his age would allow. "Hello there. I've seen you running across the streets and the streams and the fields and the farms, and I have come over to you today because I do have something, pretty important to me, that I need to say to you. The mine – it seems to be shifting here and there, and across and around the township, and now it has come very near here. You see the culvert barely holding up the bridge? As you can see, it's still broken, still smashed, still bent, still...not quite fixed, you see."

I nodded along with his concerns.

"They, the mining company, need to put a new one underneath it, to keep the river flowing and to flush out all this pooling. And now the bridge itself there, you see, even the bedrock that supports it is crumbling; I fear that when I drive to meet my nephew for Bible study, or if he comes here, that soon one of us may not make it across very well."

"I do see what you mean. That would be bad news for all of us."

"And so I'm glad you do see, because my wife is now very ill, and while we've tried to grow a good number of things, some of which our doctor would not, or could not prescribe to help her, I'm beginning to realize something that I'm not happy with at all. But that is no matter for right now, since all of our crops have been ruined by the pooling, which occurred of course, as you know, before the cold came. And, well, our farm animals, though they're far from the streams and warm inside their barns this time of year, as you can well imagine, still they – well, they've seen better days and the limited water that we do still have, which they drink..."

His words trailed off indiscernibly.

"...brings me to my main concern, but first I want to show you a photo I took with my old camera early in the fall, and which I have spent too much money to get developed in color."

He unzipped from his coat pocket a gleaming photograph of a wetland taken at the turn of the season when all things green turn ever slightly brown, with a green shape well-centered.

I held it and examined it.

"I'm sure you're an intelligent young man who knows what animal this is."

"It's a frog, an amphibian. At least it looks like a frog. But where is...and why is..."

"Look closely to see if you can spot anything wrong with it."

"You mean with the quality of the photo itself or the actual picture?"

"The animal."

The frog appeared just like any I had ever seen; a few I had observed in person, but most in my memory were from photographs just like this one, reasonably well-taken for someone whom I had little reason to believe was a professional photographer.

Its legs were in place, as were its gills. Many little black dots marked its leathery skin. Its eye looked healthy and clear, and so did its other eye, and so did its other eye.

"Oh my goodness!" I forced it back at him.

"So now you do see."

"Why...why are there three of them?"

He stepped closer. "There there, chap. Maybe you've read the book – or at least heard this poem: 'All things bright and beautiful, All creatures great and small, All things wise and wonderful, The Lord God made them all.'"

"I have heard that poem before. Many times, in fact. Cecil Frances Alexander."

"Well it sure is unusual to find someone your age these days who has any familiarity with poetry. Do you think you could show this to your company?"

"I'm not sure Murray and Affiliates typically deals with things like this. To report something, it should be connected to or at least directly associated with a stream, something I could see in real time, not a photograph, which in this case might actually be too unbelievable for them to believe."

Old Man sighed, and his shoulders fell. "As it directly concerns me then, something has been going on with my well water. It disappeared for a while and then returned, though now I fear it may be contaminated or that something has poisoned it, and I need your help because I'm afraid to drink it. Do you think this is caused by the mine?"

"It's definitely the mine."

"I know you people offer remediation services; could you possibly fix up my land?"

"My job is just to collect data, and I haven't been trained in remediation, otherwise I would get to your land immediately."

"So then can you just tell them about my well?"

"Where is it?"

"Right there." He pointed to a modest yet conspicuous structure several yards away from his house.

"I'll mention it to Amy Lane – she's my project manager. Meanwhile, I'll collect data in such a way that this issue is brought to their attention. There are these things called AOIs, Areas Of Interest, that we report to describe stream issues. Most of them are pre-written, but you can also add your own, and you can write comments as well."

"Oh, now I understand full well what's going on with your job! In that case, you ought to give them my name and number too."

"I'll write them on my JHA – I mean, my Job Hazard Analysis, along with the details of your situation. You might have told me last time we met – what did you say your name is?"

"Elias McCullough."

"In the meantime, Elias, you can call the number on the side of my truck; it's over there on the other side of your house. Let them hear your voice loud and clear."

I gestured to the intersection of New Scales Road and Venial Road, where my truck was stationed on the gravel lot; it had accumulated a thin layer of snow on the windshield and on the hood, but the phone number was still visible.

"Thanks for your help. You best be getting started on that before it's too late. I didn't mean to hold you up."

"It's alright, I'll get back to work then."

As he hurried back inside, I headed for the gate to the farmland.

"But one more thing!" I exclaimed when he was at the doorstep. "I really hope your situation improves."

Elias nodded, hand on the doorknob. "One time, our streams were our source of livelihood. The coal miners' un-waged battle against us, however, caused these streams to wither away, and my wife's health was sacrificed in order to take their place. Grieving over her malady, I disappeared for a long time into my home. I now tell you this, Richard: You must wake me, for if I too should sleep, the environment will be destroyed. I believe you are the chosen one in this regard. You must head to the fields before we both fly up to heaven. And I do hope that your actions will mark the regeneration of our groundwater."

"I'm sorry for not taking better care of things earlier."

"Don't worry about that, just do your best right now. I will pray for a solution as I always have, and I am sure it will come one way or another."

My Side Quest had come.

CHAPTER 60:

Artfully Dilapidated

My grandfather used to tease me whenever we dined at a restaurant. When I ordered a side of french-fries and squirted out a giant mound of ketchup from the upside-down Heinz bottle, he would ask me if I would like fries with that ketchup. The joke never failed to elicit a hearty round of chuckles from me, and the punchline always helped to keep matters in perspective, and to see issues from different viewpoints.

Standing right next to the well, I peered in before reporting the AOI, because I was not sure if the oily shimmering darkness was contaminated water *or* the very essence of contamination treated by a wet blanket.

Resisting the impish desire to present my superiors with a philosophical quandary, I reported the problem as 'Contaminated Well Water.'

Before entering through the gate, I stood on several points of the bridge and reported three AOIs: 'Smashed Culvert,' 'Crumbling Bedrock,' and 'Collapsing Bridge.'

I stepped back for a panoramic view of this merciless product of child's play and flashed another picture of their haphazard drawbridge.

Then I hitched the rubber strap onto the sparking gate, and proceeded onward. My leg wobbled, but I could still walk, and there was little pain after having soothed it, but the pain that did exist helped to keep me moving alongside the streams at a steady rate.

Most of the well-tilled farmland had been plundered from its former beauty, artfully dilapidated by hydraulic fracture. Nothing Leonardo da Vinci ever invented could compete with the destructive power of an underground mine, which rendered futile any agricultural production and caused the entire landscape to look like the background of the *Mona Lisa* painting.

It was time for a well-phrased comment: 'Large-Scale Degradation.'

Both the Sharmin main stem and SharC-66R were clear and well-flowing. The lucky surprises occurred along the secondary tributaries; although SharC-66R-1R flowed peacefully into the distance, 2R, 3R, and 3.2R all held the very sights that make eyes sore.

Upon reaching the upper buffer of 1R, I headed for 2R.

I traced a path strictly alongside the stream and spotted a small patch of orange staining covering a withered streambed like fresh earwax on a flimsy tissue. I reported it as 'Orange Staining.'

Heading over to 3R, I hopped a fence.

Water rested stilly in a massive brown puddle that defied all sense of boundaries; the mess resembled that of a clogged toilet, and sure smelled like one too.

The flow rate was 0.777, so I rounded it to 1 GPM. I marked it as 'Diffuse Flow' and described it as 'Turbid.' The comment to describe this disaster came as an epiphany: 'Brown Swampy Water With Foul Scent.'

Further upstream, the surprise that awaited me was a profuse splash of shiny orange staining, indicating that angels painting the sunset had spilled their art supplies. The aberration begged for remediation via the antidote of accurate description. I observed, in addition to the orange discoloration, areas festooned with both translucent and rainbow-colored diffraction complementing the giant cesspool.

"Effing gross," I muttered.

I labeled the AOI as 'Orange Staining With Sheen.'

Heading onwards to 3.2R, I gazed at the plants covering the streambed, still surviving but now resembling mere weeds. I rushed over to the streambanks, first brushing them aside; then I forcefully tore them out of the ground, and I almost barfed on my notebook.

The broad base was only twice that of the height, which was nearly that of the dreadful, dying weeds themselves. The plastic orange cone in my truck had been manufactured, but I had no idea they could occur as a natural process, otherwise I would have patented one myself and sold it on eBay. The redness climbed the slope of the pile like the blending of colors on a topographic map. It was as disgusting to a janitor as it was promising to a detective, and architectural beauty composed its sublime horror.

'Possible Acid Mine Drainage,' I typed.

I snapped a picture for good measure.

Plastic orange cones were positioned around the bridge.

I started to cross the stream the way I arrived, but then reversed. Upon shifting into park, I wrote the issue on my JHA.

The long way back would have to suffice, so I turned on the radio to soothing music:

"Who...can...say...where the *road* goes...where the *daay* flows...*only – time*.... And who...can...say...if your *love* grows... as your *heaart* chose...*only – time*."

CHAPTER 61:

Right to the Point

Amy folded her hands on the clear desk. "So, *how-did-it* go?"

"It went well for me. But not for somebody else."

"Well...what *did you write* on your JHA?"

"First of all, something that could have affected me was an unsafe area of the road that looked like it was crumbling; cones were around it, but they were not blocking the way, so I started to go across, but then realized that it actually might have been unsafe."

"So, sort *of like the* road was *chopped off* on one side?" she said, making a vertical karate motion.

"Yeah, sort of like that."

"Well *thaat's* good that you *were smart enough to* turn around."

"The other thing is that there is a landowner who says his water is contaminated or poisoned, and that his wife is sick."

Sunshine Lady furrowed her brow. "Lemme *see your* JHA."

She glared at my crumpled paper.

Subtle Serpent looked to the corner of the ceiling, then rested the paper on her desk. Her tilted head resembled a ship capsizing. "Did *he* say it was contaminated or did *you?*"

"He did."

Her eyes grew more intense as she bowed her head towards me. "And are you *sure* it's contaminated?"

"I'm sure he knows his own well better than anyone else. I even recorded it as an AOI."

"You did *what?*"

"Think about it this way: The water that flows underground from the stream and into his well is more or less part of the stream itself, if not something very close to it that would be worth taking note of."

Sunshine Lady tapped a pen to her lips, foot floundering with legs crossed. "I see *what you're* saying," she said, dragging every word.

"But it makes sense if you think about it that way, doesn't it?"

Amy smiled and placed her pen on the desk, her feet now flat on the floor. "Well *good for you for* helping him out, you *little spunky* monkey."

"You can call me the detective dog," I said as I turned away from her.

Her out-of-tune giggles persisted until I returned to my desk.

I examined the schedule for next week. No longer was I to be monitoring Sharmin Creek, as I had been transferred to part of a stream called JakCr-85. The schedule also showed the phrase 'Terrence to show Richard sampling' under next Tuesday's column. Evan and I shared the schedule for next Monday.

Jon had deserted his office.

Amy had vanished from her own as well, while the door to the vice president's was closed. Murmuring came from behind the door.

Evan's back was turned to me.

Budging Elephant Man's door, I heard only a slight creak and held up my phone.

The nail was still sticking out of the blank surface.

I put my phone back in my pocket.

"What are you doing in there?" Boiler Brain had seen me. "Are you looking for Jon?"

I nodded. "Yeah, I have a really important question for him that only he would be able to answer."

"He's in a meeting with Mike and Amy right now. He said he'll be out in a minute (I think)."

"It's not a particularly big deal. I can ask him later. We need to plan out what we're doing on Monday."

I hurried to my seat a few moments before their meeting dispersed.

Upon examining the schedule for next week, I surveyed the map to allocate the fairest share of streams for us, plotting out convenient routes that would be in both our best interests.

An email from Amy popped up offering the opportunity for anyone interested in joining the safety committee. I replied that I was certainly interested, and asked what my primary duties would entail. It was time to Level Up.

"Richard," called Amy, "I need to have *a safety meeting with you* at three."

"That's in half an hour; I'll be ready then."

"Hey Richard, can you move your rain gauge measurements to the other tab?" said Brian. "You've been recording them on my space."

He was right; I cut-and-pasted them onto the other Excel tab.

Viewing the map on CartoPac, I devised an elegant series of routes that might just work out for Evan and myself, by which we would also share a roughly equal amount of walking and measuring. "I've got something sorted out for us."

"Actually, no (I've been doing this for a while and I'm an expert at it). I'll handle it."

"Fine then, you go ahead."

In fast-motion relapse, Boiler Brain wrote notes on his

blank notepad, zoomed in and out of different stream points, and clicked here and there on an Excel spreadsheet. "Okay. I have something that will work out for both of us. I get most of the main stem, while you get this part of the main stem and almost every trib (including the tribs of tribs). It's actually less walking for you overall (since technically we're supposed to walk everything)."

"Richard. *It's* time." Amy stood at the end of the aisle.

The time read 2:48.

"Okay, I'm ready. Evan, I'll get back to you on this."

She led me down the right side of the complex. "We're going *to have a safety meeting* with Mike."

"Mike...the guy who works here?"

"Yep."

We continued to the main entrance.

"I'm the only one here who knows how to talk to him," Isaac mumbled to Zombie Woman. He looked at me like he knew what was about to happen.

Shadow Guy stepped in front of us and led us to the Conference Room.

"Why don't you have a seat?"

He flicked a light switch that illuminated the far side of the table.

I sat with an upright posture in the same spot where I had my interview, shoulders level.

"Need anything to drink?"

"I'm fine." I tapped my foot gently against a leg of the table.

"I'll be right back."

He disappeared along with Amy.

The analogue clock on the left wall ticked one eternity at a time.

When the second-hand finished its round, Amy returned and sat down on the other side of the table, soon followed by Mike who sat to her right. Last came Jon, who closed the door and locked it. He made his way over to Amy's left and took a seat.

Mike took a deep breath and held his hands together on the table. *"Let's get right to the point. We've decided to part ways and not have you work here anymore."*

CHAPTER 62:

Best Business Practices

They looked like they were about to be hit by a tidal wave. I clutched the table, preparing for shipwreck; I sought relief, but two windows on the wall opposite the door provided an outside view for them, and not for me. The bass drum of my heart pounded in my chest.

My voice was firm and professional. "Forgive me for using this term, but what kind of joke is this?"

"This is not a joke," said Shadow Guy, baring his nostrils.

With that haunting stare, Amy had become Mona Lisa incarnate.

Elephant Man tapped his foot on the floor as he coughed. "This really blindsided me. I thought I was doing a decent job. Where'd I go wrong?"

The tone of Subtle Serpent's voice would shatter glass, though she willed that the windows stay put. "You didn't *do* anything wrong. We just feel you're not a good *fit* for this company." I wanted her lips to look sincere, but her eyes smirked.

It was Elephant Man's turn to say something. "Ya just don't fit in with *aalll* the rest of us, *kid."*

"So I'm losing my job just because you've suddenly decided I don't fit in?"

Shadow Guy held his hands together again and cleared his throat. *"That's right."*

"When was this decision made?"

He squinted and crossed his hands back and forth. *"Look... it doesn't matter."*

"What could I have possibly done differently?"

Subtle Serpent's face sank into a smug grin like she was enjoying a warm bath. "You were walking too *fast* through the woods. Not asking good *questions.* Guessing at *stream* widths. Letting *leaves* get in the way. Getting stuck in the *mud.* Not keeping your *water* in the fridge. Cleaning your *sensor* at the kitchen sink. Not making sure you were in the right *area.* Using *equipment* the wrong way. And saying we were *at odds with each other."*

She exhaled and settled deeper into her resting seat. Perhaps it was the lighting, but she seemed chubbier than usual, a fallen cherub.

"So what!" I cried opening my arms, palms faced outward. "Is that stuff really such a big deal that it would require my *dismissal?* If I didn't do it right, why can't I just do it again?"

Shadow Guy shook his head, then leaned in hunching his shoulders. *"Safety. That's a* big *concern of ours with you."*

"You mean people are putting me in unsafe situations? Or is it that I'm somehow risking my own safety? Which I'm not."

"The second one," he said, finger pointed diagonally. He rested his fist on the table and held it there. *"I've heard reports of someone doing* unsafe *activities."*

"What *kinds* of unsafe activities?"

He straightened up, opened his mouth, and looked towards the ceiling. *"I've...gotten reports of someone carrying around an open* pocketknife *in the field."*

I sputtered before enunciating my reply. "That's not even true! Who? I want to know who told you that."

Shadow Guy squirmed in his seat like a worm trapped under a rock.

I looked at him directly, focusing my attention and determined to stare him down until he withered away. I didn't know he had black eyes until now.

"There are people I've known for many *years,"* he started, *"and they said they've seen someone doing* unsafe *things. I trust their judgment, and they say it was...*you." He remembered to point his finger at me just in time.

"Well, I *don't* trust your imaginary friends!"

"Don't get smart *with me."* His head shimmied from side to side.

"Hmph." I folded my arms and straightened my back. "I'm already *smarter than you."*

*"Alright you little f**k, you're* done *for!"* He shook an enfeebled fist above his livid face.

Elephant Man, now standing, tapped his knuckles three times on the desk. "Time ta git goin'." His cadence matched that of Eeyore from *Winnie the Pooh.*

I stood up and took a deep breath. "Alright, I guess it is time ta git goin'."

Subtle Serpent, her very own bottom screwed onto the seat itself, rotated her torso so that even my very slight missteps away from the door were at the center of her inhuman glare.

"I just have to pack up my stuff."

"No – you – don't!" Shadow Guy fell out of his chair with legs kicking.

I was out the door.

"I'll just need to gather my things together from my desk, locker and truck, and then I'll be out of your way for good."

Incoming rapid footsteps hammered the ground behind me and petered out in a Doppler-effect sensation. Shadow Guy knocked wayward the portrait-and-stool setup; brown paint gushed forth from a quarter-sized hole in the wall, and then trickled.

I stepped over it.

When I arrived at my cubicle, I found him standing over me. Although he was only slightly taller, the rigidity of his puffed-up stance made him seem monumental. He shook his pointer finger back and forth repeatedly, his hand vibrating.

Subtle Serpent tiptoed up to the paint puddle, and stepped as far as her little legs would carry her, and when she had crossed, her dainty stilettos were still completely clean.

In her safe haven there emanated an otherworldly cackle reminiscent of a broomstick-riding witch gliding through the night over a ghastly city by the light of a full moon.

"YAA-HAA-HA-HA-HAAA!"

Shadow Guy was still in my way, standing on his toes inside his black shoes and staring me down, breathing forcefully. I winced; there was no reason his breath should smell like leather. When I sidestepped him, he straddled his arms and legs, blocking my access.

"Take your key fob off right now."

I hesitated.

"Richard...."

His toothy grin crossed from one side to the other; his eyes were dilated in the strangest fashion, as though they did not belong to him. And while he blocked my way in a you-shall-not-pass Gandalf style, I thought for a moment he could've played a Caucasian Captain Hook; the spirit of death comprised his entire face.

"They're in there." I choked on the tension in my throat and pointed weakly.

He granted me access.

Fumbling with the keychain, I struggled to overcome the trembling of my fingers. With unparalleled concentration, I drew the key fob along one ring, and then the opposite way along the other ring.

An unseen hand swooped in, and he bent my fingers the wrong way.

"You need to go now."

"But I have to get my belongings."

"We'll box them up for you."

"Okay, then I'll just sign out."

I reached for the computer mouse, but he stood between me and the computer.

"*Richard,* get the hell *out of here.*"

Subtle Serpent's laughter consumed the background.

My coworkers held their heads down.

"It's cold outside, and I have to get my heavy coat, my hat, and my gloves from my locker!"

"*Absolutely not.*" He straddled the opening to my cubicle.

My thin autumn coat was hanging on the ledger right behind his shoulder.

I stared down the aisle, which had grown to an infinite length, and my feet were frozen like ice on the street.

Elephant Man leaned against the far cubicle closest Subtle Serpent's office; his hand was on his hip blocked from view by the cubicle itself. "Time ta git goin'." I could've set a metronome to his four-four time-signature speech.

Looking behind one last time, I jumped, and sent a flailing arm to the sleeve of my coat. My heart pounded in my ears amidst the slowdown of a time dilation, while Shadow Guy's vicious claw swept toward me and tore the fabric of the sleeve I now held.

He deked to my other side like a basketball player.

"I'm going now! Move!"

"*Then go. And if you come back, we're calling the police.*"

With knees high, he marched like a soldier to the side of the aisle.

I approached Shadow Guy and shook my fist. "No, no, no, you can't call the police when you have my stuff. I'll accuse you of theft!"

He rolled his eyes while suppressing a haughty laugh.

Elephant Man inched closer to the aisle, hand still placed on his hidden hip. "Time ta git *goin'.*" Even he now grinned mischievously.

With every forward step I made, Elephant Man retreated incrementally, his legs angled like those of a fencer.

I leapt over the widening pool of paint saturating the carpet and felt a jabbing motion in my spine. Ultimately dejected, I pressed open the glass door.

Upon making sure it was closed, I found Shadow Guy standing behind me. Contempt had thoroughly disfigured his appearance.

"What do you want?"

"Nothing from you."

He still held the door open.

"You know, you really don't seem like someone who would be a geologist."

"MWAHAHAHA!!!"

I tromped across the garden. The piercing cold that penetrated my coat forced me to bring my arms to my chest to conserve warmth, and with my arms no longer available to hasten my rush, I walked slowly across the poorly-salted parking lot, sacrificing warmth for balance whenever I was on the verge of slipping.

Upon igniting the engine, I turned on the heat, struggling to steady my breathing while swearing under my breath. I flickered the headlights and adjusted the rearview mirror. My face was reddening faster than the heat warmed my body; my brow was raised high, giving my eyes a distinctively circular shape.

Five minutes later, two indistinct figures approached from the distance.

As their forms grew closer, I identified one as Shadow Guy, who wasn't riding a dark horse. He was accompanied by Encyclopedia Brown and they were both wearing winter coats.

Kevin knocked twice on the window before I rolled it down; he bent down to speak with shoulders higher than his head. The freezing air shook his flimsy voice. "G-g-get ready. Candace will c-c-call you soon."

He stepped aside.

Shadow Guy pointed to the sinking sun and stuck his head through the open window. I scooted off the seat.

"Leave this property right now, and never *come back!!"*

His spittle never made contact with my skin. When my hand reached the window panel, he removed his wretched face.

Part Seven

CHAPTER 63:

To Speak with a Soft Tongue

The car was prone to swerving on the snowy roads. I could not relax my right foot enough to steady the vehicle, so I drove obnoxiously slowly.

Flashing high beams accompanied honking, and in giving me the finger, the driver of a brown sedan veered ahead in a semi-circle, nearly colliding as it fronted my bumpers. I ignored the ringtone of my iPhone 6 and kept my hands on the steering wheel, entirely for the purpose of personal safety.

A single open parking spot appeared in the lot of a Sunoco station. I made a sharp left and slowed into the remaining space.

I vaguely recognized the number on my phone under '1 Missed Call' and tapped 'Return Call.'

"'Hello, is this Richard Armadale?'" The voice was so soft and tender that I wondered whether she and the others had even communicated.

"Speaking."

"'This is Candace Meakard, Human Resources of Murray and Affiliates. How are you doing this afternoon?'"

"Probably worse than you."

"'I talked to Amy, and she said you did not take our decision well.'"

"As far as you would be concerned, I was professional

about it. I didn't swear or act out or anything like that – but some people did."

Candace remained chipper. "'I just wanted to review your experience with our company and give you a post-employment follow-up.'"

"Please do explain what's going on."

Her breathing and lip-smacking created static in the reception. "'You've been in a six-month probationary period during which we decide if you'd be a good fit for this company going forward. You were still in that time range when we decided that it's in both our best interests to relieve you of your duties.'"

"You mean *your* best interest. What did I do while working here that made you decide to get rid of me?"

Soft Tongue's voice paused. "'Well, there wasn't one thing that you did that led to our decision, like not turning in your JHAs, for instance. This is just a broad, general assessment of where you are in your professional development, what our needs are as a company at this time, how far you've progressed and how much you've learned, what our goals are, what we typically expect from employees, who we are as a company, who you are as an individual, what we've seen of your working style, and whether or not we're a good match for each other in the grand scheme of things.'"

Her tone indicated she had been taking muscle relaxants or painkillers and that she was lying down on a large, comfortable bed.

"That's all well and good, but what was it that I did – or didn't do – that has led you and the other staff to make this drastic decision? What could I have done differently in order not to be fired?"

"'Again, it wasn't any *one thing* you did or didn't do, and you're not being fired.'"

"It's good to know I'm being laid off."

"'You're not being laid off.'"

I brought a hand to my mouth. "How would *you* describe what's happening to me?"

"'You're being terminated.'"

"What is that supposed to mean?"

Soft Tongue inhaled. "'It means that at this time, we feel that you as an individual are not fulfilling the role we assigned you in the way that we had expected, or in the way that most people in your position would do this job, so we're just letting you go.'"

"If you're saying I sucked at my job, now's the time to tell me."

"'I'm not saying that. This is just a general feel for how you as an individual can help us as a company reach our goals, and how we can make sure that you –'"

"Okay, okay, I get what you're trying to say…. You must have spoken to the others – Jon, Mike, Amy. What was their input on my job performance?"

"'Well, I actually did ask Amy for feedback, and she mentioned some very strange actions on your part, some during your safety supervision.'"

"Like what?"

"'You were not asking enough questions, or the right types of questions in the right situations. Amy informed me that their biggest concern was you being in an isolated environment by yourself. You were carrying around an open pocketknife in the field which you dropped, creating a hazardous situation. We were shocked that you were not double-checking an area before entering it. You were speeding down the highway. A major concern of ours with you is proper use of equipment. You held a senior technician against the wall. You were rushing through the woods. You took a flow measurement in front of a pile of leaves. You were guesstimating stream widths. You drove into a mud pit. You were rude to people from Conrad Power.'"

"When you called me at first, I was actually talking to my

coworkers, and they said that I inadvertently sparked tension between Murray and Conrad when I *joked* that we were at odds with each other."

"'No, that has nothing to do with it,'" she said sharply.

"Even if the issues you mentioned are true – which they're not – then why was Mike in such a hurry to get me out of the building, and what's the deal with calling the police?"

"'He was...trying to diffuse the situation, since you seemed so eager to find out what was going on. You must understand, it was a very stressful situation for him.'"

"And probably more so for me."

"'But it was stressful for Amy, too. You had only yourself to worry about. Anyway, the main thing she told me was that this job just might not be a good fit for you.'"

"So then you admit she was lying about me?"

She hesitated. "'Oh *no,* Amy would never lie to me, I'm sure of it. I've known her for many years, and she said she's seen you doing unsafe things. I trust her judgment, especially in regards to *you.*'"

"Is it really that big of a deal if I go back – say, just to bring home my hat and gloves? And if matters are cleared up once they realize I did nothing wrong, could I possibly continue working here?"

"'Some people who've worked here have returned to our company. But for someone like you, I wouldn't count on it.'"

"My final concern is retrieving my belongings. How will I get those back?"

Soft Tongue caught her breath. "'Now that you're on the outside of things, you can't go back; you can only communicate with me, since I'm the human resources representative. On Monday, I'll drive all the way down to the Austin location, pick up your things, and swing back to your place on the round trip and set them inside.'"

"No you won't, you're not coming anywhere near my apartment! I'll contact the landlord to make sure. Actually, let's just meet at the Hartland Woods post office."

"'Okay. I'll meet you there at noon.'"

"See you then. Thanks for *reaching out.*" I hung up on her.

I honked at all the ugly brands of cars on the highway, some of which were going too slowly because old people were driving them. Bo had joined the major leagues, and I was proud to be on his team.

As I swore and cursed at other drivers, I turned on the radio to a station playing a song the real scumbags likely had never heard:

"Never gonna give – you – up. *Never gonna* let – you – *down....* *Never gonna* run...around, and, *desert you.* Never gonna make – you – cry. *Never gonna SAY* goodbye.... *Never gonna* tell...a *lie...*and – hurt – you."

CHAPTER 64:

The Sun Still Rose

At KFC, I salivated over a meal of fried chicken, mashed potatoes, biscuits, and green beans.

Terminated.

I hated that word, for it reeked of the spirit of rejection.

My password no longer worked when I tried logging in to my company email after dinner. I tried again, and it was still locked. I typed my password slowly, a third time, but to no avail.

On LinkedIn, the vast number of jobs I applied to over the summer were no longer listed. A position for Environmental/ Geologic Field Technician from the company that just dismissed me appeared in the Jobs section.

The number '2' appeared over the bell-shaped Notifications symbol; two people had viewed my profile.

One was Jonathan Wyganti; his face did not appear on his profile picture.

The other was Jack Murray, great-grandson of the man, the myth and the legend; he had changed his status from 'President of Murray & Affiliates' to 'Retired.' His photo revealed a face scored by heavy wrinkles, with dull and listless eyes that had seen my job description, that I got 'paid to explore the wilderness.'

Another notification emerged indicating that Brianna had quit Murray and Affiliates for Longhorn Engineering and Environmental Services.

In a new tab for www.murray-s.com, I perused the website, and my eyes grew weary at 'cost-effective solutions.'

I tried to reach every single contact I had acquired from work via phone, but none of them responded. Both Evan and Terrence ended calls to them before I reached their voicemails.

I faltered on my sleep schedule and stayed awake until almost midnight. A hot shower was a refreshment to my weary mind, but when I lay in bed, sleep eluded me.

To find solace in the outside world I turned on the news, but neither CNN nor FOX could speak to what I had endured.

"AAAAAAAAAARRRRGGGHHHHH!!!!!!"

I got out of bed and hurled my slippers like javelins, one against the wall to the side of the TV, and one onto the floor. An infant started crying on the upper floor. My voice was still on full blast.

Exhausted, I collapsed onto the carpet, arms and legs trembling wildly, with my torso banging against the hardwood floor, as if doing *the worm* upside-down. Frothing at the mouth, I grunted and groaned in deepest anguish.

Choking on spewed saliva, I bolted upright and headed to the kitchen, lips parched and mouth dry.

The cool glass of water soothed my throat, and I slid back into bed, only to undergo an episode of what all men do at some point when they are all alone.

I let out a keening, wailing howl that reminded me of my old dog Migsy whimpering outside just before dinnertime, and flipped the pillow when tears had soaked one side.

The bathroom light made my eyes water even more, so I dimmed them until my reflection in the mirror became visible.

My hair was frazzled, and distinct red marks were on the

parts of my cheeks where I felt most of the heat. The whites of my eyes were entirely pink with certain blood vessels prominent. All in all, I looked like Klaus Baudelaire from *A Series of Unfortunate Events*, and a melancholy violinist might as well play Game Over music.

I lay in bed yet again, motionless, and though I slept not a wink, the sun still rose at dawn.

CHAPTER 65:

This Wonderful Land

Only four pieces of bread were in the bread box, and in the fridge two slices of ham and three of cheese. The milk container was half empty – not half full.

With substitute rubber boots on my feet, I grabbed a spare coat, filled an empty water bottle, and raced out the door; it was warm for a wintry day.

I ran all throughout Hartland Woods, finding streams here and there, following them until I had discovered all areas of the neighborhood, running like a bandit chasing the wind, tromping across neighbors' yards, if that was where the streams led.

Heeding neither their occasional complaints nor answering their asinine questions, I ran and ran, never stopping even when I became tired or hungry, exploring every last nook and cranny of the suburban wilderness, relishing the joy that was so sweet and so complete that let me know, at least for today, this wonderful land was mine.

And by the end of the day when I was exhausted not from stress but from physical activity – as every day should end – I felt as if I owned the whole world.

Satisfied from the wonder of exploration, and with my water bottle empty, I hiked a shortcut through the hilly woods to my apartment.

The mother of the crying baby spoke to me about the racket

I created; I simply told her I had slept through a nightmare, and because it happened seldom, she need not worry.

My keyboard standing by the windowsill reminded me that music – quality music – had always enabled me to find peace. As I heard the opening lyrics of 'Alde Lang Syne,' the rhetorical question resounded mightily:

"Should *alde*...ac*quaint*-ance beee *for*got aand nehh-ver brought *to mind?*"

At day's end, I returned to my resting place and found the blessings of sleep.

CHAPTER 66:

Words from the Father

The following morning, I attended Saint Francis of Assisi Parish. Father Matthias slid down the pew nearer me.

"If you do not change your heart, you will be no better than they are," he warned in a gentle tone.

I appreciated his steady speaking pace and his avoidance of the Common Speech. He stroked his gray beard as he observed me, deep eyes filled with care.

"The only escape from your pain is complete and unconditional forgiveness, as difficult as it may be."

"But wouldn't revenge also make me feel better?"

"All three of them probably have experienced something very similar to you. They have most certainly obtained their revenge – their reward – many times over, and they are still in a state of revenge. You see..." He leaned in closer "...once you choose to descend a slippery slope, you cannot easily return to where you started, nor can you decide where to stop. Is this not true in your experience, or in your intuition?"

He held his thumb and index finger together, raising and lowering his hand.

I nodded slowly. "They never gave me a real reason why they terminated me. I guess it would be easier to forgive them if I could just understand what was going on."

Matthias parsed his tongue and shook his head softly with

eyes closed. "But you cannot have it both ways. God may be hiding a truth from you which you cannot handle. There are many things in life that will consume you; anger is only one, curiosity just as much, for once you know why you were dismissed, you will likely feel no better than you do now, and your quest for knowledge beyond your purview will consume you just as much as unbridled wrath. Forgiveness and compassion for your fellow man *is* the way forward."

"How can I forgive them when I'm a completely innocent person? I want to grind that pathetic Murray and Affiliates into the ground! I was granted the title of 'Environmental Field Technician.' I was almost a member of the High Life."

"Richard, I don't want you to disappear along with them. I want you to be happy. Yet even after it's all over, you still suffer from your anger."

"It's alright. It's not your fault."

"What do you mean?"

"I loved that job, then they interfered and forced me out. I was handed over to the misfortune of unemployment. I was trying to do the right thing all along, to follow my heart. What were they trying to create out of me?"

"It seems so. But their ambitions failed."

"I fulfilled my promise as an employee to them. All of the fields and pastures above the mines should be *mine*. I want my job to be returned to me!"

"You surely succeeded in what you did. It would seem as though they failed you as a company."

"Wh-what?"

"They were not compatible with you."

"It worked just fine for several months."

"Richard, don't destroy your soul."

"I-I can't. I would never do that."

"It's because God loves you that He wants you to move on. He delivered you from them in order to save you. It was the only way."

"I guess so. I'm so glad you're here in the end. Maybe there's no reason for regrets."

"So please, Richard, stop punishing yourself."

"But with my own hands, I –"

"I need to disappear very soon. So please, don't give me anything to worry about. You don't need the shackles of your past memories. You've suffered enough."

"I lost the job I love. There was no crime, yet this was the punishment!"

"You don't need that punishment anymore. Please, Richard."

"..." I was speechless.

"As I have said, they must have experienced the same thing you did. And I can also imagine what it must have been like for them. They have become monsters, and they didn't like it that you struck them down. They must have suffered as well."

"But would they have done the same thing if they were in my position?"

"I don't know if the decisions they made were correct, but I don't think God would want to punish you and make you live this way."

"Is that true?"

"Yes. It's just as the Bible says. At least, I don't want you to live like that."

"Alright. But I will never again use coal as a tool of death. I swear that to you. To you and to God. And once we have defeated those who use coal to toy with people's lives, I shall remove my bonds of hatred."

"Thank you, Richard."

"I think I can finally be at peace. Please destroy my rage before I am totally absorbed in misery."

"Why is that? Are you saying you can't stay like you are now?"

"I will stay like this. I will live on and do what is right. But now I'm an isolated person, unable to even speak up for myself. What if my unforgiveness lasts an eternity? It would be a veritable hell."

"Richard, what will you do?"

"Please. Pray to set me free."

"Yes. Goodbye, Richard."

"Thank you."

"Richard, please forgive them. Please."

"I should have come to you right away. I feel terrible, but they're the criminals."

"You've confessed; your former employers are the ones going to hell of their own will."

I took a deep breath. "So it would seem."

"Now I don't mean to minimize what you are going through. But do keep in mind that the Lord has a terrific sense of humor."

The priest promised to arrange a mass on my behalf. I thanked him for his time and left the parish. I clenched my fists while facing away from the rising sun above the building.

Driving home, I listened to the same song from the same station as I did on my last day of work:

"Who...can...say...why your *heaart* sighs...as your *love* flies...*only – time*.... And who...can...say...why your *heaart* cries...when your *love* lies...*only – time*."

I unlocked the door and sat on the couch with the television off in a dark room. Then I went out and watched the sky.

CHAPTER 67:

Perfectly Fake

I arrived at the Hartland Woods post office before she did, and at ten minutes past twelve, a black car pulled in smoothly, and was parked in reverse.

Candace opened the trunk, and inside were several large, tightly sealed cardboard boxes with a few smaller ones.

"Wonderful place you have here!" she peeped.

"Lovely, isn't it?"

As she unloaded the boxes, I examined Soft Tongue.

She wore a tan pantsuit that fit her slim figure elegantly enough, and her light yet shiny brown hair was curled into a bun. Her complexion was unnaturally smooth with teeth that made the snow look gray, and her flat brown eyes resembled graham crackers. There was an abundance of makeup on her face with classic bright-red lipstick, her most outstanding feature and the only part of her not well color-coordinated.

Her posture was peppy, and she lifted her knees when she walked, with every step of her black high heels tapping the pavement like those of a ballet dancer.

When she finished unloading, she turned to face me with a flawless fake smile. "Here's all your special stuff, dear. I hope I'm not forgetting anything. Let me know if I am." She held her palms together tightly below her chin.

Each item was written in magic marker on the sides of the cardboard boxes.

I brought out the list I made of everything I could remember, pencil in hand, and checked off my personal belongings. By the time I had examined each box, some items were left unchecked.

She lifted her knees and swiveled her hips. "You science people are so smart and organized with all your handy lists. I don't do science, I do *people.*"

"I don't know what 'doing people' means, much like you probably don't know what science is all about. But to be frank with you – now that my job is over – I never felt like I was actually doing science at your company."

Soft Tongue held her hips to the side, both hands on her waist, and smacked her lips. "See, that's how smart you science people are! You think you're not doing science even when you're doing *science.*"

"Let's just say I'm doing science right now. There are some things on my list that you failed to bring."

She held her palms up to her chin and opened her mouth in an O-shape. "I'm so sorry, I thought I remembered everything that I told myself not to forget, but I knew I was going to forget something, so I tried not to forget, but I still forgot. What did I forget?"

I rolled my eyes. "An army blanket, my phone charger, two pens, tick-spray, a black umbrella, a heavy blue coat, protein bars, and a pork rinds container."

Her jaw dropped. "Ooh, I'm so sorry, I should have remembered them. Amy looked in your truck and opened the back and said, 'Are these pork rinds?' But I told her, 'Just assume everything that isn't ours is Richard's.' So I'm glad that they are yours, and not somebody else's." She shrugged while holding her hands to the sides.

"Wait, why was Amy – oh nevermind, it doesn't matter. I'll give you this sheet and you can collect all the things without checkmarks."

Soft Tongue high-stepped on her toes. "Why don't you just email them to me, and I'll make sure they're in the mail by this afternoon. I have a meeting to catch."

She walked backwards to the front door, waving a palm like one would clap with a single hand. "Have a *wonderful* day, dear!"

"You too," I grumbled.

CHAPTER 68:

The Unknown Caller

The Monday was a snow day for the kids in town. The snow rapidly accumulated in a heavy white sheet on my driveway.

Upon dressing into winter gear – long underwear, winter coat, fuzzy hat, and wool gloves – I grabbed the wide-rimmed, sharp-bladed yellow snow shovel hanging by a broad, long nail in the garage. Energetically, I heaved mounds of snow off the driveway and piled them on the front yard.

My phone ringed, and I reached into my pocket: 'Unknown Caller.'

I dropped the shovel, and rushed inside tracking snow all over the entrance mattress and onto the wooden floor, where it quickly melted.

"Hello?"

"*Greetings, is this* Richard Armadale to whom I am speaking?'"

"Yes, who are you?"

"*It is quite possible* that you are perhaps already familiar with me as an individual.'"

"Who are you?"

"'Emily.'"

"You mean Emily, Ron's friend?"

"*I am* rather acquainted with him.'"

"Why are you calling me?"

"*What was it* precisely that you were thinking?'"

"What do you mean, 'What was I thinking?' You're the one who called me."

"*Are you familiar* with the word 'ultimatum,' *and do you* understand its definition thereof?'"

"Yes, I am, and I do."

"*Have you not* ever read or heard the phrase, *doing your job too well?*'"

"No, I haven't. Just tell me why you called me, please."

"*The only fact of which I am presently aware* is that they are attempting to sue a landowner for deliberately contaminating his very own well water and in turn blaming it on them.'"

"You mean at Murray?"

"*Of course,* you silly goose; *who else* but them and Conrad?'"

"Right, of course."

"*Now this is a term* which I do not often use in my own writing and seldom in my speech with other individuals because I find it to be quite uncouth, *so as* the saying goes, *'pardon* my French.' *Mike and Amy* seem to be in some rather deep shit for hiring you. *With regards* to your time of employment, *were you attempting* to overthrow the entire organization?'" asked Revolution Girl exasperated. "*You continually* bombarded them with negative information. *My personal recommendation* therefore is to blow the whistle a little more gently next time if you wish to maintain employment within a company.'"

"Thank you so much."

"*Well,* what can I say? *You are* very much quite welcome. *But Richard,* do not ever lose hope.'"

"Wh-why do you say that?"

"*Because.*'" Several moments of unbreakable silence passed. "*Very soon* there will be a revolution.'"

"Emily, what's your last name?"

The phone clicked.

As I drove to the grocery store, I turned on the radio to a song expressing sorrow joyfully:

"It's the hard-knock life, for us. It's the hard-knock *life, for us.* Steada treated...*we* get tricked. Steada kisses...we *get kicked."*

When I returned and put the groceries away, my refrigerator was full.

Grinning, I dialed Old Man's number.

"'Hello?'" His voice seemed clearer on the phone.

"Hi, this is Richard from Murray and Affiliates. Is this Elias McCullough?"

"'Mmm...speaking.'"

"Last Friday, you told me that your well water was contaminated and that your wife was sick, correct?"

"'Yes, still the case sorry to say.'"

"I was *laid off* because my efforts to help you were outside my specified job duties, so I can no longer assist you in my former role. I suspect that Murray is colluding with Conrad Power and that they will not remediate your property. Your best bet at this point is to contact the Department of Environmental Protection and tell them what's going on."

"'But they always take a long time to get here and do anything, you see. They're so lazy. I've seen your work ethic, so that's why I asked you.'"

"You could at least tell them, and they may eventually help, even if they don't respond until next year. Tell them all about your ruined crops, the flooding on your property, your sick wife, the collapsing bridge with the smashed culvert, the strange-looking animals, and tell them that there is shiny orange staining on some of the streams near your land. Tell them everything, and that these conditions have persisted for months on end. Also, tell your neighbor Mallow not to let anyone from Murray onto his property until they've cleaned up the mess."

"'Thank you.'"

"Goodbye and good luck."

CHAPTER 69:

Part of What We Share

In the week leading up to Christmas, the following articles emerged on Google News:

'Southeastern KY projects get DEP funding for clean energy.'

'PFAS contamination not widespread in KY.'

'KY rule to tackle water pollution from oil and gas wells advances.'

'Georgetown County of KY temporarily raises taxes by 13% to clean up groundwater.'

In my room I danced like an Irish tap-dancer.

Murray and Conrad were definitely at odds with each other in the midst of their business charade, and despite all I had done for them, I would always be remembered for the last noteworthy thing I said. And they hated me for saying it, because they knew it was true, and because it posed a philosophical problem for them. But the most pitiful part of it all is that they wanted to convince themselves that it wasn't such, that the two organizations could see eye-to-eye on everything.

Terminated.

I embraced the word as a badge of honor, because it meant they could find nothing wrong with me. Soon I would have to begin my job search anew, and make the rubber hit the road again, but for the time being I was quite satisfied with myself, and at peace. The grass could very well be greener on the other side, as long as Mike Matthews would refrain from ripping it up.

On my iPhone I listened to the beginning of his representative song:

"When the *days*...are cold and the *cards*...all fold and the *SAINTS* we...see are all made – of – gold. When your *dreams*...*all fail* and the *ones*...*we* hail are the *WORST* of all, and the blood's run stale.... I wanna *hide – the – truth, I wanna* SHELTER YOU, but with the *beast inside,* there's nowhere *we – can – hide.* NO MATTER WHAT *we breed, we still are MADE* OF GREED. This is my king-dom come, *this is my king-dom come.*"

Through it all, the rise and fall, there were no bodies in the streets, and now that they were dead and gone to me my memory would help me carry on. Shadow Guy was the last person I forgave, and I was looking forward to moving on with my life, as long as he wasn't already on the move destroying my reputation amongst other employers, his haunting shadow lingering far and wide....

To soothe my ongoing concerns, I grabbed my picture book from the shelf one last time, just to look upon the words of that special poem: *Every drop of water, Every breath of air, Every ray of sunshine, Is part of what we share.*